LADY MAKES
HER MARK

BOOKS BY SUSANNA CRAIG:

Goode's Guide to Misconduct

Nice Earls Do

The Lady Knows Best

The Lady Plays With Fire

The Lady Makes Her Mark

Love and Let Spy

Who's That Earl

One Thing Leads to a Lover

Better Off Wed

Every Rogue Has His Charm

Rogues & Rebels

The Companion's Secret

The Duke's Suspicion

The Lady's Deception

Runaway Desires

To Kiss a Thief

To Tempt an Heiress

To Seduce a Stranger

THE LADY MAKES HER MARK

GOODE'S
GUIDE TO
MISCONDUCT

Susanna Craig

ZEBRA BOOKS
Kensington Publishing Corp.
kensingtonbooks.com

ZEBRA BOOKS are published by

Kensington Publishing Corp.
900 Third Avenue
New York, NY 10022

All Kensington titles, imprints, and distributed lines are available at special quantity discounts for bulk purchases for sales promotion, premiums, fund-raising, and educational or institutional use.

Special book excerpts or customized printings can also be created to fit specific needs. For details, write or phone the office of the Kensington Sales Manager: Kensington Publishing Corp., 900 Third Avenue, New York, NY 10022. Attn. Sales Department. Phone: 1-800-221-2647.

ZEBRA BOOKS and the Zebra logo Reg. U.S. Pat. & TM Off.

First Printing: June 2025
ISBN-13: 978-1-4201-5483-2
ISBN-13: 978-1-4201-5484-9 (eBook)

10 9 8 7 6 5 4 3 2 1

Printed in the United States of America

The authorized representative in the EU for product safety and compliance is eucomply OU, Parnu mnt 139b-14, Apt 123
Tallinn, Berlin 11317, hello@eucompliancepartner.com

Chapter 1

London, November 1810

Constantia had learned through experience the importance of avoiding trouble. In a lifetime of reinventing herself, she had learned when it was time to walk away from whatever name she had claimed, the identity she had built, the place she called her own.

When the note arrived informing her of an urgent meeting of the staff of *Mrs. Goode's Magazine for Misses*, she had felt the familiar prickle of apprehension.

She had wanted, unaccountably, to ignore the warning.

Well, not *unaccountably*. Leaving her present position would be difficult. She would feel the loss. She was six-and-twenty, and the other young ladies who worked for the magazine were the closest she had ever known to friends, though they would undoubtedly be surprised to hear themselves described as such.

Experience had also taught Constantia reserve. She knew better than to trust people. To let them in.

Or perhaps she was prickly and standoffish by nature. At a certain point, it became impossible to distinguish between what she *was* and what circumstances had forced her to become. At a certain point, such differences ceased to matter.

Nonetheless, she had trusted Lady Stalbridge, the magazine's founder and editor, at least as far as she had trusted anyone for twenty years. She had made herself vulnerable, shared her art, but explained that her family situation made it unwise for her to reveal many details about herself. She had concocted a new surname, *Cooper*, on the spot.

And now, almost a year later, just when she had started to relax, to let herself walk out without glancing over her shoulder, the letter had come. A letter about a staff meeting she had not expected, directed to Miss Constantia Cooper at this address, written in a hand she did not know. That single, folded sheet of paper had slipped into the narrow sliver of unguardedness she had allowed to open and cut her to the quick.

Half an hour before the meeting began, she gathered up her meager possessions. Her artist's tools first, as usual, the brushes, tiny pots, and half-finished pieces tucked neatly in their places inside the cleverly designed wooden box that served as both carrying case and easel. The rest of her things were always already half-packed: her mother's picture and letter beneath the valise's false bottom, her undergarments folded neatly on top to discourage anyone who might be tempted to pry.

And then she took what was likely to be her last look around the room she rented from a modiste whose French name, Madame D'Arblay, Constantia suspected would be as unlikely to hold up under scrutiny as her own. The modiste's shop occupied a former townhome near Oxford Street. The public areas of the shop were on the ground floor; the shop work was done on the first floor; and the modiste lived above that. Constantia paid a pittance to occupy what had once been the house-keeper's quarters belowstairs, a spacious apartment with one significant drawback for an artist: It had only one window, covered over with bars and a scraggly shrub, and in any case too small to admit more light than just what made it possible to tell night from day. The remainder of the cellar was used for storage.

Out of habit, she counted the stairs as she climbed, so as not to stumble in the darkness. One could not always be carrying a candle; certainly not now, with her artist's case in one hand and her valise in the other. She considered walking through the door at the top and out of the shop. Away from the meeting and the little life she had managed to build. Best to make a clean break of it.

But the apprehension fluttering around in her chest had a curious way of disguising itself as hope. Perhaps Lady Stalbridge had hired a new secretary, which would explain the unfamiliar handwriting. Perhaps the meeting had been called to share good news, not bad.

As a compromise between those two warring impulses, she left her bags resting on the thirteenth step, one from the top, easy to access if she should have to leave in a hurry after the meeting, but enough out of the way that if Madame D'Arblay should send one of her shop girls down to the cellar for something in the meantime, no one would stumble over them.

After dragging in the sort of breath that could not help but pin back her shoulders and lift her chin, Constantia emerged into the dressmaker's shop.

She hated the momentary disorientation produced by the sudden transition into light and warmth—the inevitable shiver and spate of rapid blinking, the few seconds of defenselessness, when she might be seen before she could see.

But it was November and the shop was no longer bustling, not even at midday. Madame D'Arblay was directing a woman's notice to an open pattern book, and two younger ladies, probably the woman's daughters, were fingering a display of ribbons. None of them paid Constantia any mind as she slipped out the back of the shop.

Navigating the warren of alleys and side streets and mews, deftly avoiding the puddles, not all of which had been left by that morning's rain, she made her way to the rear of Porter's Antiquarian Bookshop on Bond Street. Lady Stalbridge had arranged for the staff of the *Magazine for Misses* to have access to a back room there for meetings. Whenever the shop was open, any one of them might retrieve the key stowed behind the front counter.

Constantia had arranged her own access to the room the rest of the time. In exchange for dusting shelves when the shop was closed, she had been given a key to the back door. Though the room in question was crowded with furniture and books, it—unlike the cellar at Madame D'Arblay's—had the advantage of a large window. A large, dirty window. Shockingly dirty. But still, it permitted sufficient light to draw by.

While working at the scarred oak table, she had been surprised countless times by the staff of both the bookshop and the magazine. She was aware they all found her odd, but she was indifferent—well, *almost*—to their impertinent stares and whispers.

Today, as usual, she was the first to arrive. She looked around the room, at the modicum of organization she had been able to impose: less dust, fewer books stacked on the floor, a complete run of the *Magazine for Misses* along the window ledge. It had grown into a habit with her, this neatening and straightening, something to balance the chaos of her circumstances and a certain wildness in her soul.

Another corner of the little world she had built into a sort of nest and would have to abandon—or tear down.

But it wouldn't do to give in to sentiment. Slipping a blank sheet of paper from the drawer of a rickety desk and plucking a pencil from the knot of her simple coiffure, she took up her post at one end of the oval table, across from the place Lady Stalbridge usually commanded, and began to sketch.

Out of habit, her pencil swept across the page in the exaggerated style of the magazine's satirical cartoonist. Her monthly contribution, "What Miss C. Saw," had been rechristened the Unfashionable Plates by readers, who delighted in her sharp critiques of London's elite— much to Constantia's surprise. Surely a fair number of those readers belonged to the very set she mocked?

But she supposed there was a certain entertainment in discovering one's ballroom adversary had been skewered, a certain relief in ascertaining one's own fashionable foibles had been spared—for this month, at least.

The pencil was dull and the picture that emerged from its tip equally so. One could only bear to draw so many ridiculously high collars or absurdly tall hair plumes. Ordinarily, she would already have finished a pair of panels for the next issue. She preferred to work well ahead of deadline. But this month, every effort had found itself kindling for the fire.

Still, she supposed she ought to try, as it was likely to be her last contribution to the *Magazine for Misses*.

Once, she had gone so far as to imagine herself slipping into Lady Stalbridge's shoes as editor, whenever the countess decided to step aside from that role. But that had always been a foolish dream—not least because Constantia knew better than to plan for a future that could never be anything but uncertain.

Before she could do more than place indistinct figures in a scene, Lady Clarissa Sutliffe arrived, slightly out of breath. "Oh, Miss Cooper. You're here." She slid into a chair along one side of the table, her back to the window. "That must mean—oh. Well, I'm not really sure. What *does* it mean, do you suppose?"

Constantia did not answer, did not even look up from her work, though the blunt tip of her pencil was creating more smudges than lines. She had her suspicions about this meeting, but it would do no good to share them with the petted and indulged daughter of a marquess. What could *she* know of danger or treachery?

To her relief, Lady Clarissa did not press for conversation. Next to arrive was Miss Theodosia Nelson, who was clutching the fateful note in her hand. Upon seeing the other two women, she smoothed the scrap of paper against the table and laid it in the center. Miss Nelson's grim expression did not invite confidences, but it told Constantia she understood the letter's import.

Detractors of *Mrs. Goode's Magazine for Misses*—known variously among them as the *Magazine for Mischief* or *Goode's Guide to Misconduct*—would give much to discover the identities of the contributors. And now it seemed that someone other than Lady Stalbridge was in possession of their names and addresses. The significance of the letters summoning them all here was as clear and chilling as any threat.

With a nervous sound, which might under other circumstances have passed for a laugh, Lady Clarissa reached into her reticule and laid her letter beside Miss Nelson's. For no reason that she could explain, Constantia retrieved hers from her bodice and added it, still folded, to the pile. Silence hung over the three of them like a pall, and beneath the dull pencil, Constantia's sketching grew less and less legible.

Miss Julia Addison was the second to last to appear, sinking into the chair beside Miss Nelson and sliding her letter across the table to join the rest.

Lady Clarissa greeted her arrival as another opportunity to strike up a conversation. "I wonder why Lady

Stalbridge needs to see us on such little notice? I had to say that Thomas, my cat, had run away—even though the poor old thing is asleep under my bed." Her violet-blue eyes were always wide, but Constantia's quick glance over the tops of her spectacles revealed them to be even wider than usual, fixed with alarm on the growing pile of notes. "Papa let me join some of the servants in a search for him. I gave two footmen the slip and came here. I figured, it worked for Daphne," she finished, calling to mind the sudden appearance of a cat at one of their meetings last spring, and with it, Miss Daphne Burke, who had become the magazine's advice columnist, against Constantia's wishes. Miss Burke had meddled shamelessly in the lives of one of their readers and, to make amends, had thrown herself away on a rake and was now Lady Deveraux.

"I had been wishing for another meeting," Miss Nelson ventured after a pause, "so that I could tell you all that I'm to have an article published in *The Times*."

"Theo," exclaimed Lady Clarissa, reaching across the table to grasp her fingers. "That's marvelous. I knew you could do it."

Constantia twisted the pencil between her first finger and her thumb. The walls of this little room were closing in. In the face of bad news, surely they were entitled to seize this last chance to share something good?

"I've submitted a watercolor to an exhibition," she announced. She preferred to work in oils, but Madame D'Arblay had feared the odor of mineral spirits would offend her customers.

As triumphs went, it was a small one, hardly worthy

of the name. But if she didn't speak of it with these three women, she might never have an opportunity to speak of it with anyone at all.

"Anonymously, of course," she added—unnecessarily. She never did anything that wasn't anonymous, to one degree or another.

Miss Nelson was the first to congratulate her: "Excellent news!"

The others seemed not to know what to say. Nearly a decade Constantia's junior, Lady Clarissa was obviously intimidated by her, though the girl's own artistic gift was nothing to sneeze at. If her father could be persuaded to allow it, she would surely achieve her goal of becoming a concert pianist.

As for Miss Addison? Well, her tendency to bubble over with enthusiasm, her apparent indifference to the potentially serious consequences of behaving rashly or saying something outrageous, had often put her and Constantia at odds. She was free in a way Constantia would never be, and perhaps she was having difficulty mustering felicitations for someone she did not like.

And in fact, when at last that young lady spoke, it was not to praise Constantia, but to contribute another confession of sorts to the pile: "I'm going to marry Lord Dunstane."

Constantia narrowly restrained a gasp of astonishment. Miss Addison's biting theatrical reviews had earned the attention of notorious playwright Ransom Blackadder, who had subsequently written a play, *The Poison Pen*, that threatened both her and the magazine's reputation. At Lady Stalbridge's urging, she had

established a tenuous connection with the Earl of
Dunstane, Blackadder's patron, to see if the situation
could be defused.

How had a plan to keep the magazine from being
destroyed led to an engagement? Constantia couldn't
decide whether Miss Addison had sacrificed herself on
their behalf or thrown them all to the wolf. After all,
how could she be expected to keep her secret—all their
secrets—from the man who would be her husband?

Or might she already have said too much?

Before Constantia, or anyone, could speak, Lady
Stalbridge appeared in the doorway.

"Oh." The countess's disappointed gaze traveled
the room. "I had hoped . . ." Then, spying the papers in
the center of the table, she sighed, opened her reticule,
and tossed two more letters to join the rest. "Oliver
received one as well."

Oliver, Viscount Manwaring, was Lady Stalbridge's
stepson. He was also the person behind Mrs. Goode,
author of the famed *Guide to Homekeeping* and the
figurehead of their magazine. Penning domestic manuals
and managing ladies' magazines were not the sorts of
activities that did credit to a gentleman's reputation,
however. Lord Manwaring had a great deal to lose if
those behind the *Magazine for Misses* were exposed.

But not more than Constantia.

Lady Clarissa expressed some childish hope that the
letters had been sent as a joke, which Lady Stalbridge
was quick to deny.

"But—but," Miss Nelson stammered, "this means

someone else knows who we all are, even where we live!"

At those words—the truth that Constantia had known from the first but had come today hoping to hear denied—she pushed back from the table, her chair scraping noisily across the floor. "You'll excuse me, please," she said with a nod and a curtsy, leaving the half-finished sketch behind.

Experience had indeed taught her when it was time to walk away from a situation.

Today, it was time to run.

Leaving through the front of the shop might have been a tactical error, she realized, as she glanced from customers to clerks to whoever might be disguised behind that bookcase crammed with books, as tall and solid as a wall. But the distance from Porter's front door to Madame D'Arblay's was shorter, two points on a straight line.

As she passed the counter, she laid her key on it before striding out into the gray afternoon. She did not hurry her steps—at least, not noticeably so. She did not cast a suspicious look at every passerby. She knew by now how to stay vigilant without showing fear.

That did not mean, however, that she did not *feel* it.

Her heart pounded, working to move blood half-congealed by the combination of chilly air and the icy terror that had overspread her veins. The magazine's foes were legion. Rakes who objected to Miss Busy B.'s advice. Playwrights and actors who found fault with Miss on Scene's reviews. Parents and governesses and a larger society who wanted young ladies to remain ignorant and thus easier to control. The letter writer could have been any of them. And what a clever way, just the names and directions on a series of notes, to show the staff of the magazine who had the upper hand now.

Constantia had no reason to assume that Miss C.'s cartoons were the particular target of the letter writer's ire. But that arrow had pierced her fragile bubble of security and contentment all the same.

When she burst through the door of Madame D'Arblay's, a bell jangled harshly. Though the shop was empty of customers, the modiste sent Constantia a reproving look. She was to come and go through the back, not the front.

"I won't trouble you or your clientele again," Constantia assured her, after leaning for a moment against the doorframe to catch her breath. Then she slipped through the shop, snatching up her bags from the stairwell as she passed, and left for the last time through the rear.

This time, her feet traced a different route through the alleyways, northwest toward the nearest coaching inn. She would take the next available stage, whatever direction it might be bound. She couldn't afford to wait and choose her destination.

She only prayed she had enough money left in her purse to start again wherever she ended up.

The rumble of wheels and clatter of hooves, muffled by the rows of houses and shops between her and the streets of London's West End, grew louder as she approached the point at which she would have to emerge to cross the thoroughfare.

"Where 're ye off to, miss?"

The man's wheedling voice made her whole body jerk, coming so close behind and just loud enough to be heard over the patter of her own hurried footsteps and the pounding of her heart. Almost as if he had spoken right in her ear.

Probably just some servant or shop assistant. No one sent to pursue her.

Nonetheless, startled, she leaped away from him into the relative safety of the busy street.

Sound and sensation blurred around her, inside her. The shouted oath of a coachman. The hot snort of a frightened horse. Sharp pain, everywhere, as the cobbled street rose up to meet her. Both valise and artist's case flew from her hands.

Then everything went black.

Chapter 2

Roused by the commotion outside his library window, Alistair Haythorne, Earl of Ryland, glanced down in surprise at the book in his hand, as if *Observations on the different breeds of sheep, and the state of sheep farming in some of the principal counties of England* had been responsible for the noise.

Long ago, he had claimed the room as his sole preserve from a household otherwise overrun with women. The housekeeper, Mrs. Swetley; a cook; maidservants who came and went with the seasons; and his sisters. So many sisters. Seven of them, to be exact. Not that they all resided at Haythorne House anymore. The two eldest were married with households of their own, and some portion of the younger five were sometimes with one of them, or with Aunt Josephine in the West Country.

Still, it was a great deal of . . . *femaleness* for one house to contain, and a man occasionally needed a reprieve from it. A space to which he could retreat for some much-needed peace and quiet.

Peace and quiet which were evidently to be in short supply today.

Another shriek rose from the street, followed by a shouted exchange between two deeper voices. With a sigh, Alistair closed the book on sheep farming and heaved himself from the chair, threading his way across the room to peer through the window. "Let's see what all the ruckus is about," he said aloud, though he was alone in the house.

It wasn't madness to talk to oneself, he reasoned. Only madness to expect an answer. And people rarely listened to him anyway—even if he was the earl.

Below, a woman lay sprawled on the cobblestones, struck evidently by the carriage that now lodged across the road, stopping traffic. Nearby, two men argued— the coachman, by his livery, and a passerby. Beneath his window, a fashionably dressed lady slumped in the arms of her maid, packages strewn about them on the pavement. One of them, he surmised, had shrieked. And a brave lad had taken it upon himself to catch the team of horses by the tack. Still skittish from the accident, they pranced and pawed a good deal too close to the fallen woman.

Then again, perhaps she was already dead.

"What a senseless tragedy." With a grimace, he let the curtain drop and turned away from the window. Half a dozen crates lay scattered about the floor. He was meant to be sorting through the last of his personal books and papers, determining which would accompany him, which ought to stay with the house or with his solicitor, and which could be disposed of.

As he strode from the room, he tossed *The State of Sheep Farming* onto the nearest pile, entirely indifferent as to whether it landed in a crate bound for Devonshire or the scrap heap. Downstairs, he snatched his greatcoat from a rack near the door. But he did not don it, though the November air had teeth. From the top step, he once more surveyed the scene on the street. Nothing much had changed in the intervening moments, beyond a slight increase in the size of the gawking crowd.

"Has no one thought to summon a physician?" he called out. Whatever Marylebone's comparative deficiencies to Mayfair in other respects, it was positively crawling with medical men. Two onlookers accepted the charge and hurried off.

Passing the defensive coachman and the wilted lady, he walked up to the boy, whose arms strained with the effort of containing the skittish team. "You there," he said to a pair of young bucks standing a row or two back in the semicircle of bystanders. "Help him. Unhook the horses and walk them. Shoulder the carriage out of the way."

Those orders roused the coachman to his duty and he came to assist, still protesting his innocence. "Came out of nowhere, she did. Darted right under the horses' noses. Naught to be done—no way I could have stopped them."

Indifferent to the man's excuses, Alistair knelt beside the fallen woman, who lay against the cold stone, breathing shallowly. He sent up a silent prayer. Her body was twisted, her right arm tucked beneath her at an awkward angle, her face half-hidden by a tangle of golden-red hair. Her bonnet was nowhere to be seen. A delicate brush of his fingertips revealed a bruise already beginning to form on her temple, a gash along the cheekbone below, skin pale, eyes closed. Her clothes were of modest quality without suggesting poverty. Difficult to determine her age in her current state, but certainly not yet thirty, he thought.

A shadow fell across her face, and he looked up to find the lady's maid standing over them, a vinaigrette in her outstretched hand. "Will she be all right, sir?"

A hopeful question, and one he could not honestly answer in the affirmative. With a tight smile, he thanked her for the smelling salts, sparing a glance for her employer, who was now slumped weakly against the area railing in front of his house. "You'd best go back. Take your mistress inside to warm herself, if she can climb the steps." He gave a nod toward Haythorne House, the door of which still stood open.

"You're very good, sir."

Once, twice, he passed the small silver vial of hartshorn beneath the young woman's nose, which was sprinkled whimsically with freckles, their ginger color stark against her pallor. Her eyelids fluttered but did not open. She showed no other signs of rousing. He did not think he dared to do more until the physician arrived.

Carefully he spread his greatcoat over her body, murmuring a string of soothing nonsense, the sort of patter one perfected with five younger sisters who often demanded comfort over one thing or another.

Something familiar about her delicate profile niggled at the edges of his memory. He tried to imagine her face with color in her cheeks and animation in her expression.

Had he nodded to her on the street? Or perhaps even met her once?

The arrival of two physicians, from opposite directions, put an end to his speculations over her identity. A quick, assessing scan of the two men decided him in favor of the one more humbly dressed, whose ungloved hands were clean but showed signs of having done actual work. "Do what you can for her," he demanded.

Then, taking the other physician by the elbow, he led him—older, portlier, almost certainly costlier—up the steps and into his foyer, where the fainting lady sat in the nearer of two Chippendale chairs. The chairs were positioned on either side of a demilune table, over which hung a pier glass already draped in holland cloth in preparation for his departure. The cloth also thankfully disguised a bit of the faded wallpaper behind. The chairs, too, had been covered; one still was. He supposed the lady's maid had swept the dust cover aside for her mistress's comfort.

"This lady witnessed the accident and was taken ill from the shock," he explained to the doctor.

She had recovered enough to be eyeing Alistair with speculative curiosity, making him suddenly aware that crouching over the injured young woman in the street had left scuffs on his boots and mud on one knee of his pantaloons. Doubtless such a sight would have given his valet palpitations.

Fortunate, then, that he employed no such person.

"I rang for tea," the maid explained. "But no one answered the bell."

"You've caught us in the midst of closing up the

house for the winter," he said. "I suppose, amidst all the bustle, none of the servants heard. Allow me."

He strode to the back of the house and downstairs to the kitchen, which was empty. The servants had left that morning, the housekeeper and one maid for Devonshire, the rest to other posts in Town. He was meant to follow the next day, with the last of his books and personal things.

But first, he would surrender the key to his solicitor, who had found a tenant for Haythorne House for the winter. And the spring. For as long as they would take it, in fact; Alistair could no longer bear the expense of a London residence.

The tenants were a man—most would balk at the term *gentleman*, as he had made his fortune in trade—and his wife and their only child, a daughter of eighteen, who was to enjoy her first London Season, "once the house has been fitted up in the proper style," the solicitor had added rather sheepishly. Assorted craftsmen were to begin work first thing in the morning.

It was unusual, certainly, to allow a tenant to redecorate. But Alistair saw no reason to doubt the merchant's wife's taste; anything would be an improvement on the house's current state of genteel shabbiness.

Alistair's only hesitation, and it had been a slight one, was whether he mightn't be better served by staying in Town himself and courting the girl, who was rumored to have the sort of dowry that washed away a man's troubles and made him forget whence the money had come.

But in the end, he had decided in favor of Rylemoor Abbey with his sisters. Mrs. Swetley, the housekeeper, had protested the thought of his spending even one night in the house without servants. Alistair, who had craved a rare evening of silence, had countered with a promise to dine at a chophouse, rather than light a fire in the stove himself.

Which made the offer of tea rather difficult to fulfill. Less because of the lack of fire than the lack of tea leaves. If Mrs. Swetley had left any in the house at all, she would have left them under lock and key—and taken the key with her.

But Mrs. Swetley, it seemed, had anticipated some sort of emergency. She'd left the tea service on a table in the kitchen, covered by a linen cloth, with a spirit lamp and sufficient tea for two brewings, if he were frugal. And while Alistair was not in the habit of making his own tea, he certainly understood the necessity of frugality.

By the time he ascended the stairs again, tea tray in hand, more than a quarter of an hour had passed. He returned to a foyer not markedly different from when he had left it, although someone had also uncovered the pier glass so the lady could assess whether her faint had done irreparable damage to either her coiffure or her bonnet. Her maid relieved him of the tea tray, deposited it on the table, and poured a cup for both the physician and her mistress.

He had intended the second cup for her, but no matter.

"I say, sir," said the lady, in a voice whose haughtiness suggested she had fully recovered from her earlier bout of delicacy, "are you alone in the house?"

"What an unusual question, ma'am." He glanced

around the increasingly crowded foyer; in his absence, they had been joined by the coachman and another burly fellow. So much for his evening of quiet. "I hope a gentleman might be excused for wondering what prompted you to ask it."

That reply earned him a hard look along the not insubstantial length of the woman's nose. She reminded him of his aunt Josephine. "For one thing, a *gentleman* does not fetch his own tea." She punctuated the sentence with the soft *clink* of china against china, as she returned her cup squarely to its saucer. "And for another . . ."

The physician, having made quick work of his own cup, was now fastening the clasps of his leather satchel. "It wouldn't do to leave the girl here unchaperoned."

"The . . . girl?"

At that moment, the second physician appeared in the doorway of the library, wiping his hands on his handkerchief. "I wasn't sure what else to do with her, sir. These two"—he nodded toward the driver and the other man—"helped me carry her in."

"Were you able to rouse her?"

The younger doctor hesitated for a moment before shaking his head. "Not to speak of, no. She took quite a knock to the head." Alistair tried to read the man's expression. Did he have his doubts she would ever come around? Did he expect her brains would be scrambled if she did?

He handed over a small vial, wrapped in crinkly paper that revealed its contents as surely as any print upon the label could: laudanum. "No bones broken, as best I can tell. But internal injuries are more difficult to assess. At the very least, she'll be sore when she wakes. And likely . . . confused."

"How am I to—? Surely, you don't mean to—?" As he dropped the little bottle into his coat pocket, Alistair glanced around to discover that the coachman and the other fellow had slipped out, and the other physician was hard on their heels.

"It's here or a hospital, sir," said the younger doctor, pocketing his dirty handkerchief, his voice matter-of-fact. And a hospital, as anyone of sense knew, was as good as a death sentence for an unidentified and unconnected young woman in her condition.

"Who is to nurse her?" Alistair could not keep the note of bewilderment from his voice as he watched the physician slip his arms into his coat, clearly preparing to depart. Alistair was reminded of his own intention—nay, the necessity—of vacating Haythorne House first thing in the morning.

"If, as I take it, you're a bachelor gentleman, and there are concerns over propriety," he said as he tipped his head toward the grande dame, "perhaps that lady, or her maid—"

"Certainly not!" exclaimed that lady, straightening her rather bedraggled bonnet. "The gentleman claims to have a legion of servants hiding belowstairs. I daresay they'll manage." She took her maid by the upper arm and all but pushed her toward the door.

"Stay a moment," Alistair insisted, but to no avail. The lady and her maid swept out, and the young physician slipped past him, too, refusing payment for his services. Another moment and Alistair was alone again.

Or as good as. In his library, the young woman lay perfectly quiet, her eyes closed, her head propped on the arm of the worn velvet settee in lieu of a pillow, her body still mostly covered by his greatcoat. The physician had unbuttoned her pelisse and removed her torn gloves and her muddy ankle boots. Her right wrist was bandaged and there was a plaster on her cheek, but he could see little other change in her condition.

A draft of cold air alerted him to the fact that no one had bothered to close the front door. When he stepped to it, he discovered a boy standing on the uppermost step, his outstretched arms sagging beneath an indistinguishable burden. "She dropped these when she, er, fell," he said, eager to off-load the battered bundle of what looked to be carpet and kindling. "An' I found these in the street where she'd been," he added, adding a broken and twisted bit of metal and glass to the top of the pile once he had deposited it into Alistair's hands.

Spectacles. She'd been wearing spectacles. That shadow of memory flickered across his mind's eye once again but disappeared before he could prod it into some recognizable shape.

"Wait a moment," he told the boy, then turned to place what he'd collected on the nearby chair. He fished in his waistcoat pocket, glancing past the lad into the encroaching twilight. Afternoon was giving way to evening. He dropped three coins onto the child's mittened palm. "Go to the Barley Mow and fetch round some dinner for me. And—and beef tea for the lady," he added, though it felt like a futile gesture, to provide nourishment for one who thus far had shown no sign of regaining consciousness.

The boy's eyes widened at the sum with which he'd been entrusted. "Aye, guv."

Alistair closed the door behind him and leaned against it for a moment, warily regarding the pile on the chair of what remained of her possessions. With something like a sigh of resignation, he pushed himself upright, carried the items into his library and deposited them in the middle of his otherwise empty desk, then set about lighting candles against the deepening gloom. The woman never stirred.

He started with the mangled spectacles, though what they might tell him he could not imagine. One lens was gone, the other cracked, a spiderweb of fractures branching out from the upper-right corner. The opposite earpiece was bent downward, like the handle of a lorgnette. From the lad's description, she must have landed atop them when she fell.

He held them up, regarding her through the cracked lens, trying to imagine them on her nose, how they might change the look of her face. He raised and lowered them twice, three times, before realizing that the spectacles did not distort his view of her in any way. The glass was—he fetched a book from a nearby crate and studied the print through it to be sure—why, the glass was clear!

Carefully, he laid the spectacles aside, puzzling over why any young lady, especially a reasonably pretty one, would wear them if they weren't needed, and turned his attention to the next item: a battered carpet valise, which did not look to him as if it had been in the finest shape before the accident. It bore all the hallmarks—scuffed corners, worn handles, a fraying seam—of a bag that had traveled many, many miles. Reluctantly, he withdrew its contents: two dresses, of much the same quality as the one she wore, or as he imagined it had been when she had donned it that morning; undergarments, unharmed but wrinkled, and nothing a man with seven sisters hadn't seen dangling from the washing line or draped haphazardly over a clothes press; and another, somewhat less practical, pair of shoes.

Thinking the bag empty, he moved to lay it aside. But it weighed more than an empty bag ought. Upon further investigation, he found a small compartment beneath what had seemed to be the valise's bottom. In it were tucked a letter, obviously old and often read, and a rectangular leather case, like the sort that contained a small picture.

He hesitated over them. These two items were things she had obviously wanted to keep secret, given that they had been hidden. He didn't like to pry. But until the young lady woke, which he was beginning to doubt she would ever do, he had no other means of discovering anything about her situation or her history.

He opened the letter enough to discover that the salutation had been torn off—a fact that only increased his interest.

He glanced down the page, as if reading quickly lessened the intrusion on her privacy. A letter of parting, full of the sort of regretful effusions that might have some meaning to the person to whom they were addressed, but which told him little enough. A feminine hand, he thought, the ink faded with age. The letter broke off in mid-sentence, as if a second page had gone missing. Nothing to identify either the sender or the recipient, not even a date. Nothing at all to help him in his quest to identify the young woman.

He folded the letter again and set it aside.

Could the picture prove more helpful? With his thumb, he flicked open the clasp on the case to reveal a portrait of a young woman with red-gold hair tumbling over her shoulders. Not a painting of the young woman lying in a similar posture on the sofa opposite, though there was a resemblance.

Enough of a resemblance that a blush heated his cheeks.

The portrait was a nude. Skillfully done—*artistic*, one felt obligated to say. Though from the way the brushstrokes caressed the woman's curves, Alistair had a hunch the artist had not been entirely free from lascivious interest in his subject.

He closed the case and laid it near the letter and the useless spectacles.

That left the pile of kindling—which had once been a box, he determined upon further investigation, now spattered with ink. Ruined paintbrushes and glass shards and broken ends of pencils stuck out from the wreckage at odd angles. Evidently it had been a case for art supplies.

So, the mystery woman was an artist?

"Better and better . . ." he muttered beneath his breath.

He moved pieces out of the way until he came to a stack of partially finished sketches, the uppermost rendered illegible by spilled ink. The next sheet, protected by the first, bore the outline of a pen-and-ink sketch in a style he had seen before. A cartoon, really. A caricature of the fashionable set, contemptuous of their clothing, their conversation.

Just left of center in the scene stood a dark-haired gentleman with a dour expression, ill-suited to the occasion. *He* looked very familiar indeed, as well he should—Alistair faced him in the mirror over his washstand every morning.

Where and when the artist had seen him in anything resembling such a situation or such a pose, he couldn't guess. But now he knew when and where he had seen *her*.

He peered over the top of the paper at the figure beyond, sleeping, perhaps never to wake.

"Miss C.," he murmured. "We meet again."

Chapter 3

Alistair had met her, briefly, in the spring of that same year. He had accompanied his friend Miles, Viscount Deveraux, on the sort of outing that might have seemed ordinary to rakish Miles, but which Alistair would always remember as an adventure: a breakneck ride from Hertfordshire to London—chasing after a girl, of course. Miles's second reluctant fiancée of the Season.

At the end of the journey, a discovery had awaited them. Miles's name was once more to appear in the scandal sheets. The author of the piece had been Miles's bride-to-be, Miss Daphne Burke—who, as it had turned out, was also the advice columnist for *Goode's Guide to Misconduct*. Alistair's sisters were faithful readers of the notorious periodical, despite his protests.

And this time, the exposure of Miles's rakishness was to be accompanied by a less than flattering illustration of *that devil, Deveraux*. The artist had been none other than the hand behind the magazine's monthly mocking cartoon, "What Miss C. Saw."

None other than the young woman now lying before him.

Miles and Alistair had intercepted the scandal sheet at the printing house before the damage had been irreversible. And after an explanation—and an embrace—had set all to rights between Miles and the author, it had fallen to Alistair to accompany the artist home.

Half an hour alone with her in Miles's curricle ought to have been sufficient time to discover something about Miss C. Her name, for instance. Where she'd come from. How she had joined the staff of *Mrs. Goode's Magazine for Misses*.

Why he—dull, generally inoffensive Alistair Haythorne—had been a frequent target of her satirical pencil.

But asking questions was an awkward business, and Miss C. had not been forthcoming on her own.

The only information she'd imparted had offered no more of a clue about her identity than that old letter. Her few words had been quietly and coolly spoken; above the rattle of wheels and the noise of the street, he had heard too little of her voice even to speculate about her accent. She had instructed him to deposit her in the vicinity of Bond and Oxford Streets, a bustling shopping district into whose impersonal throngs she had quickly disappeared.

He hadn't liked to leave her there, unaccompanied and unchaperoned. But she had seemed to regard her independence as unremarkable. Whether she lived nearby with her family in one of the elegant mansions of Mayfair or alone in a room above a shop he would never know. At least, not without prying in a most ungentlemanlike manner.

Now, though, what choice did he have but to pry?

Laying aside the cartoon, he explored the remaining pieces of half-completed artwork. The deeper he went into the pile, the better the pictures had fared in the accident, their style varied but the hand that had made them invariably skillful.

Her hand?

The available evidence pointed to one conclusion: Miss C. was an extraordinarily capable artist, whether working in pen-and-ink, watercolors, or oils. But that only begged another question. Why would someone with such a gift squander it on satirical sketches for the *Magazine for Misses*?

Alistair knew of one person who might be able to answer that question, other than the artist herself. In their quest to find Miles's fiancée, he and Miles had inquired of Miss Burke's chaperone, Lady Stalbridge, and been directed to the *Magazine for Misses*' printer by Lady Stalbridge's stepson, Lord Manwaring. Manwaring had admitted that Lady Stalbridge knew Mrs. Goode. Impossible not to speculate that she might in fact *be* Mrs. Goode. But of course Alistair had never acted on those speculations or vouchsafed that secret to another soul. To have done so would have been very bad *ton*, and Alistair was no gossip. It was one reason he and Miles, so different in most every respect, had been able to rub along so well for so many years.

Truth be told, despite Alistair's vocal misgivings

about the magazine whenever he happened upon a copy, the identity of Mrs. Goode was a matter of supreme indifference to him. His three youngest sisters—Lady Frederica, Lady Georgiana, and Lady Harriet Haythorne, known in the family as Freddie, Georgie, and Harry— had been just shy of unmanageable long before *Goode's Guide to Misconduct* had come on the scene.

But if Lady Stalbridge, or Mrs. Goode, also knew Miss C., what choice did Alistair have but to make use of a connection he ought properly to have forgotten? The packed valise and artist's case, the sturdy shoes and woolen dress, all hinted at a woman undertaking a journey. Running away from home? Why, at this very moment, Miss C.'s family might be frantic with worry, with no notion of what had become of her.

He scrounged up a half sheet of paper, dipped his quill, and scratched out a few lines of explanation and inquiry, worded in such a way that he hoped would not reveal more than either Miss C. or Lady Stalbridge would like.

The seal had only just hardened when he heard a rap on the outer door. He went to answer it and found the lad returned with the food. Another coin from Alistair's waistcoat pocket, almost the last. Another set of instructions, and the boy was on his way to Berkeley Square with the letter, while Alistair returned to the library and sat down to his dinner.

Not that he had much appetite. Nor did his desk make a terribly genial dining room, though this was not the first occasion on which he had resorted to it.

Tonight, however, his attention was all for the figure reclined on the little sofa on the other side of the room.

Was it his imagination—his misplaced hope—that a hint of color had returned to her face? Perhaps it was nothing more than the reflected glow of candlelight.

But no, her breathing was steadier too. Deeper. With a sigh, he pushed away his plate, rose, and approached the settee, his thoughts a jumble of concern and frustration and perhaps even a flash of irritation.

Readers of the magazine had dubbed Miss C.'s cartoons the Unfashionable Plates. It was true that Alistair was often careless about what he wore. He had no aspirations to join Beau Brummell's set, that dandy who seemed to imagine the funds for fine tailoring grew on trees. But Alistair was hardly alone in his indifference to fashion, and certainly not the only gentleman without a fortune to go along with his title. What had he done to draw Miss C.'s eye—to say nothing of her ire?

Last spring, he had not even ventured to ask her.

Now he wondered whether he would have another chance.

He stood looking down at her. Her hair was all in a tangle, as one might expect, given her ordeal—though he remembered it having been rather disordered the first time he had seen her too. Its tendency to curl—*to frizz*, his sisters would have said—made it rather ungovernable, he supposed.

The Miss C. of last spring had carried herself with the air of a woman who would bristle at the notion of being governed.

Well, and look where that independent streak had

got her. Once more, he brushed a few strands of hair away from her face, carefully avoiding her bruised and bandaged cheek.

Last spring, he hadn't suspected how soft those curls were. As fine as copper-colored silk.

He hadn't noted that scattering of freckles before either. The spectacles had disguised them, he supposed. Her eyelashes were fair, but thick enough to cast a wispy shadow over her cheekbones.

Was that a flicker of movement? Or only a trick of the light?

Another rap at the front door distracted him. He opened it to find the now-familiar boy, who thrust a note into his hands with a sharp nod before disappearing into the rapidly thickening gloom. Alistair returned to the study and broke the seal on the letter—his own letter, refolded and resealed. Beneath his query a few lines had been added in Lady Stalbridge's elegant script.

I regret to say that I can be of little assistance. Mrs. G. has reason to believe that the name Miss C. provided to her is a false one, and we know nothing of her family. We are glad to know that she is in your capable care, however, as her precipitous flight and other circumstances hint that the young lady may be in some danger.

He sank down onto the crate nearest the settee and read the note twice more. Words leaped out at him.

Danger and *false* and, most alarming of all, *capable care*. He was practically penniless and alone in an almost empty house.

What had he to offer a damsel in distress?

The phrase brought a little snort of wry laughter to his lips. Miss C., he felt certain, would not appreciate it—neither the label nor his laughter.

Tossing aside the paper, he took her uninjured hand between both of his. The beds of her nails were paint-stained, her fingers roughened by frequent scrubbing. Not the hand of a lady. Absently, he chafed his thumb across her knuckles.

We know nothing of her family.

The young lady may be in some danger.

Had the terrible accident with the carriage been no accident after all?

Had she been running from something? Some*one*?

Last spring, he had dismissed her as a frowsy spinster who had taken an irrational dislike to him—no, to his *appearance*. She didn't know *him*.

Now, having seen the pictures in her artist's case, having glimpsed skills far beyond those of Mrs. Goode's satirical cartoonist, he felt a flicker of regret at the realization he might never know her.

He thought of the portrait hidden in the bottom of her valise. Too old to be her own work. But precious to her, for some reason. Miss C. was a woman with a secret. A woman who guarded even her name. Mrs. Goode believed that the name by which she knew her was a fabrication. But Miss *C.* . . . surely there was some clue in that?

"Charlotte?" he ventured, searching her slack face for some hint of reaction. "Caroline?" Still nothing. He patted the back of her hand. "Christine?"

Useless, really. He might run through dozens of names without striking on the proper one. And what if it were the first initial of her surname instead? After all, Miles's bride, the former Miss Burke, had written under the name "Miss Busy B." Surnames beginning with *C* were legion indeed.

Still, he felt compelled to try. "Miss Cleves?" he called out in a singsong voice, the sort one used to wake a sleeping child. "Oh, Miss Crawford! Dear Miss Camden."

Nothing.

What in God's name was he to do?

Tomorrow, his tenants expected the key to an empty house. He tried to picture their reaction to finding an injured and unconscious young woman sprawled on the settee in the library.

No, he couldn't leave her, of course. But the alternative—taking her with him to Rylemoor—seemed equally ill-advised. Carting her across the country in a jouncing coach was worse than any hospital—and might just constitute kidnapping.

"Oh, my dear Miss Clara Cartwright," he exclaimed, increasing the volume of his voice and patting the back of her hand more vigorously, "you simply must wake up."

Again, that flicker of shadow beneath her eyes, so faint he put it down to his imagination.

Well, at the very least, he could make her more comfortable. She was tall, almost as tall as he, and the angle

of her head against the arm of the settee was giving his
own neck an empathetic crick.

He stood and peeled away his greatcoat to reveal
her slender form. A reticule—it had perhaps been
dangling from her injured wrist—lay nestled in her lap.
He picked it up to place it with the rest of her things,
noting its heft and then recalling for no particular reason
how when Harry was a little girl, she had often stuffed
hers with rocks.

Miss C.'s practical, almost coarse, woolen dress, he
decided as he slid his arms beneath her shoulders
and knees, was just one more layer to her disguise, for
the figure it hid was, like her hair, softer than he had
expected. Standing, he cradled her against his chest.
Despite his annoyance with some of her artistic choices,
he could not help feeling a surge of protectiveness at her
current vulnerable state.

The slightest whimper eased from her lungs as he
started toward the stairs, but she gave no other indication of waking. He thought of the physician's parting
words about her injuries; perhaps he ought not to have
tried to move her. But surely a bed was the proper place
for an invalid.

Two floors above, arms aching and suitably winded,
he toed open the door to his own suite of rooms and the
last bed in the house that had not been stripped of its
linens. It was a spartan chamber, even without the evidence of his imminent departure. But the mattress was
soft. He deposited her on the center of the bed, covered
her with the quilted counterpane, and turned to light a
fire in the hearth.

Its crackle and snap at first muffled the sounds of movement behind him. The more convinced he became that what he heard *could* be noises of wakefulness, the more reluctant he grew to turn and reveal them once again to be the products of nothing but his own fancy.

"Where—? Who—?" The mumbled questions were quiet, laced with confusion and edged with pain.

He spun on his heel to face her. She was trying to lift her head from the pillow and wincing with the effort it required. "You're alive!"

Confusion streaked across her face. Then, as the firelight illuminated his features, a flare of what could only be recognition. And finally, her eyes squeezed shut and she slumped against the pillows once more.

Chapter 4

Constantia had a headache. Not a garden-variety headache either; not the sort caused by concentrating too long on one detail of a sketch or forgetting to open a window when mixing paints. Not even a megrim. This pain was bone-deep. No, deeper. As if her very brain was bruised.

And not just her brain either. Every bit of her hurt, from her hair to her toes . . . She wiggled them experimentally. The movement made her wince and also wonder:

When had she taken off her shoes?

She remembered lacing up her ankle boots, knowing she had a long walk ahead of her, though she hadn't the faintest notion, now, where she'd been headed.

Or where she'd ended up.

The tips of her toes brushed against the covers, and she dared to crack one eye. Yes, definitely a bed. Not *her* bed, however.

Which made the prospect of a dark-haired man approaching her as she lay in that bed all the more alarming.

Especially when that man was the Earl of Ryland.

Of all the rotten, no-good luck . . .

They had met face-to-face only once, but she had observed him at other times, trying but never succeeding to make sense of a fundamental inconsistency in his character. Ryland kept close company with Viscount Deveraux, the most notorious rake in all of Christendom. Yet he dressed and behaved and spoke as stodgily as a clergyman who considered style a sin.

In public, he abstained from vice, or even much in the way of comfort, but obviously, given his choice of friends, he must indulge in private, or at least smile on those who did. Since he was a titled nobleman and not unattractive, the most likely explanation for the disparity was that he shared his friend's rakish proclivities but did not want the world to know.

Perhaps it was hypocritical of her to be bothered by another person pretending to be someone he wasn't. But a duplicitous man could do untold damage to others, while she only lied about her identity to keep herself safe.

Of all the people Constantia did not trust, she did not trust two-faced men the most.

Flight, though instinctive, was out of the question. Her painful limbs recoiled at the prospect, and she had to settle for shrinking back into the pillow and squeezing shut her eyes, praying that he did not notice that slight movement.

Her luck, it seemed, had not improved.

She listened to his footfalls against the carpet, counting the steps until he reached the bed, then willed herself to limpness when he picked up her hand where it lay against the coverlet and patted it vigorously. "No, Miss C. Don't go back to sleep." She longed for the strength to jerk her fingers away, to resist even that gentle command. "I know it's tempting, but you've had quite a blow to the head, and I think it would be better for you to stay awake."

A blow to the head? Well, that would explain the dreadful ache. But . . . "How?"

Even to her own ears, which were ringing, the question sounded muffled. Almost indecipherable.

Decipher it he did, however. "How did you hit your head? An accident. Onlookers said you darted into the roadway from an alley and met with a passing carriage. A wonder you weren't struck by a wheel. Or trampled beneath the horses' hooves. But it must have been a glancing blow—knocked you down, onto the cobblestones. Physician says you haven't broken any bones, at least, though your wrist may be sprained."

She remembered none of it. Even in her current state, she was appalled by her own carelessness. Darting into the roadway? Without looking? "Why?" she managed, though her jaw ached, too—she must have clamped her teeth together when she fell.

"Why? That's a question I can't answer, I'm afraid. It seems as if you were in a hurry and weren't looking where you were going. Or do you mean, why did you fall? Because that would be a question for Sir Isaac Newton." He had the nerve to chuckle. "You know, *gravity* . . ." He sat down beside her, still clutching her hand, and she winced again at the dipping of the mattress. "I'm sorry. This is no time for jokes."

No, it bloody well isn't.

Though one corner of her mouth wanted to quirk all the same. The feebleness of his attempt at humor somehow made it even more amusing.

Evidence he could wield rakish charm when he chose?

Refusing to reward him with even the wryest of smiles, she countered the involuntary twitch of her lips by screwing her eyes more tightly shut, as if that could block out the sound of his voice. She had the vaguest memory of running . . . running away . . . but from what?

Pain was a wall between the present and the recent past, and she hadn't the strength to scale it.

"Fortunately," he went on, his tone and his touch gentle, "the accident happened in a place where you have friends."

Friends.

So he *had* recognized her.

Worse and worse.

She recalled Lord Ryland's stubborn insistence, last spring, in seeing her home, when she had been perfectly content to hail a cab—and when her "home" was the last place she'd wanted him to see.

After that day—and the cartoons she'd drawn of him—how could he possibly imagine they were . . .

"*Friends?*" she echoed, intending to convey her skepticism at such a description.

But when pushed from between clenched teeth and

parched lips, the word came out sounding . . . uncertain. Confused.

"Don't you remember me?" A laugh, dry as dust. With it, he somehow managed to convey both incredulity and self-deprecation. "That is, I—I felt certain you would . . ." Now a pleading note edged his words, and in her astonishment, she could not resist another glance at him. "I'd swear that a moment ago, I saw a flash of recognition in your eyes."

His own eyes were dark, searching, and more than a little desperate. She had to dip her chin to avoid the intensity of his gaze.

The gesture seemed to persuade him he'd been wrong. He paused, evidently gathering his wits, before continuing in a calmer voice. "I suppose it's not to be wondered at, after that blow to the head." The bed shifted again as he rose, though he did not release her hand. "Ryland, at your service."

Then she felt his breath on her knuckles and realized he was bowing over her hand. The sort of utterly ridiculous, mock chivalrous nonsense one might expect of a rogue.

So she supposed it was no great surprise she found herself, in her present weakened state, ever so slightly charmed.

She shut her eyes again, though an outline of the image remained etched on her eyelids for a moment. The fire behind him had limned his figure in gold.

He had a better profile than she remembered from that awkward ride across Town. One might be almost tempted to describe it as handsome.

Doubtless, that impulse was merely an effect of the flattering firelight and her own addled vision.

"And you," he went on, releasing her hand. ". . . Well, perhaps it would be easier to show you."

He was gone before she could explain or protest.

In his absence, she took stock of matters as best she could:

1. No matter how badly her head hurt . . . or her wrist . . . or any other part of her body . . . if what Lord Ryland had said was true, she was lucky to be alive.

2. But she was alive in a bed in the home of the one man in London with whom she had the misfortune of a prior acquaintance.

3. That prior acquaintance seemed to have behaved with propriety so far, but she was certain he hid a devilish nature. She counted herself lucky to be still dressed, though the missing shoes might pose an obstacle to her escape.

4. And speaking of escape . . . the accident had befallen her because she had been hurrying, he'd said. To something? Or away from something? It must have been something big and important enough to make her careless. But what?

He returned before she had a prayer of answering that question. In one hand, he clutched a sheaf of papers, and in the other, a valise. *Her* valise. Whatever her destination, she'd packed a bag . . .

"When the, uh, the accident happened, you must have been carrying this." He lifted the battered satchel and deposited it at the foot of the bed. "And you had an artist's traveling case too. It didn't fare well against the cobblestones, I'm afraid. These sketches are all that survived," he explained, rather sheepishly, as he started to hand them to her, then paused. "Unless you require your spectacles for this?"

"My—spectacles?" She reached up as if expecting to find them still on her nose. If she had thought of them at all, she would have assumed—*hoped* might be the better word—they had been lost during the accident. Otherwise, the plain glasses lenses might have aroused his suspicions. "No. I, um, I see close up well enough without them."

"Good," he said, handing over the pictures, though still with a hint of reluctance. "Because they're broken too."

Relieved, she began to shuffle through what he'd given her and soon lighted on a sketch of him in a less than flattering pose.

The sort of pose in which she'd always drawn him, since that day she'd first seen him and chosen him for her model of a typical nobleman, roguish to the core but trying to trick Society by donning the air of a staid and stuffy gentleman of virtue.

Suddenly, she understood what had motivated the question about her spectacles. He must wonder whether the keen eye behind these sketches had seen through his straitlaced front.

When she tilted her chin upward, as if comparing him to his likeness, he cleared his throat and snatched up two or three of the pieces she'd laid aside.

"You—you're an artist, as you can see," he said, nervously placing them on top of the sketch she was holding uppermost, the picture of him. "Of no small ability. You illustrate a periodical called *Mrs. Goode's Magazine for Misses*, under the name 'Miss C.' We met, once, because of it." He gave a grudging nod toward the papers, acknowledging the picture of him. "But I'm afraid I can't offer much more in the way of enlightenment."

"Enlightenment?" she echoed.

"I can't tell you more about yourself, who you are, not even what the *C* stands for, because . . . well, you didn't say."

Oh. Oh, dear.

He didn't just imagine that Constantia had forgot *him* when she'd hit her head.

He imagined she'd forgot *herself*—even her own name!

He left the bedside and returned to the fireplace, as if what came next made it advisable to put a bit more distance between them. "We do have a mutual acquaintance. The Countess of Stalbridge. She is, uh, connected in some way to Mrs. Goode. I took the liberty of writing to her about your . . . situation."

Little flickers of memory began to penetrate the fog that had settled over her mind. There had been a meeting of the magazine staff . . . She recalled a room. A table. Alarm coursed through her, though its root cause was still shrouded in mystery.

"And what did this Lady Stalbridge say?" she prompted, momentarily grateful for the discomfort that let her disguise the anxious clench of her teeth as pain.

"Very little. That she did not know your real name either. And that . . ."

"Yes?"

His next words required effort. "That she believed you to be in danger."

The final word crashed around inside her like her artist's case against the street, until it was dashed to pieces and nothing but jagged edges remained. All at once, she remembered. There'd been a letter. A pile of letters. Hand addressed with their names and directions. Someone knew. Someone was after her—after all of them. She had left the meeting and run . . .

The realization sent papers flying as she tossed aside the coverlet and scrambled to sit upright and thrust her legs out of bed. "I have to—"

"Certainly not." He stepped toward her.

The whole room spun, and kept right on spinning, even after she closed her eyes. "No," she mumbled, part resistance, but mostly reluctant agreement. A whole battalion was taking target practice in her head.

Then his hands were on her shoulders, bearing her back to the welcome softness of the pillow. His cologne, a woodsy scent that no doubt made all the young ladies swoon when they got close, filled her nostrils.

She wanted, quite irrationally, to draw a deeper breath.

"If you're in danger—"

She was. She couldn't remember a time when she hadn't been. And at present, with a man pinning her to a bed, her danger seemed only to be increasing.

Then, to her shock, he shot upright and withdrew his hands.

"—then you must consider yourself under my protection."

The protection of the Earl of Ryland? She wanted to laugh.

But his voice was serious and warm, comforting in spite of her instinct never to trust.

"At least," he went on, "until you get your memory back."

Her memory. A chill settled over her, restoring her to herself. He'd taken pity on her, in spite of her drawings of him. But whenever she revealed that she knew who she was . . . well, then she would be out on the street.

Given that she presently couldn't even stand up on her own, she obviously needed time to recuperate, and also time to formulate a plan for getting away and covering her tracks. Again.

Any way she looked it, she was at his mercy. And she didn't dare tell him the truth.

"That's very kind of you, sir," she gritted out. "To let me stay here, until I recover."

An expression flitted across his face—a gracious smile, or at least an attempt at one, undermined by an awkward tension. He backed away from the bed and retreated to his post at the hearth, where he busied himself once more with prodding unnecessarily at the fire. When he spoke, he did not turn to face her. "That, um, that brings us to a small difficulty. The, uh, the fact of the matter is . . ." A thrust of the poker sent up a shower of sparks. "This house has been leased to someone else. My sisters are already gone into Devonshire and the household staff has dispersed. Every chamber but this one has been emptied of its furnishings, in preparation for some renovations."

Every chamber but this one . . . She glanced toward the window, at draperies she had, a moment ago, taken for rose pink. She'd assumed she'd been deposited in one of his sisters' rooms.

But if the fabric was merely faded . . . if those draperies had once been a deeper shade, scarlet or wine . . . then this might, she supposed, be a man's bedchamber.

His bedchamber, in other words.

And if that was the case, then . . . well . . . she was lying in his bed.

Somehow, that made matters even worse.

She dragged in a steadying breath. With it came the scent of him, lingering on the sheets. Something sparked along her spine, something she chose to call apprehension.

Gradually, the rest of his speech sifted through her aching head. No sisters. No servants. "Do you . . . do you mean to say we're here . . . alone?"

Her voice was as weak as the rest of her, the last word barely a whisper. Yet it rang in the room's stillness like the call of the night watch.

"I'm afraid so, yes. I do beg your pardon. And worse yet, first thing in the morning, my solicitor expects to retrieve the key for my tenants and workmen will begin to arrive."

She plucked uncertainly at the coverlet. "You're leaving. Tomorrow."

He didn't answer; it wasn't really a question. If the house had been leased, then of course he must vacate it.

And so, perforce, must she.

Though she would not have thought it possible a moment ago, her head began to throb harder. How would she manage on her own until she recovered? She had to wet her lips to get the next words past them.

"Wherever you're going, will you take me with you?"

The question astonished even her. Because, for almost as long as she could remember, she had relied on no one but herself.

She closed her eyes and waited for him to make another joke, to mock her predicament, to reject her desperate request.

"To Devonshire? That—that hardly seems wise."

She couldn't disagree.

"It's a long journey for someone in your condition. And besides, there must be someone here who will miss you. There must be somewhere better for you to go," he insisted, though his voice was gentle. "Lady Stalbridge, perhaps—"

Sharply, she shook her head and instantly regretted the movement. The fresh stab of pain made her stomach roil. Given the imminent exposure of everyone associated with the magazine, Lady Stalbridge had trouble enough to be getting on with, without Constantia visiting more upon her doorstep.

Sensing her discomfort, he did not complete the thought. The fire crackled, filling the silence.

"Supposing even that I were willing to take you so far, how would we explain to everyone . . . ?" He didn't finish the thought, but she knew what he meant nonetheless.

How would they explain—to his family, the servants, anyone they met along the way—who she was, where she'd come from, and what she was doing in the company of the Earl of Ryland?

Excellent questions—perhaps her supposed inability to answer them, even for herself, would prove useful. In any case, she took comfort from them, and from the note of uncertainty in his voice. They meant he was considering the matter. She had to get away from London, and he might yet prove persuadable.

"You . . . you mentioned sisters? Younger sisters?" she asked, though she knew the answer.

"The youngest is not sixteen."

"Still a teachable age, then."

He made a noise that might have been a snort of laughter.

She gathered up the sketches now scattered across the bed, the movement made more difficult by her bandaged wrist. "Could you—would you employ me as you sister's drawing master?"

The suggestion made a muscle twitch along his jaw, as if he had gritted his teeth. Nevertheless, he appeared to consider the matter for a moment, then shook himself brusquely as if to drive the idea further off. "Even if it were possible, there is still the matter of traveling nearly two hundred miles together."

Unchaperoned.

He did not speak the word aloud.

He did not have to.

"Surely two persons situated such as we find ourselves need not be concerned overmuch with propriety. Without a name, what reputation have I to lose?" She carefully did not raise the issue of any potential loss of virtue, not wishing to give him ideas. "And surely you cannot think I would do anything to damage yours?"

One dark brow shot up, and he looked pointedly at the papers in her lap, the unflattering sketch she'd made of him unfortunately uppermost. "Is that so, Miss C.?" he asked, a wry edge to the words.

Warmth prickled her cheeks. "You've really no idea what the *C* stands for?" It was a bald attempt to deflect his attention from the picture, to manage his displeasure.

It was also a genuine question. He hadn't asked her name last spring, that much she recalled—or at least, he hadn't asked *her*. But with very little difficulty, he could have uncovered the name by which she was known at the magazine.

"None, I'm afraid."

She believed him, which meant that he hadn't asked anyone else, either—not Lady Stalbridge nor Miss Burke, now Lady Deveraux and the wife of his good friend.

Constantia had drawn Lord Ryland half a dozen

times since that day, at least, but she seemed to have inspired very little curiosity in him.

"It's not merely the fact of our traveling together," he explained after a moment, returning to the previous subject against her will. "Though that would be unfortunate enough. It is the means by which we would undertake such a journey. I sent my sisters ahead in my traveling coach with my housekeeper, you see, while I—well, I intended to take a public conveyance. The, uh, the mail coach, in fact. But I can't ask it of you—certainly not in your condition."

She did not nod, but inwardly she agreed, not merely because of the discomfort involved, but mostly because to travel in such fashion would expose her dreadfully and leave her at the whims of those who wished her ill.

Then he drew a deep, fortifying breath before the next words rushed out. "And regretfully I must confess that I gave my sisters what little ready money I had, to ensure their comfort, and I do not have the funds at hand to secure another means of transportation."

She could have sworn he blushed at that, but his dismay could not have been greater than her own shock. No funds? A lack of money was, she supposed, what had prompted him to lease his house.

But why should an earl be poor? Had he gambled his fortune away? Did he keep six mistresses, one for every day but Sunday?

It was really no business of hers what Lord Ryland did with his money, of course. But at present, it had become her concern. What use was his offer of help if he hadn't a penny to his name?

Agitated, she shifted her feet beneath the coverlet, and something heavy slid from the bed and landed on the floor with a *thunk*.

Lord Ryland had resumed staring into the fire, but the sound roused him, and he turned to retrieve what had fallen.

"My reticule," she gasped when she saw it in his hands. Now she knew she'd truly been knocked senseless, for she hadn't once wondered about its whereabouts since she'd awakened.

Wordlessly he laid it beside the pictures on her lap. Relief surged through her. She picked it up and weighed it thoughtfully on her palm before unpicking the knot with the assistance of the fingertips of her bandaged hand and spilling some of its contents onto the bed.

Gold and silver coins gleamed in the firelight.

"Is it enough?"

"For what?" he asked hoarsely, his eyes fixed on the money like a starving man before a bakery window.

"To secure a private post chaise."

He nodded slowly, and then started, as if the movement of his own head had caught him off guard. "No, Miss C. That is to say, it would be more than sufficient, but I cannot accept—" He paused, cleared his throat. "I could, however, reserve a suite of rooms for you at the finest London hotel."

"I don't want to stay in London," she insisted. "Not alone." Until she was stronger, more sure of herself, better able to evade the dangers that surrounded her, she dared not risk her customary solitude, dared not rely on her well-honed independence. "And you wouldn't be accepting anything. You would merely be securing a mode of travel more suited to the comfort of an invalid."

Still, he hesitated, and she reached for the last tool at her disposal, the bluntest instrument of all, uncertain of its effect. How determined was Lord Ryland to play the gentleman?

"You did promise me your protection."

"I did." She heard hesitation, a questioning note in those words, as if he couldn't quite believe he'd made any such promise. Then he nodded once more, sharper this time, a sign of reluctant agreement. "I did. Until your memory returns." The caveat felt like a warning. "Rest now, and I'll see what arrangements can be made."

With a bow, he left her to the heavy silence of his bedchamber

Dear God, what had she been thinking to ask Lord Ryland of all people to take her away? She had put herself entirely into his hands.

His gentle, surprisingly strong hands.

She closed her eyes against the memory of his touch as worry and pain and a strange sense of relief tumbled over her in waves.

Chapter 5

A listair had some experience with young ladies who told untruths.

He had immediately seen through his sister Freddie's explanation for her ten minutes' absence during the Montlake ball—and her feigned surprise at his observation that Lord Cowell had been absent for the same interval. And after the girls' governess had left them for a better situation, he had known better than to put much stock in Harry's claim to still be studying her German every day.

He felt certain Miss C. was lying. About several things.

She remembered him. And herself. But she wouldn't admit to either. She was keeping secrets—her name, the little painting, and something more besides. Given that he suspected her of dishonesty, he would have been well within his rights to laugh off her suggestion of accompanying him to Rylemoor.

Three things had pointed him in the opposite direction.

The first was Lady Stalbridge's letter. The word *danger* still burned in his mind's eye like a brand.

The second was Miss C.'s obviously desperate state. The sight of her bruises and the bandaged wrist, along with the memory of her limp weight in his arms, were as difficult to brush aside as Lady Stalbridge's words.

The third was her invocation of his promise. Not, he was almost ashamed to admit it, the promise itself, though he generally prided himself on acting as a gentleman ought to act. But her expression as she'd reminded him of it . . . impossible to know, of course, where pleading ended and performance began. Still, he could tell it had cost her something to ask.

And if the disparity between the state of her belongings and the contents of her purse had told him anything about her at all, it was that she was accustomed to hoarding everything of value she possessed until she had no other choice but to surrender.

So, against what was probably his better judgment, he had done as she had suggested. He'd hired a coach and driver, both serviceable if a bit worn. He'd haphazardly finished sorting his belongings, overseen the loading of the last crates and trunks, and turned over the key to his house to his solicitor. And he'd urged her to accept three drops of laudanum in what had been an abominably weak cup of morning tea before assisting her into the carriage and signaling to John Coachman to be off.

She was lying now on the seat opposite, her legs curled to accommodate her height to the length of the forward-facing bench. One honey-colored curl had escaped its pins and fluttered with her breath as she slept through the first hours of their swaying, jolting journey.

Having hardly slept the night before, Alistair almost envied her repose. But a sense of unease, mingled with curiosity, kept him from closing his eyes.

Where had she acquired such a sum of money? Had she stolen it? Hocked the family jewels—or perhaps their paintings?

Done something more scandalous yet?

In spite of the potential for disaster, instead of insisting on the truth, he'd gone along with her wild scheme. He was taking her to his ancestral home, where she— a stranger with a sketchy past—would be in the company of at least four and probably more of his sisters for some indefinite tenure. Worst of all, he'd agreed to let her teach them to draw and paint.

He liked to think that he had done it out a sense of gentlemanly duty. Noblesse oblige, or some such stuff.

A less noble part of him was worried that he might have done it for the sake of his backside. Even a hired post chaise was preferable to the travails of being tossed about like so much Royal Mail.

And if a sliver of him had done it because he found Miss C. . . . . *intriguing*, well, it was only a sliver and didn't bear acknowledgment.

She slept through the first two changes of horses. He was glad to see it; she'd rested relatively peacefully the night before, too, which he knew because he'd checked on her three times, in between stuffing books in crates and pacing the entry hall. Her color had improved. And when they'd left the house, he had not needed to carry her. She'd walked away under her own power—leaning heavily on his arm and moving stiffly, to be sure, but without limping or other signs of pain.

If he had dozed, too—either the night before or during the first forty miles of their journey—then it could not have been for more than a few minutes. The pink of her cheeks and the bounce and flutter of that unruly curl were too familiar for them to have been out of his sight for long.

"Will you be studying me this intently for the next hundred and fifty miles?" she murmured as the next change of horses approached.

Her eyes were still closed—or appeared to be. Her question was the first hint he'd had that she might not be sleeping quite as soundly as he'd assumed.

"I beg your pardon." He dragged his gaze to the window, though a sleety sort of rain had rendered it all but opaque. Not that it mattered. He knew what lay beyond the glass as well as he knew the back of his own hand, having made the journey between the metropolis and Devon many, many times in his twenty-eight years.

A stretch of silence followed as she pushed herself into an upright position and made a futile attempt to neaten her hair. He did not look away from the murky window, but he was aware of her movements on the periphery of his vision and in the shadow of their reflection in the glass.

"It's I who should apologize," she said at last in a surprisingly conciliatory tone. "I daresay I've been guilty of the same at some point. I suppose artists must do more than their fair share of staring."

She spoke of her work as if she couldn't quite believe that the sketches he had shown her were her own.

"If it helps, I wasn't thinking about you," he replied, the slightest edge to his voice.

A tinkle of laughter broke from her lips. "I'm cut to the quick, Lord Ryland." It could not have been clearer that she did not believe him.

It was, he supposed, only fitting. After all, his answer hadn't been entirely truthful.

And he didn't believe her either.

"Well, perhaps I was thinking of you, indirectly." He turned his eyes from the gloomy landscape and settled them on her. "In truth, I was wondering what possessed me to go through with this mad scheme."

A momentary silence filled the carriage, broken only by the rumble of wheels and the creak of wood and iron and leather. Her bandaged right hand lay nestled in her lap, palm upward, fingers relaxed, but the other hand was tightly curled around the front of the seat, as if she were trying to counter the coach's unpredictable movements but not quite able to hold herself steady.

"And what conclusions did you reach?"

He gave it another minute of thought. "Chivalry?" The note of self-mockery in his voice was clear; it made one corner of her mouth kick up in a crooked smile.

Was crookedness its ordinary state, or an effect of her injuries? It pained him, somehow, not to know.

"Or perhaps curiosity," he added. "I really can't decide."

"Curiosity . . . about me?"

"About a great many things, Miss C."

Including myself.

That answer failed to satisfy, of course. He really had not intended that it should. The color rose to her cheeks, darkening that delightful array of freckles as well as the edge of the bruise that had begun to bloom beneath the plaster, and she snagged her lower lip between her teeth and began to gnaw.

As it turned out, making her feel worse did not make him feel any better.

"Or perhaps," he went on lightly, "I simply hoped that some portion of my sisters would acquire at least a single accomplishment they might tout to prospective suitors."

One eyebrow arced in disbelief.

She met his every attempt at humor with an expression that suggested she doubted his capacity for it. Evidently, she expected him to be as somber and sour in person as she made him appear in all her sketches. He weighed whether to be offended. Was that hint of incredulity at the notion he might have a sense of humor more proof that she remembered him? Or was it based solely on impressions formed during a few brief conversations over the last twelve or so hours?

"The daughters," she began and then corrected herself, "the *sisters* of an earl . . . haven't they numerous accomplishments?"

He considered for a moment. "That depends entirely on how such things are accounted. Danny has a smattering of Italian, which she uses to swear without Aunt Josephine comprehending it. Harry can catch a trout when even the most skilled angler would vow no fish were biting. As for Freddie and Georgie? Well, I suppose they *have* elevated troublemaking to an art form. So, accomplishments . . . of a sort. But no previous instruction in drawing—it was not an interest I thought desirable to encourage."

Miss C.'s eyes grew wider with each example. "Danny? Freddie?"

"Mm, yes. The Ladies Bernadette, Charlotte, Danielle, Edwina, Frederica, Georgiana, and Harriet Haythorpe." He ticked off the names on his gloved fingertips. "And no, I am not the eldest, though I am named after my father. I do believe he would have started the alphabet over again with sons, if he had been able to bring them into the world. Instead he had to content himself with Bernie, Charlie, Danny, Eddie, Freddie, Georgie, and Harry."

Her mouth popped ever so slightly open and a sound escaped that might have been "ah." Or "oh." Some non-committal noise conveying quite clearly that she didn't know how to react. She leaned forward, as if her next question were better asked in confidence. "And do they—are they all . . . under your care?"

She sounded as if she believed him incapable of caring for them . . . of caring, at all.

Or perhaps she was simply daunted by the prospect of having to teach seven pupils at once.

"The two eldest are married. Lady Brinks and the Honorable Mrs. Jefferson Powell, now. Eddie prefers country life and busies herself with managing the household at Rylemoor, which is why she rarely joins us in Town." He did not mention her understanding with the curate of the parish; under ordinary circumstances, it was a match far beneath her, but it was also evidently a love match, and in any case Alistair, who had had frequent cause for wishing for someone to help him with his sisters, could not afford to protest. "Danny lives with Aunt Josephine near Bristol," he went on. "That leaves—"

"Just Harry, Freddie, and Georgie," she supplied, sounding vaguely stunned.

"Those three are faithful readers of the *Magazine for Misses*," he warned her.

He had found two issues stashed among his books and papers as he'd hurriedly sorted through the last of them late last night. No notion, now, whether he'd hidden them there to keep them out of his sisters' hands or whether his sisters had been hiding them from him.

In any case, he'd packed one in the crate destined for Rylemoor, on the off chance Miss C. really had forgot everything and he needed something to prod her memory.

The other, he'd mischievously returned to the bookshelf, leaving it for the daughter of his tenant to find.

"That's the magazine you said I draw for. Will you— will you tell them?" She swallowed. "Who I am?"

How can I, when you *will not tell* me?

"That seems ill-advised, for any number of reasons," he said.

"I—I suppose so, yes. It will raise questions I cannot answer."

Or will not *answer.*

"If I revealed to them that you draw the Unfashionable

Plates," he said, using the familiar name for Miss C.'s popular cartoons, "which is naturally their favorite feature in the magazine, it would only set a certain expectation as to the style of drawing in which you will instruct them." It was his turn to lean toward her, as he favored her with a wry smile. "And I assure you, they are accomplished enough already in the fine art of teasing their brother."

Something flickered in her hazel eyes—guilt or amusement, he could not say. He had the distinct impression that she had never before considered the private fates of those she skewered so publicly.

In his case, laughing sisters had been the least of his troubles.

A thump from outside drew his gaze once more to the window, though he did not immediately adjust his posture. He supposed it had been the coachman, alerting them to their imminent arrival at the next post of their journey, though Alistair had not thought them due to stop so soon. And indeed, the carriage had already begun to slow and seemed to turn toward their destination.

The stop after this one would be the end of the day's travels, at a coaching inn he favored for its economy more than the comfort of its accommodations. By post chaise, it was a three-day journey from London to Rylemoor Abbey, with two nights on the road, and though on this occasion he would have been more than willing to endure further discomfort to shorten it, both for his own convenience and the sake of Miss C.'s purse, he knew that given her injuries, she also needed rest.

At just that moment, a wheel struck a rut in the road, or seemed to. Something gave a frightful *crack!* and all at once, the carriage dropped and lurched to a stop.

As he'd already been leaning slightly forward, the sudden motion threw him toward the back of the coach. He raised his arms to arrest his movement, planting his palms against the worn squabs, one on either side of his traveling companion. Miss C. gasped—either at the abrupt stop or at the discovery that she was pinned in something dangerously close to an embrace.

The sound drew his attention to her mouth, her soft peach-pink lips only inches from his own.

It had been an age since he'd enjoyed anything like intimacy with a woman. And he felt strongly that carrying an unconscious woman to his bed, or urging her back there when dizziness caused her almost to fall, should not count.

Yet he could not deny that those circumstances had acquainted him with information no mere acquaintance should possess: the texture of her hair (finer than embroidery silk), her scent (a piquant mixture of something vaguely floral and the sharp note of mineral spirits), and the precise number of freckles in the constellation across the bridge of her nose (eleven).

Before he could react, even to apologize—and that was not, to his chagrin, the present direction of his thoughts—the hired coachman wrested open the door. Alistair dropped back into his seat and Miss C. smoothed a trembling hand over her hair, which still bore a few traces of a simple coiffure, or what had remained of one after her accident and a night of sleep, now knocked further askew by her nap. If her bonnet had survived yesterday's misadventure, it had not been among the possessions returned to her.

"Looks like t' axle broke, sir," the driver grunted, doing a passable job of masking his surprise at the compromising position he appeared to have caught them in. Only his eyebrows revealed any trace of speculative interest. "Happen there's help to be found in t' village." He jerked a thumb over his shoulder and Alistair peered past him. A scattering of buildings were just visible in the distance through the mist. To call it a *village* might be a bit grandiose.

"Will we wait here?" Miss C. ventured.

As if in answer to her question, something shifted and the bottom seemed to fall out from beneath them again as the body of the coach dropped a few inches more.

"I think, ma'am," Alistair said, mustering a wry smile, "we'd better not."

She was already halfway out the door, her good hand balanced on the coachman's shoulder as she made the leap to the ground, now rather closer than it had been.

Alistair followed a moment afterward, snatching his hat from the seat and squaring it on his head. Its brim did little to shield him from the rain, which rather seemed to swirl around them than pelt down from the sky.

There was nothing for it but to walk.

Miss C. sent a baleful glance toward the luggage. "What about our things?"

"The trunks will be safe enough," he promised, though he had no real cause for certainty beyond the generally worn state of their traveling things—nothing to tempt some highway robber. "And John and I will bring the valises." He'd packed his own for the overnight stays, while hers contained just what it had when the urchin had deposited it into his arms, with the exception of her sketches, which he'd placed in one of his own trunks for safekeeping.

The coachman took the hint, grabbed both carpet-covered bags in his two ham-sized fists, and set out toward the village at a faster clip than Miss C. could manage. The strip of last summer's grass, which lay between the grooves carved by innumerable wheels of carriages and carts, was wide enough for two people to walk abreast. Alistair offered her his arm. Instead, she used her good hand to gather her skirts and lift them above the mud—though privately he thought that avoiding a muddied hem was hardly worth the effort, given that it was the same dress in which she'd lain on the cobblestones and then slept in his bed, and its once-neat woolen respectability was now little more than a memory.

The distance was not great, at least. But still, it was farther than anyone might have wished, given Miss C.'s injuries and the chilly rain. Wordlessly, he shrugged out of his greatcoat and draped it over her shoulders, which earned him a frown of surprise and a murmur of something that might have been thanks.

Eventually they had gone far enough that the mist

could no longer disguise the few gray houses and shops, stone church, and two pubs that constituted the village. One of those pubs, the Coach and Cask, had a stable at the back and took advantage of its position on the post road to supply horses and a hostler for the convenience of those traveling through.

But it was not, Alistair realized as soon as he had ducked inside, an inn.

The walls of the Coach and Cask had last been white-washed so long ago they now bore more resemblance to a cup of chocolate than a glass of milk. Stubs of tallow candles in tin sconces gave off a smoky light. He counted just two doors—the one through which they had entered, and another at the back, which must lead out to the stable yard.

He swept off his hat, and despite a scattering of customers and a fire roaring in the hearth, it was suddenly quiet enough to hear the rain droplets patter from the brim onto the flagstone floor. "Do you have rooms to let?" he asked, stepping closer to the bar, a simple, well-polished slab of oak, and addressing the ruddy-cheeked, balding man behind it. He did not hold out much hope, but it was too late in the day to expect the axle to be repaired while sufficient daylight remained to resume their journey.

"Not to speak of," the barkeep said. "I told your coachman he was welcome to bed down in the stable." A pause, just long enough for Alistair to wonder whether he was to expect a similar invitation. "S'pose I might make a place upstairs for you and"—his gaze slid past

Alistair to take in Miss C.'s bedraggled, bonnetless state—"your missus."

Ordinarily, Alistair would have protested the assumption. But this time, he had the presence of mind to keep his mouth shut. With slightly widened eyes, Miss C. managed a curtsy. "We're much obliged."

The man jerked his chin toward a table near the fire. "Take a seat, and I'll see what's to be done. S'pose you'll want tea, Mrs.—"

"Cooper." She spoke the name without the slightest hesitation, so quickly he wondered whether she had meant to do it, or whether she had inadvertently revealed more than she had intended. She pressed her lips together—a moment too late, perhaps. Then she nodded. "Tea would be lovely."

Alistair helped her to a chair and settled himself in the one opposite her. They sat without speaking to one another as a murmur of conversation rose once more around them and thoughts raced through his head. The idea of presenting this stranger to his sisters as their new drawing master, gut-churning as it was, seemed positively harmless when compared to their present perilous charade as husband and wife.

He tried not to think of the worn but comfortable inn that had awaited them down the road, or to wonder whether "upstairs" was in fact the hayloft above the stable. After a while, a boy brought a pot of tea and a single cup without a saucer. Alistair, who would have been glad of the same, wordlessly accepted the mug of ale that was presented to him instead. They drank together, she from china, he from pewter, still not speaking and only accidentally meeting one another's eye.

An eternity later—and yet long before he was ready to face what lay ahead—the barkeep reappeared and gestured for them to follow. They rose with a creak of wooden chairs and the snap of a coin laid on the table— her money, but from the sum he had retained to pay their expenses on the road, in order to avoid drawing further attention to their unconventional arrangement.

"After you, Mrs. Cooper," he said with a bow made more than usually stiff by the cold and damp, a gesture she regarded with something like smugness. Then she stepped toward the rear door and Alistair followed her out.

Chapter 6

T he day had already been so gray that twilight had
hardly changed the color of the sky. Only colder air
heralded the impending arrival of nightfall. Constantia
could see her breath as they huffed up a set of rickety
stairs, attached with dubious firmness to the exterior
wall of the pub and only partly sheltered beneath the
building's eaves.

On the landing was a nail-studded oak door that
opened into the publican's living quarters: a low-ceilinged
room in which the man did whatever eating and sitting
could not be done below, and on either end of it, an area
divided from the main space by a faded calico curtain.
Behind one curtain, she supposed, lay the man's bed.
To the other, he led them.

He drew it aside to reveal a small space, hardly
bigger than the bed it concealed. One side of the bed
was pressed up against the wall that, by her swift calcu-
lations, housed the chimney from the fireplace below.
What little room remained along the end of the bed had
been given over to storage. The bedside table was a cask
stood on its end. Their valises sat on the floor beside it.

"'Twere my sister's." The explanation was little more than a grunt as the barman swept the light of a candle into corners that might better have remained unlit. "'Til she up and eloped with Jem."

The flickering light danced over the craggy lines of his scowl as he thrust the candlestick into Lord Ryland's hand. "There's meat and cheese in the larder. Be obliged if you didn't eat it all." And with a brusque nod, he left them and returned to his duties below.

Constantia sat limply down on the edge of the bed and fought back a laugh that she feared might be rising hysteria. "Who do you suppose Jem is?"

"A local farmer?" Lord Ryland suggested as he squeezed past a few crates to place the candlestick in the center of the barrel-table.

"Did you see his expression? No, I think . . ." She racked her brain to concoct something amusing to diffuse the tension. "I think the fellow must be the owner of the rival pub across the way. Probably knew a hardworking, unappreciated woman when he saw one."

That earned her a small, tight smile. Then he turned away, putting his back between her and the light. "I'll leave the bed to you, of course. I'm sure I can sit up downstairs, or join John Coachman in the stable."

To say that his offer took her by surprise would be an understatement. She'd expected him to leap at the chance to indulge in rakishness, here where no one in Society who thought him a gentleman would be the wiser.

Or perhaps he understood the flaw in his proposal

perfectly but expected her to point it out—to make it seem as if the fateful decision were hers.

"You can't." She pushed the necessary denial past lips gone suddenly dry. His shoulders tautened in a remarkably good simulation of surprise. "It would only raise suspicions," she dutifully explained, "and our host is skeptical enough about us already. We might find ourselves without a roof over our heads at all."

Her words met with one curt dip of his chin. Agreement, but to all appearances grudging. She would give him credit: His gestures, however insincere, were believable.

He sidled back along the bed toward the makeshift doorway without meeting her eye. "Are you hungry?"

"A little." She pushed to her feet as he swept the curtain aside. "Do you suppose there's water for washing up?"

"If not, there's a fire in the stove, and I spied a pump outside." He picked up his hat from where he'd laid it beside their valises. "I'll fetch some."

"Wait."

That word at last brought his eyes to her face. To her surprise, his were dark and convincingly troubled.

She shrugged her shoulders free of his greatcoat and held it out to him with her good hand.

He took it from her with another nod, less stiff this time. "Thank you."

While he was gone, she explored the main room, which contained a small stove, a cupboard with food and the means of preparing and serving it, and a drop-leaf table, with one straight-backed chair tucked squarely beneath it. The rug on the floor was the only concession to comfort and homeyness.

Had the barman's sister taken the other chair with her, or had she been worked to a frazzle and never allowed to sit down?

Constantia washed her hands with the water remaining in the teakettle and then set about preparing a simple repast of bread and cheese and cold meats. It would be a humble meal in humble surroundings, but she had endured far worse, and she was glad of the glow emanating from the little stove, which someone obviously took care to polish.

When Ryland returned, rain dripping from the tip of his red nose, she wordlessly surrendered its warmth to him. The kitchen, such as it was, was too small for two, so she sat on the chair and watched as he shrugged out of his wet greatcoat and hung it on a peg by the door, laid aside his hat, and chafed the feeling back into his ungloved hands.

She did not expect a display of practical skills. Whatever the cause of his current money woes, he had surely been raised with a bevy of servants, or at the very least sisters, to tend to his every need.

But he surprised her. With deft movements, he filled the teakettle and another pot with water and set them to heat, then rinsed the teapot and added a scant few fresh leaves to those that had already steeped—heeding the barkeep's caution to be sparing, she supposed. Or perhaps the earl liked his tea weak. Certainly that morning's evidence would suggest as much.

In companionable silence, he laid the table, brought

the food, and poured the water when the kettle sang. When she made as if to rise and give him her seat, he scanned the room for the missing chair.

"It would seem our gruff friend doesn't entertain much," she explained.

"I imagine after entertaining the village all day, he likes his quiet."

Then, to her shock, the Earl of Ryland sat down on the floor, balancing a plate of bread and cheese on one knee while cradling a steaming cup in the opposite hand.

"You are in sympathy with him, I'm sure," she said. "With seven sisters to plague you, you must understand the terrible plight of such a man, surrounded by chatter all day."

He slanted a glance toward her. "Then you would be astonished to know how very much I miss them whenever we are apart."

She was not astonished. She was incredulous.

But she disguised her reaction behind a choking cough. "I—I think I must not have any siblings," she offered when she could speak. "Though of course I'm not really sure." It wasn't even a fib. Her mother had had no other children, but her father might have. If those siblings existed, they were nothing to her, however. She'd grown up quite alone. "I have a sense I've often been left to my own devices."

Lord Ryland chewed over her answer along with a bite of cheese, and then took a long gulp of tea to wash it down.

"My friend Deveraux hasn't any brothers or sisters.

When I was younger, I used to envy him his peace and quiet."

Peace and quiet? From what she had heard, Lord Deveraux took every available opportunity to raise as much of a ruckus as possible. And Lord Ryland's friendship with the man must reflect some weakness in the earl, some complicity with Deveraux's notorious troublemaking.

Mustn't it?

"And now?" she managed to ask.

"From time to time I make a great show of annoyance at my sisters' incessant babble and retreat to my library, but the truth is . . ." He paused for a long moment, thoughtful. His next words were underscored by the silence of the room. "Too much quiet drives me mad."

Gradually, though, Constantia became aware of all the little sounds around them, the drip of rain from the eaves and the crackle of the fire and the low hum of voices from the pub below. A certain amused wistfulness settled over his face. "Besides, silence is almost always a sign that trouble's afoot."

That meshed, she supposed, with his earlier description of his sisters and their dubious accomplishments. But whatever she had expected this journey to reveal, it had not been anything like genuine affection for his mischief-loving sisters.

Despite the inevitable rumples of travel and the fact that he was seated on the floor, the Earl of Ryland still managed to look the picture of a proper English gentleman. Except for the way the knot of his cravat had loosened. And a lock of dark hair that persisted in falling forward, requiring him to toss his head occasionally to keep it out of his eyes.

Her fingertips itched with longing, the unexpected desire to make another sketch of him, as he appeared to her in that moment, nothing like the man she thought she knew.

"Speaking of your sisters," she said, jerking herself away from a precipice that had been the death of many an unwary woman, "what can you tell me about their artistic inclinations? Will I find them eager pupils?"

At that question, his body went from relaxed to stiff, though he hardly moved. Every suggestion of softness disappeared, every hint that the true Lord Ryland might be neither rigid nor rakish. "I'm sure you'll find that many of them, perhaps all, have some ability. Harry in particular may even have a gift."

"But none of them have had any prior instruction?" she asked, recalling what he had told her in the carriage and making no effort to disguise her surprise. "Why did you not ensure that Lady Harriet at least had the benefit of a master?"

For answer, he stuffed the last bite of bread and cheese into his mouth, freeing one hand so he could push to his feet—a clear refusal to answer. "I am in danger of forgetting my manners," he said, his back to her as he returned his cup and saucer to the kitchen. "You must be tired from the journey and yesterday's ordeal."

Both of them were keeping secrets. But his might not be the one she'd assumed he hid from the world.

"Yes, I—" She shot a glance toward the curtain, behind which lay the bed they would share, then gazed down wistfully at her own empty plate, wishing suddenly for some excuse for delay. "I suppose I am."

"Then I'll go down and see what report the coachman has to make, while you . . ." He made an aimless gesture with one hand and glanced over his shoulder just enough that she could see his cheek was pink. "The water's warm, if you'd still like a wash."

"Oh." Heat surged into her own face. "Thank you. But I—" Never having had a lady's maid, she had always kept her clothing simple enough to manage on her own. Present circumstances had created a new set of challenges, however. She held up her injured wrist. "I'll need some assistance, I'm afraid."

He turned away before she could see whether her words had made him blush harder, or blanch. But she could hear him drag in a ragged breath. "Of course."

No steel-spined butler had ever moved with the precision and propriety he exhibited as he poured water from the pot into a shallow washbasin, gathered a few rough towels, lit a tallow candle, and carried it all behind the curtain.

Dutifully, she followed him. He made a makeshift washstand on the upturned cask, then turned as if to go.

"If you could just—" With a wiggle of bandaged fingertips toward the nape of her neck, she indicated the fastenings of her dress. She could not bear to think of another night in that same dirty, and now damp, garment.

When he did not meet her eye, she turned her back to

him. For just a moment, she thought he meant to refuse. Then she was aware of the tug of his fingers slipping loose the short row of buttons along her spine.

When the last button slipped free, she felt the fabric sag and gape open. Instinctively, she wrapped one arm across her chest to keep the dress from slipping to the floor. Her plain cotton shift, dingy with washing, must now be on display, along with the fact that she wore no corset. Fortunately for her independence, she'd never really required one. Her figure was straight as a stick, and no amount of tight lacing could have coaxed a cleavage from her bosom.

Would he say something disapproving?

Would he trace one warm fingertip down her spine?

She shivered at the imagining of it.

"I'll give you time to settle in," he said, the sudden gruffness of his voice somehow eliciting another shiver, which she chose to blame on the cooler air dancing across her skin.

"Th-thank you."

He edged his way past the bed, managing neither to look at nor to touch her, and was beyond the curtain before she could muster the strength to speak another word.

What on earth ailed her? Had she been struck by a fever after a quarter-mile walk in a drizzling rain?

How otherwise to explain her own strange longing, that twinge of regret when he made no attempt to practice his secret rakish charms on her?

But of course, he had every reason not to trust her either. Not to reveal his true self. She was, at best, a burden to him. An annoyance. Even the comforts of a private coach were insufficient recompense for the added trouble of traveling with a woman who'd made it her mission to mock him. And now, even those modest comforts had been swept away, replaced by the discomforts of accommodations that didn't deserve the name of *inn*.

She waited until she heard the latch of the outer door before she let her dress drop to the floor, then undid the ribbon of her shift and shed that as well, along with her shoes and stockings. One-handed, she wet a cloth, wrung it, and bathed as best she could, grateful for the steaming water, particularly in the absence of soap.

Once she had freshened herself, she opened her valise in search of a nightdress and discovered that her sketches were missing. By themselves, they were no great loss; she could hardly blame him for having thrown one of them, at least, into the fire. But the painting . . .

She began to rummage, employing both hands despite the discomfort, pushing aside linens, making a tangle of all her remaining possessions, until her fingertips found the familiar edge of a leather case in its usual place, beneath the valise's false bottom. Relief shuddered from her in a sigh. Perhaps Lord Ryland didn't even know it was there.

Carelessly, she stuffed the contents back into the bag on top of it, all but the nightdress, which she donned with a struggle. Afterward, she picked up her clothes from the floor, shook them out, and draped them over the crates to air and dry. The boots she tucked beneath the bed so that Lord Ryland might not trip over them when he returned.

Then she blew out the candle and crawled into the bed, hugging the chimney wall for what little warmth radiated from it. The mattress rustled beneath her, but the sheets were clean and the straw reasonably fresh. The barkeep's sister must not have been gone long.

The quiet sounds around her—dripping eaves, the murmur of voices below—ought to have lulled her to sleep in a moment. She was exhausted. But she was also sore, and the laudanum was in Lord Ryland's pocket. The steady patter of rain made her worry about the condition of the roads and how long they would be delayed here. And the fading conversations, as night wore on and patrons called out their farewells, only made her wonder when Lord Ryland would return.

At long last, she heard steps on the outer staircase and the creak of the door. Then the rattle of dishes, the clatter of someone washing up. The barkeep, her drowsy mind insisted. Surely not the earl.

She screwed shut her eyes all the same.

Then, moments later, footsteps—unbooted—crossed the floor in her direction. The fabric of the curtain whispered as it was drawn aside. And she was no longer alone.

She forced herself to breathe slowly and evenly, to feign sleep. Her performance must have been convincing. Ryland spoke not a word to her as he washed in the water that remained, surely now not even tepid, and slid into bed beside her, his back to hers. She wondered how much of his clothing he had removed—and then chided herself for her curiosity.

She couldn't possibly sleep like this, tense with cold and uncertainty, everything strange and improper and wrong.

But the heat of his body was welcome, softer and warmer certainly than the wall to her other side. The rhythm of his breath was unexpectedly soothing—she'd grown accustomed to being alone, but also to denying the loneliness she sometimes felt. Even the raindrops, which earlier had drummed out an ominous warning, threatening to strand them in this intolerable situation, dwindled down to nothing more than a gentle lullaby.

Incredibly, she slept.

When she awoke some hours later, she could have blamed her interrupted slumbers on the gray sunrise filtering around the curtain.

But she rather suspected the culprit was the aroused male pressed against her backside.

The sensation was not entirely outside her experience. When one moved through life as she had been driven to move, without the protections of parents, an elder brother, a governess, a chaperone, then one discovered that men—so-called gentlemen included—imagined themselves entitled to women's figures, their scent, their smiles, their . . . attention. They groped in the guise of helpfulness, and rubbed themselves against unwitting and unwilling victims in crowded shops and passageways.

Such knowledge was surely *unladylike*. But Constantia had never claimed to be a lady.

She was not really surprised to awaken with the Earl of Ryland's arms around her and his, his—*organ* nudging the small of her back. After all, he was a man— evidently, a virile one—and she had willingly shared a bed with him.

But she was still . . . unsettled.

Unsettled most of all by the discovery that she had no great desire to wriggle free.

For one thing, the morning air was cold, the quilt was thin, and he was warm.

For another, he was quite obviously still sound asleep—the weight of his arm and the steadiness of his breathing revealed as much. And even he ought not to be blamed for what his body did when he was not conscious of it.

For yet another, just as she had begun to think that the man in question might be . . . not entirely objectionable, she was now discovering that the sensation of his proximity was . . . not altogether unpleasant.

That realization spurred a sharp intake of breath, which for a moment only propelled them closer together. Without waking, he nestled closer still, cinching his arm tighter, drawing in a deeper breath that stirred the hair at her nape. And then a sleepy murmur, half sigh, half groan.

The sound made her stiffen. The sudden tautness of her body caused him to draw back a fraction. A momentary flex of his hand around her middle, as if in drowsy disbelief of the situation in which he found himself, or as if he couldn't quite bring himself to let go. Then he stiffened, too—every bit of him that hadn't been stiff already, that was—fumbled free of the linens, and shot from the bed like a bullet from a pistol. "Good God! I— I'm so—"

Holding her breath, she did not turn but listened to the frantic rustle of him gathering his clothes, the swish of the curtain, and finally, the slam of the door.

Leaving her to contemplate the possibility that, rather than linger another moment in bed with her, the man had rushed out into the cold, damp morning in nothing but his drawers.

Either she'd been wrong to suspect him of hidden roguery, or he despised Miss C. a great deal indeed.

Chapter 7

Beneath the meager shelter of the eaves, Alistair stood overlooking the stable yard, his boots in one hand and greatcoat in the other, grateful for the second time that morning that he'd gone to sleep still decently clad in buckskin breeches and a shirt.

Some would surely quibble with the word *decent*. They would say it hardly applied to a gentleman wearing neither coat nor cravat. And regardless of his degree of dishabille, *decent* certainly did not comport with his behavior.

Well, *almost* decently, then.

Besides, no one need know about any of it. He had no intention of regaling his family and friends with the details of this journey. They need never hear how he had shared both a carriage and a bed with a woman he barely knew and did not trust. A woman he felt certain was something shy of respectable.

A woman against whose . . . *person* he had mindlessly rutted while she slept.

Good God.

Fortunately, nothing wilted an unwelcome cockstand like cold rain and self-recrimination. Effective even—perhaps *especially*—when one's mind persisted in recalling the unexpected and undeniably pleasant plumpness of an otherwise slender woman's bottom.

Shivering in the dawn air, he slipped his arms into his greatcoat and stepped into his boots. What ought he to do next? Return and apologize to Miss C. for his boorishness? Rouse the coachman and see what could be done to hurry the resumption of their travels?

If she were willing to continue, that was, or willing to continue with him. She might demand to be left in sole possession of the coach for which she had paid.

Jaw clenched, he descended the steps and crossed the yard. The horses had already been fed, and both the hostler and the coachman were also at their breakfast. Alistair hailed the latter. "What news about the repairs?"

"Good news, sir," the man insisted with an encouraging nod, though Alistair heard a note of uncertainty in his voice. "'Tweren't the axle. Blacksmith says he can forge a new wheel pin that oughter last us the rest o' the way. And th' rest o' th' damage ain't naught but what this chap"—he jerked his thumb over his shoulder toward the hostler—"and me together oughter be able to fix."

There were rather more *oughter*s in that sentence than Alistair would have liked, but he nodded encouragingly. "That is good news. How long?"

One muscled shoulder rose. "Midday. Mebee."

Each word rose slightly, like a question. A guess, then.

But Alistair could only trust it was a guess borne of long experience. A midday departure would put them well behind schedule, and it might yet be delayed further by any number of things, particularly the weather. The sky, rather than growing lighter as the sun rose, had begun once more to darken. Nevertheless, the coachman's words offered a spark of hope, and he would present it as such to Miss C.

When the time came, and he had no choice but to face her again.

"Very good, then. Keep me apprised of your progress. I'm going to stretch my legs."

He was still not dressed for going out in public, but as the village streets were all but empty and he had no intention of doing more than walking down the main thoroughfare, he calculated that the state of his clothing was unlikely to matter to anyone.

Down the street a short distance and on the opposite side stood the village's other pub. A shingle hung above the door, bearing a worn picture of a goose and some lettering he could not decipher at this distance. As he drew opposite of it, a young man with a shock of straw-colored hair and wearing an apron came out to sweep the step.

Alistair recalled Miss C.'s speculation that the rival barkeep had won the heart of the sister of the Coach and Cask's proprietor. Before that moment, he had not suspected her of harboring romantic notions in her breast.

Then again, some degree of fantastical nonsense was to be expected from an artist.

The blond man paid him no attention and Alistair

went on his way, up the street and past a few houses, a butcher's shop, and a handsome stone church. When the buildings began to thin, he crossed to the other side and paused in front of a general store. *Price's Mercantile* had been painted in gilt on the front window, which framed a display of gloves, ribbons, cologne in pretty cut-glass bottles, and a small wooden box containing an assortment of charcoal pencils and pastels, cunningly arranged beside a pad of heavy paper.

While he stood there, a young woman appeared behind the glass, feather duster in hand, and danced it over the items as she hummed some unfamiliar tune. He stood contemplating for a long moment, not really watching her, though it must have seemed so, he realized, when she finally saw him, gasped, and dropped the duster in the middle of the arrangement, just out of reach of her fingers.

There was nothing for it but to assist her.

He stepped to the door, found it still locked, and had to wait for the young woman to let him in. She turned the key with both hands, wearing an expression of suspicion.

She could not have been more than fifteen, his sister Harry's age. "Did you want somethin', sir?" She did not immediately step back from the door and make way for him to enter.

He gestured toward the window. "Your duster. You dropped it because I startled you. I thought perhaps I could assist you by retrieving it."

"Oh!" She blinked up at him, stunned, then gestured him inside. "That's awf'ly kind."

With ease, he leaned over the modest display, fished the duster from the front of the window, and held it out to her.

She accepted it with a grateful curtsy and he turned to go.

His hand was on the door when she spoke again. "Was there somethin' in the window that caught your notice, sir?" He glanced over his shoulder, uncertain of her meaning. Nothing about her demeanor could be described as preening or flirtatious. But it was clear she wanted to make a sale. She looked him up and down, a dubious expression on her face as she took in the state of his attire. "A new pair o' gloves, p'rhaps?"

A reasonable suggestion, since he wasn't wearing any at present. He'd left his behind with his hat, in the room above the Coach and Cask. Since the morning was cold, he'd been strolling with his hands stuffed in the pockets of his greatcoat, until his assistance to the shopgirl had required otherwise.

He looked past her, into the well of the window, where the odd assortment of wares was laid out, some items more eye-catching than others.

"The crayons, actually," he said.

He hadn't exactly been thinking of Miss C. as he'd stood on the street looking in. Except to the extent that since yesterday, he seemed always to be thinking of her, his thoughts bouncing from one extreme to another: from pity to annoyance, from distrust to—as of this morning—a most uncomfortable twinge of desire. How ludicrous for either of them to imagine they could make this journey without incurring any harm and then, at the end, pass her off as—of all things—a drawing master to his sisters.

Particularly given the fact that she no longer possessed any art supplies.

He tilted his head to one side, considering. Would it go better for him if he returned bearing gifts?

Surreptitiously, he slipped one hand back into his pocket and fingered the coins remaining there—the last of his own, which he had stubbornly kept separate from hers. "How much?"

"Two and sixpence," she replied promptly—almost as if she could count through the heavy wool coat. "With the paper."

Was it a wise investment of his remaining resources? Or a foolish one? Not that two shillings would get him far on his journey if Miss C. elected to leave him behind.

"Sold." He withdrew his hand and proffered the coins.

She beamed, then tucked her duster behind her back, in the ribbon of her apron, and carefully lifted the box from the window and handed it to him to hold while she retrieved the pad of paper.

He was no judge of the quality of the implements. He only hoped they would not give further offense.

"I'll just wrap these up, shall I?" Before he could reply, the girl took the small box from him and carried it and the paper deeper into the shop. "Are you an artist?" she asked when she returned a few moments later bearing an awkwardly shaped package tied with string.

"Certainly not."

He spoke his denial more sharply than he had intended, as if she had flung an insult his way. The wariness returned to her eyes. "It's only," she explained, "that some folks do come here just to make pictures of the church."

"Do they?"

"Aye. My papa ordered that paper special from London—took a notion someone might need it someday. But no one ever has."

"Until now." He lifted a hand to tip the hat he'd forgotten he was not wearing, then gestured lamely with the package instead. "Much obliged, miss."

Tucking the art supplies under one arm, he stepped into the street, glancing back at the church before turning toward the Coach and Cask. With somewhat quicker steps than a quarter of an hour ago, he passed by the other pub, which he now saw was called the Jolly Gander; the blond man—Jem, perhaps—nodded to him as he polished his windows. Alistair crossed to its rival and went inside.

The small, low-ceilinged public room was empty and dim. He gazed with longing toward the hearth, though it was cold, before skirting the tables with chairs stacked atop them and making his way out the rear door. The stable yard was also quiet, and for a moment, he fancied he had been left behind.

But of course that was nonsense—the carriage could not have been repaired in time; not a single conveyance had passed along the roadway in the time he'd been gone; and Miss C. could not walk far.

Squaring the package and straightening his spine, he marched up the steps and into the barkeep's quarters, which appeared at first glance to be empty too. The curtain around the man's bed had been looped back, revealing a narrow, neatly made cot. The fellow successfully managed at least a few domestic tasks without his sister's help, it seemed.

When the door clicked shut behind Alistair, Miss C.'s head peeked around the curtain at the opposite end of the room. Then, after a quick, assessing look at him, she stepped fully out and stood, unsmiling, with straight back and lifted chin. "My lord," she said, not curtsying, her voice nearly as cool as the air outside.

Thanks to the even simpler styling of her second dress, she had managed to don it without his assistance. He fought down a surge of disappointment, along with the forbidden memory of the pale skin of her shoulders, the intriguing dips and hollows of her spine—all left shockingly unguarded by the usual cage of a corset.

Not that her present posture seemed to require any assistance.

Only her red-gold hair, tucked securely behind her ears but hanging in loose waves down her back, bright in spite of the gloom, offered any proof that his imagination hadn't conjured the soft, sleep-tousled woman he'd awoken to find in his arms.

Suddenly concerned that his cold walk through the village hadn't been sufficiently, er, *quelling*, he thrust the package behind his back and bowed stiffly. He *would* get the better of these unseemly thoughts. He focused on her bruised and scraped cheek, a visible reminder of the accident that had brought them together. *Danger,* his mind whispered. "I hope I didn't disturb you when I went out this morning. I should have warned you that I am an early riser."

She dropped her gaze, but not before he saw her lips twitch. "Indeed."

Oh, dear. Had she taken the phrase *early riser* for a reference to his . . . ?

"Tea?" she asked, smoothing one hand over her skirts and stepping toward the kitchen.

"You needn't—" he began, but she seemed to want something to occupy herself. A few short moments later, she approached the table beside which he was standing, a cup of tea in her uninjured hand, a thick slice of buttered bread balanced on the saucer.

He refused the chair. "I have something for you. An—an—" *An apology,* he wanted to say. "A peace offering," he said instead.

Now she glanced up into his face, a golden glimmer in her hazel eyes. "I wasn't aware we were at war."

"War?" Warmth crept into his cheeks. "Well, no . . . That is—" He laid the package on the table beside the teacup and took an overlarge bite of bread and butter to keep himself from saying anything more.

She approached a step closer and plucked uncertainly at the string that held the brown paper in place around the rather crumpled package, but she did not slip the knot. "From the shape, I gather it's not a bonnet."

"A bonnet? Er, no. That would have been—"

Improper.

Intimate.

Such would have been his answer just two days earlier. But given their present circumstances, the old rules for gift-giving, the conventional excuses, hardly seemed relevant.

"I was going to say that such a purchase would certainly have been *practical*," he lied, mortified. "A pity I didn't think of it. But I'm not accustomed . . . that is, my sisters would protest the notion of me picking out their headgear. I haven't much sense for such things, you see." She was studying the movement of her own hand as she wound a loose end of string around her forefinger. "You might have a look for yourself, though. The shop's just past the Jolly Gander—"

"The Jolly Gander?"

"The pub across the way."

"Jem's place, you mean."

"Well, now, we don't really—"

She sent him a sidelong glance, full of amusement. Teasing again.

At that, his lungs couldn't seem to decide whether to heave a sigh of relief—she wasn't furious with him, then, though she had every right to be—or to suck in a breath of . . . well, not surprise, exactly. *Wonderment,* perhaps? She really was quite clever.

And lovely.

Unable to both inhale and exhale at once, he sputtered and coughed instead, a predicament which only served to amuse her further. "It isn't far," he managed when he had recovered. "And we've ample time, I'm afraid. John Coachman says it will be midday at least before the carriage is repaired."

"Oh." Once more, the bit of string, now frayed, occupied all her attention. Clearly, the delay distressed her. "I've never really been one for frittering the hours away with shopping. But I suppose it will be something to do."

He was struck with an idea. "Open it," he urged, with a nod toward the package.

With a decisive tug, she slipped the knot free. One-handed, she peeled back the wrappings to reveal what was inside. She lifted the lid of the box to inspect its contents, then dragged a fingertip over the pad of paper, as if judging its quality. "You—you bought me art supplies."

He did not know how to interpret the tone in which those words were spoken.

They wore an air of displeasure.

"I'm sorry if they're the wrong thing. Or, or not the quality to which you're accustomed. I only thought—"

Her chin rose, though she did not quite meet his eye. "You thought it would be easier to perpetuate the ruse of my being your sisters' art teacher if I possessed at least some of the accoutrements of an artist."

He'd considered the matter along those lines, it was true.

But in the end, just as he'd said, the purchase had not been inspired by practicality.

"There's a church in the village." The seeming non sequitur made her tip her head in his direction. Perhaps she was expecting an offer of marriage after his shocking conduct this morning—though not, the sharpness of her movement made clear, with anything like enthusiasm. "Quaint," he pressed on. "Not far to walk. The girl in the shop said that people come to this village expressly to make sketches of it." He paused again, weighing the many explanations for his conduct he could offer, up to and including the truth. "I thought it might make you feel better—more yourself—to draw."

"More . . . myself," she repeated. "You thought it might jog my memory, you mean."

It wasn't at all what he'd meant. He'd momentarily forgotten that she was still claiming not to know her own name, rather than simply keeping it from him.

"Surely you must wish that too?" he prompted.

"I—" Then she bit off whatever she had been about to say, sinking her upper teeth into the curve of her lower lip until the peach-pink color leached to white. "Of course," she went on, once she had mastered whatever wayward thought had almost crossed her lips. "I'll just fetch my pelisse." She walked away, still moving stiffly—which might, he supposed, have as much to do with her feelings toward him as with her injuries.

She was back a few moments later wearing the aforementioned garment, shabby with the signs of her fall and too thin for the raw weather. No bonnet, of course, and no gloves either. They'd been shredded on the cobblestone street in front of his house, and what scraps had remained had been cut away by the physician to inspect her injuries. His plan, such as it was, seemed suddenly more likely to give her pneumonia than pleasure.

He'd intended to fetch his own hat and gloves before going back outside. Instead, he picked up the paper and box of crayons, tucking them in the breast of his greatcoat to protect them from the elements—and, perhaps, to keep himself from stretching out an arm to her and inviting her touch. Then he opened the door and bowed. "After you."

Chapter 8

A true artist, Constantia had long believed, distinguished herself by the skill with which she manipulated perspective. One must be able to find the angle, the shadow, the unique focal point that transformed the ordinary into art.

For instance, she knew at first sight that to transform the little stone church into anything more than merely picturesque, it would be necessary to impose some distance between it and the viewer.

Ideally, several miles.

At that distance memory, or imagination, could render anything it liked from smooth, gray regularity: a rough and interesting ruin, perhaps. Or an edifice charged with gothic grandeur.

Distance, of either the physical or temporal sort, was not within her means, however, and she did not fancy standing longer in the drizzling rain. So when Lord Ryland opened the nail-studded oak door and ushered her into the rear of the nave, she began immediately to consider where she might best position herself to make a passably interesting sketch of the interior.

Why this drawing mattered to her, when the earl was likely the only person who would ever see it, she could not entirely say. Perhaps it was simply a matter of stubborn artistic pride. She didn't like to waste her time on bad drawing.

Perhaps she did not wish to seem ungrateful. He had given her a present, after all, and paid for it out of his own limited funds—which she knew because, after he'd gone out that morning, she had tried to busy herself with straightening their things and his little leather purse full of her money had fallen onto the floor.

A peace offering, he had called the gift. An apology of sorts? For touching her?

Ironic, then, that she had found the gesture itself touching.

At least, until he had mentioned his belief that the act of drawing might restore her memory and, by implication, free him of his responsibility to her.

With a twitch of her shoulders, she shook away the last vestiges of anything that resembled sentiment. He might choose to describe paper and crayons as an impractical gift, an extravagance, but she was—or at least had been, until recently—a working artist. Why should she view the items he'd chosen as anything *but* practical? They were tools, such as any tradesman might require for a job.

Their footsteps echoed in the empty church, though it was not large. She could not recall the last time she

THE LADY MAKES HER MARK   99

had been inside a church; closed-door gatherings of strangers made her nervous. Lord Ryland, however, moved as if he were right at home in this quiet, holy place, and not at all as if he had reason to fear the strike of a lightning bolt.

After a moment, she heard the scrape of a door across stone as someone entered from the far end. A grizzled older man in rough clothes approached and swept off his shapeless hat in deference.

"Mornin', sir. Ma'am. Tolliver, sir. Sexton." He bowed his introduction. "Be there aught I can do for 'e?"

"I hope we're not intruding?" Ryland approached the sexton. "We were charmed by your little church, and my, er, my wife wished to take a sketch or two." He gestured with the art supplies before handing them off to her.

"Oh, aye." The sexton favored her with a smile. "Newlyweds?"

It was, she assumed, Ryland's hesitation that had prompted the question. She parted her lips to form some reply, but the earl interrupted with a stilted nod and a noncommittal "Hmm" that the other man seemed to regard as sufficient confirmation.

"I'll jus' leave 'e be, then, shall I?"

It was Constantia's turn to nod, more eagerly this time, and Lord Ryland's to speak. "I, er, I wondered if you wouldn't show me around a bit while she works. You strike me as the sort of fellow who must know all the interesting history of the place."

"Oh, aye," Mr. Tolliver readily agreed, and with a

wave of his arm he ushered Ryland deeper into the little church and began to explain the miraculous provenance of some scrap of tapestry that hung on one side of the chancel.

While the sexton held forth in respectful tones, Constantia took several slow steps down the aisle, evaluating the architecture, the quality of light and shadow it produced. After weighing her options, she eventually settled on a pew on the left-hand side, four rows from the back, and slid almost to the middle, where a pillar obscured most of the view of the pulpit but also forced an unexpected angle on the altar. Then she slid open the small wooden box and traced a fingertip over its contents.

Charcoals. She hadn't used them in ages. Her own art teacher—or the closest she'd ever come to having one, in that wretched girls' school where she'd been more scullery maid than student—had dismissively told his pupils that charcoal left behind dirty hands, making it unsuitable for ladies' use. That, of course, had only made Constantia more determined to master the medium.

But the teacher had kept his supplies under lock and key. And sometime before she had managed to pick that lock, well before she had had to leave the school under cover of darkness, she had learned how to wield a brush instead.

Nothing had been the same since.

After so long, she was eager to try again. But she didn't immediately select one of the thin black sticks.

As always, she swept her empty fingertips over the paper in a pantomime of sketching, calculating without conscious thought the necessary mathematics—division, geometry—and rehearsing the gestures by which the little church's interior would take shape beneath her hand. Though the page remained pristine, she could see the outline, knew where the first stroke must be laid, before she ever picked up an implement.

A movement in the corner of her eye pulled her gaze away from the altar. To her left was a row of three windows, each made up of nine rectangular panes of wavy glass. Through the middle one, she watched as the sexton and Lord Ryland picked their way through the churchyard, stopping now and again to study a moss-encrusted grave marker. Behind them, the dark sky threatened rain.

It looked a rather unpleasant history lesson, to her way of thinking.

She turned back to the scene she was meant to be drawing and selected one of the pieces of charcoal, carefully prying it up from the box with her fingernail. How fortunate that the fall hadn't injured the hand she drew with. Tilting her head ever so slightly to one side, she touched the charcoal to the paper and laid down one sweeping line of black, so stark against the creamy white that she gave an involuntary gasp.

The thrill of creation would never cease to amaze her.

Another line, and another. She tried to imagine how the altar would look with more light, on a day that the sun shone through the windows. Her gaze wandered leftward once more, while with the tip of her middle finger, she rubbed a shadow into place.

Charcoals would certainly be a suitable medium for depicting the gloomy churchyard. The cloudy sky and gray granite stones. The human figures in the foreground, a stark contrast to the moribund scene.

Instinctively, her hand shifted to a blank space on the left side of the paper.

Four hasty lines established the window frame. The charcoal slid so smoothly across the paper she was hardly aware of making them. A smudge on the horizon, to convey the lowering clouds. Then a collection of curves and angles to suggest the stones in the churchyard—so many of them, clustered so tightly together, that she wondered whether there had been some long-ago epidemic. How had the little village weathered so many losses?

Of course she must include Mr. Tolliver, too, in his drab, practical attire. He was as necessary to the picture as the graves that he—and his father, and his father's father—had dug.

Once she had placed the sexton in the scene, she paused to assess her work. Not her finest effort, but passable, given how little recent practice she had had in either the medium or the style.

Of course, the composition would be improved, more balanced, if she included Lord Ryland. The charcoal would work exceptionally well to capture his not-quite-black hair. And the slight stoop of the sexton's shoulders—a natural consequence of the man's melancholy trade, she supposed—would be better set off by contrast with the earl's always erect posture.

Were her wayward fingers looking for an excuse to trace his shape?

That desire in itself was reason enough not to do it, though she had ample experience in making pictures that reflected nothing of her own feelings toward the subject. Art was the trade she had learned to ply to ruthlessly practical ends, no different from laying stone. Or digging graves.

Still, it would be far better if she were never caught drawing Lord Ryland again.

With a sharp breath, she dragged her attention away from the window and devoted herself to adding more details to the sketch of the altar. The perspective forced by the pillar made the space disjointed. *Interesting*, she told herself as she forced herself to focus on the picture she was expected to make.

She succeeded well enough that when a droplet of water splashed onto the sketch, she started. Looking up, she found Lord Ryland leaning slightly over her shoulder; she had not heard him approach.

"Forgive me," he said as she flicked the moisture away before it could soak into the heavy paper. "I only wanted to watch you work."

Rivulets of rainwater traced the sharply hewn edges of his cheekbones and jaw and carved unexpected waves into his dark hair. At the end of every curved lock, a droplet swelled and sparkled.

Clearly, he had been standing there long enough for one of those droplets to slip free.

"Did I spoil your drawing?" Worry shadowed his charcoal-black eyes.

She shook her head.

But he had. Or rather his absence had. The place in the sketch of the churchyard where he should have been, the space she had left empty, stared up at her now, stark as a gaping wound.

She had not fully understood something until that moment: What an artist chose *not* to include could sometimes reveal as much as what she drew.

"It's quite remarkable," he said, looking between her and the picture, "how a bit of charred wood can become the perfect implement to capture stone—in the right hands, of course." His gaze traveled up the pillar then out across the nave. "I would not have thought this a promising vantage point. But you have made me see it all differently."

She ought to have some reply at the ready for such remarks. She wanted, perversely, to point out to him all the things she'd done wrong. The hesitations and misplaced lines. The smears.

But no words came. The best she could do was incline her head, half in acknowledgment and half in demurral, a gesture of modesty he no doubt thought false.

After returning the charcoal to the box and closing the lid, she tucked the picture away between two other sheets and handed the whole to him to stow inside his greatcoat. Rising, she thanked Mr. Tolliver for the opportunity. Lord Ryland likewise expressed his gratitude and followed her out.

The rain had, for the moment at least, stopped. Across the street stood a shop selling all manner of goods—*Price's Mercantile*, the window proclaimed. Was that where Lord Ryland had made his purchase earlier that morning? She stepped almost involuntarily toward it.

The interior of the shop was warmer and drier than the church, the gray midmorning light assisted by several highly polished lamps.

"Back again, sir?" a girl called as she bustled forward from the rear, confirming Constantia's suspicion.

"You must be the one who told my husband about the church. Thank you." Constantia dipped into a shallow curtsy. She took care not to falter in the lie about their relationship, a quiet reprimand of Lord Ryland, who had stopped a pace behind her.

"Oh, *you're* the artist. I'm sorry we haven't anything more in the painting and drawing line." The girl looked around the shop, as if hoping something might materialize. "Might there be something else I can get for you?"

"As it happens, I could use a great many things," Constantia said, trying to sound airy. "We're on our honeymoon"—best to keep the story consistent throughout the village—"and our carriage broke a wheel."

"Oh, dear," said the girl, looking her up and down, lingering over the bruised cheek and rather battered pelisse. "And some of your things were spoiled in the accident, I suppose."

A not entirely inaccurate surmise, to which Constantia nodded.

"Well, here's gloves." She waved with one arm to a display of narrow boxes.

"Ooh, lovely." It had felt strange, to say nothing of chilly, to go about without gloves. Eagerly, she stretched out her hand, then snatched it back when she glimpsed her own fingers black with charcoal.

Thankfully the girl, who had turned away to consider what else she might offer her customers, did not seem to have seen.

But Constantia's predicament had not gone unnoticed.

"Allow me." Lord Ryland's voice was gentle, as it had been last evening. She heard a shuffle behind her—the sound of him laying aside her sketching implements—and then he appeared beside her, hand-kerchief in one hand and the other outstretched, palm upward. As if he intended for her to put her hand in his.

Instinctually, she wanted to protest. But her band-aged hand was an impediment to cleaning up. As with so many things at the moment, she could not easily manage on her own. Still, she hesitated, glancing upward, her gaze landing first on his cravat, which was slightly askew, having been tied that morning without benefit of valet or mirror. At last, she looked into his face and found it unperturbed. Resigned. Perhaps ever so slightly amused.

This was not, in her experience, an expression rakes often wore.

She recalled what he had told her about his mischievous sisters—or rather, not *what* he had said, so much as *how* he had said it. With affection. And good humor.

Gnawing surreptitiously on the inside of her lower lip, she surrendered her hand to his ministrations. His touch was gentle and comparatively warm as he curled his fingers around the breadth of her palm and began to swipe at her blackened fingertips.

There was nothing suggestive in his touch, nothing at all to remind her of that morning's embrace, however unintentional—or unintentionally libidinous—it had been. All the same, heat rushed into her cheeks and she had to make some effort not to allow her fingers to tremble in his grasp.

"Your handkerchief will be ruined," she warned.

He rubbed a bit harder at a particularly stubborn spot. The charcoal had embedded itself around the callus on her middle finger, where countless pencils and paintbrushes had rested. "You can buy me another," he suggested, a faintly wry curve to the corner of his lips.

Would that be an inappropriately personal gift? Or an eminently practical one?

When he released her hand, still rather stained but no longer likely to dirty whatever she touched, she hastily set about examining the gloves while he stuffed his ruined handkerchief into his pocket and turned to look at items on another shelf—almost as if they both knew that it would be best to put the intimacy of the moment behind them.

By the time the girl returned, Constantia had settled on a pair of kid gloves in a shade of dove gray that would not show wear, but which were still suitable for her present masquerade as a lady and a new bride. Then, after a quick peek over her shoulder to confirm that Lord Ryland was otherwise occupied, she chose a bar of perfumed soap for herself and a gentlemen's handkerchief of narrow-hemmed cambric.

"What I should really like," she told the girl, "is a bonnet. Mine was such a silly frippery of a thing," she went on in a slightly louder voice, so that her supposed husband might overhear and their stories would not contradict, "would you believe it blew right away?"

The girl looked suitably surprised—or perhaps suitably disbelieving. "No. Nothing like that, ma'am." A glance toward Lord Ryland's similarly bare head. "Neither for ladies nor gentlemen." She gave another searching look around the little shop, then a light flickered in her eyes. "Wait. I have an idea." She bustled away and returned with a paper-wrapped bundle, which she opened to reveal a hooded mantle of moss green wool, lined with tobacco-colored silk.

In spite of herself, Constantia gave a little gasp of greedy pleasure.

"I suppose it's not the sort of thing a fine, elegant lady such as yourself would usually wear," the girl said, misinterpreting Constantia's reaction. And perhaps she was right; Constantia hardly knew, because she had never before pretended to be a fine, elegant lady. "The barkeep's wife ordered it for herself—came just yesterday. But you've the greater need, ma'am. If you like it well enough, I'll just tell her it hasn't come yet and order another."

Guilt needled her. To take such a lovely garment from the poor, put-upon sister of the proprietor of the Coach and Cask . . .

But she has Jem to keep her warm until a new one arrives, Constantia rationalized. While she herself must face cold rain and a drafty carriage and who could predict what else in the wilds of Devon—or wherever she ended up, once she could no longer hide that there was nothing wrong with her memory and Lord Ryland either seduced or abandoned her. Or both.

Footsteps heralded his approach. He fingered the material, appraising its quality, then lifted the garment from its wrappings, shook out the folds, and draped it over her shoulders.

Warmth settled around her, but was it the wool? Or his touch?

He raised the mantle's hood to cover her head, then tucked in a few stray curls here and there. "Perfect."

Constantia knew she wasn't pretty. She had freckles, an angular face, and a stick-straight figure. She didn't need a looking glass to tell her that an assortment of scrapes and bruises, surrounded by hair made frizzy by a morning stroll through the damp air, were unlikely to have improved matters.

But in that moment, under the warmth of his gaze, she felt that she *could* be pretty—when viewed from the proper perspective.

Two days past, she would have regarded the look in Lord Ryland's eyes as proof of his duplicitous nature.

Now, though, she found herself wanting to believe that he was kind and generous, the sort of man who valued practicality over fashion, but who also knew that young women sometimes needed to feel beautiful. Even when they really weren't.

She understood the dangers of London and had done what she must to escape them.

But she had not anticipated the dangers of a simple carriage ride into the country. She did not know how to escape the treachery of her own thoughts.

"I'll t-take it. Yes. Th-thank you," she stammered as soon as his hands fell away, turning back toward the girl with hot cheeks and fumbling beneath the added layer of fabric for her reticule.

Once the purchases had been rung up, paid for, and wrapped, Lord Ryland stepped forward to pick up the bundle—everything but the mantle, which she still wore.

The girl nodded toward the array of packages. "Much obliged, Mrs.—"

"Cooper," Ryland supplied, without hesitation this time.

They did not speak again until they were on the street. "Fortuitous, wasn't it," she said, mostly to keep from having to speak of anything else, "that she had this cloak waiting? But perhaps we ought to cut across before we reach the Jolly Gander. It might be recognized." She glanced upward to see if Lord Ryland had smiled at her little joke.

His expression was abstracted, as if his thoughts were far away, though he did steer them back to the other side of the street with his free hand.

"*Is* it Cooper, I wonder?" he mused, once they had gained the opposite pavement. "The name came to you so readily last night, I began to wonder."

"I, uh . . ." She pretended to test its familiarity in her mind. In reality, she was recalling the day Lady Stalbridge had approached her while she had been sketching in the park. Some nearby children had been laughing and rolling an iron hoop. Constantia had thought of the cooper who had made the barrel from which the hoop had been salvaged and wondered whether he would have been gladdened by the sight. "No," she told Lord Ryland firmly. "No, I don't believe it is."

But he didn't appear to have been waiting for, or even listening to, her reply.

"Then this morning, as I watched you draw in the church, I thought that 'Miss C.' might be a reference to the artist's critical eye. You *see* what others do not."

The idea was surprisingly poetic, and more flattering than she had any right to expect, especially given the previous drawings she'd made of him.

"Perhaps," she conceded, as they walked on toward the Coach and Cask. "Art does require perceptiveness."

In the distance, she saw that their carriage was waiting in the stable yard. The repairs must be complete, for the horses were even now being hitched. A curious mixture of relief and apprehension surged through her, and she glanced up again, studying the contours of her companion's visage, grateful for the shielding edge of her new hood.

In the case of Lord Ryland, had she failed in the past to perceive the real man?

Or was she now so desperate she was seeing only what she wished to see?

Chapter 9

Beneath Alistair's watchful gaze, the familiar terrain slid by. He couldn't remember the last time he'd made the journey staring out the window. Usually, he read. Occasionally, he slept. But this time, all his books were packed away, and he had made a private vow not to fall asleep in Miss C.'s presence again.

Another mishap like the one this morning and it would take more than a box of crayons to make amends. If he weren't careful, he would have to do the honorable thing—*though at least then,* he thought with a private laugh, *I would finally learn her name.* She would have to sign it in the parish register.

No, no. He mustn't joke about it, even to himself. Marriage was no laughing matter.

And marriage to this woman was a mistake he could not afford to make.

She had spent the last two hours sketching, silent but for the occasional *scritch-scritch* of her pencil across paper, the quiet sound rising above the rattle of the carriage. When they had stepped inside the pub to settle their bill before leaving, the proprietor had been standing at the bar, grumbling over his bookkeeping. She had, with surprising deftness, talked him into giving her the stub of a pencil he'd had tucked behind his ear. "So I can draw and you don't have to ruin another hand-kerchief," she'd explained to Alistair.

He couldn't see enough of the paper to identify the subject of her picture. He wasn't even certain he wished to know. After all, he was more than aware of both her capabilities and her propensities. And he couldn't decide even now whether the box of crayons and an hour in the church had disposed her to forgive him for his bad behavior. Her gaze, whenever she looked at him, was always a little too sharp for comfort.

"Have you a knife?" she demanded without look-ing up.

"I beg your pardon?"

"A knife—a penknife," she added by way of expla-nation, a slight twist of annoyance to the words. "This pencil is dull."

"Not on my person, no. Sorry."

She flicked a cool glance toward him, sighed, and touched the tip of the lead to her tongue.

He'd lost his mind, clearly. She was the cartoonist who had made his life a mockery and a misery. Yet he'd agreed to bring her to Rylemoor to instruct his sisters—in art! He'd even bought her paper and charcoals.

And he found the sight of her wetting a pencil—whetting her weapon, more like—somehow arousing.

"We'll be stopping to change horses before long." She had resumed sketching and gave no indication that she heard him. "I would've mentioned it before, but I didn't want to disturb your work." *Scritch-scritch*. "It's the inn where I usually stop. A pleasant enough spot. We would have stayed there last night but for the unfortunate problem with the wheel."

The pencil stopped. "They know you in this place."

"Yes."

"No more masquerading as Mr. and Mrs. Cooper, then."

Was she relieved? Disappointed?

"No," he said.

She applied one final flourish to the paper, then closed the pad and tucked the pencil somehow into her profusion of coppery curls. "I hope there's food."

"The best steak and ale pie I've had anywhere, as a matter of fact." At the mention of it, his stomach rumbled in anticipation.

A smirk ghosted across her lips.

Somewhat to his surprise, she had left him out of her sketch of the churchyard. Then again, it had been done in another style to what he was accustomed to seeing from her, and her usual depiction of him would have been quite out of place. But now that she had had the opportunity to observe him closely, he could only imagine the ridiculous figure he was going to make in her next cartoon.

Well, by the time the next issue of the *Magazine for Misses* saw print, it wouldn't matter anyway.

"We'll eat quickly," he cautioned, "then push on to make up for lost time. With any luck, we can be at Rylemoor tomorrow night, only a little later than expected."

"You are eager to be home."

Eagerness, he almost said, *is beside the point.*

It was time for things to return to normal.

He was not naïve enough to imagine that there would be no further frustrations on this journey. But from this point forward, he would be recognized as Ryland; his role would be clear. No more assumed name or presumed bridegroom. One more night on the road, in a suitable inn this time, with a room and a bed of his own, and then he would be back at Rylemoor. His life would return to its predictable patterns. Its typical troubles.

Namely:

Five unwed sisters.

A crumbling estate.

And insufficient funds to take care of either, to say nothing of both.

Problems that did not—could not—involve the woman who had, inadvertently or otherwise, made them more difficult to solve.

No, Miss C. would not be disturbing the predictable patterns of his life for much longer. Already, she was mostly recovered from the effects of her fall; her bruises were beginning to change color and would soon start to fade. She seemed already to be growing tired of playing the patient, and his sisters would soon cure her of any desire to be a teacher. She would continue on to whatever her destination had been and leave him in peace.

Or what passed for it, anyway.

"At the moment," he said, realizing he had been

looking at her and that she was waiting for him to speak, "I'm eager to stretch my legs."

When the carriage stopped, he did not wait for the steps to be lowered but opened the door and leaped to the ground. While she busied herself with raising the hood of her new mantle, he spoke to the hostler to urge haste and moved about as if to ease the fatigue of his muscles. At last he helped her down, much as he would've if she had been one of his sisters, and preceded her into the inn.

"My lord." The proprietor approached and bowed. "How good to see you again. A room for tonight?"

"Much obliged, Meachum, but no. Just two pies, a pint, and a pot of tea for the lady."

"Very good, sir." He gestured them toward a table in the bustling dining room. If he found their traveling arrangements unusual, he was savvy enough to say nothing of it. "The ladies Haythorne were in fine spirits when they stopped the day before yesterday."

"And when are they not?" Alistair joked, his attention somewhat distracted by the way Miss C. was craning her neck to peer about the room. She had not lowered her hood. "But I thank you for the report. This is their new teacher, Miss Coo—"

"A pleasure to meet you, sir," she spoke across him and curtsied.

Even after they were seated, she kept her head covered. His face must have reflected some surprise at that, for she explained, otherwise unprompted, "I find it chilly in here, don't you?"

He didn't demur, though it was surely warmer inside than it had been in the carriage. But perhaps she was tired of the way her bruised cheek tended to attract notice.

"This is a market town," he offered after a few moments of awkward silence. "If there's anything you require for your stay at Rylemoor, now would be the best time to acquire it."

She was busy working loose the fingers of the glove on her uninjured hand. He considered offering his help, but after that morning, the assistance he'd given in the shop, it might seem as if he were rather too eager to touch her. "There's nothing I can think of, my lord," she said, once she had succeeded. She did not remove the other glove, which disguised her bandaged wrist. "I assume your sisters have paper and pencils available?" she countered.

He nodded.

"Then that will be more than sufficient to begin."

"*More than* sufficient?" he echoed skeptically. "I should think paper and pencil the bare minimum of requirements."

"A work of art does not begin with the act of applying paint to canvas, my lord. One must first understand the principles of composition."

"Learning to *see*, as it were."

Her expression was in shadow, but he knew from the way the firelight caught her eyes that she had shot him a look. "Precisely. I find it useful to begin by examining the techniques used by other artists, to consider the choices they have made. Rylemoor Abbey has, I hope, some paintings we can study for the purpose? From my understanding, it would be unusual if such a large and ancient estate did not."

Did Rylemoor Abbey have paintings? Alistair set his teeth together to contain a bitter laugh. "More than sufficient," he told her, making his best effort to disguise those clipped words as a little joke. Never had he been so glad to see a servant approach. A lad wearing a coarse apron placed a pot of tea and cup and saucer in front of Miss C. "What happened there?" As Alistair reached up to accept his pint, he nodded at a nearby pile of kindling, the remains of a broken chair. Both the boy and Miss C. turned to look. "Not a fight over the last steak and ale pie, I hope?"

"No, m'lord." The lad grinned as he tucked his now empty tray beneath his arm. "'Twas a fight over summat else."

Alistair paused with his mug halfway to his lips. He'd never known this unassuming posting inn to attract the sort of customers who brawled. Had his sisters been in danger?

"A fight over what?" he demanded.

"A fight over how much oak it takes to hold up a mountain," he answered with a laugh. "Some oaf come in, lookin' to find someone. Insisted this was the spot. Swore he'd sit right here and wait. And 'e mighta done it, too, if the chair hadn't broke. Fell apart right beneath him, it did. After that, he skulked off."

Alistair laughed along with him, but the spout of the teapot rattled against the edge of Miss C.'s cup, as if she didn't see the humor in the story. "My goodness. Looking for whom?"

"Dunno, ma'am. But Cook says he had the eye of a fellow whose girl had run off and left 'im."

Her gaze swung once more to what remained of the chair. Alistair could see no more than the tip of her nose past the edge of her hood. "If he was given to such displays of stubbornness and petulance, who could blame her?" she observed coolly.

The boy left, returning a few moments later with the pies. At first, Miss C. poked at hers with her fork, as if she had no appetite. But after a moment—hardly time for the pie to cool—she squared her shoulders and made efficient work of finishing her meal, which kept her mouth far too busy for further conversation. Given the direction of their previous exchange, he wasn't sorry.

After a few minutes of nothing but the sounds of eating, she laid her fork aside, then drained her teacup. "Ready when you are, my lord," she said, returning the empty cup to its saucer with a decisive *clink*. Her hood had remained in place throughout her hasty meal, but he could see now that she looked pale.

"Are you in any discomfort? Should I fetch the laudanum from my valise?"

"No." The answer was too swift to be entirely believable. "If you'll be a few moments longer, I'll wait for you in the coach." She snatched up her glove from the table and rose. "My lord."

She had not been in the habit of *my lord*-ing him until now, but evidently she had taken her cue from the servants in this place. It established a certain distance between them, to be sure.

He didn't like it.

With her injured hand clasping the mantle closed, she was gone before he could get to his feet. In a hurry for the necessary, he supposed—she had drunk a whole pot of tea. He quickly finished his food, paid the bill, and met her in the carriage before five minutes had passed.

"Is something amiss?"

Her hood was pushed down around her shoulders again, and she had already resumed sketching. "Not at all." The taut set of her lips hinted that she was not being entirely honest. "You said it would be a quick stop. I did not wish to be the cause of any delay."

He could not restrain a slight huff of something like amusement at her sudden consideration for his traveling plans. Swinging into the seat opposite her, he tapped on the ceiling. The coach rolled into motion. In short order and in spite of his earlier determination, the combination of an early morning, a full belly, and the soft sounds of her pencil lulled him into a gentle doze.

"Did she say what sort of danger?"

The question jerked him back to full alertness. "Did who—what?"

"The one you wrote to about me. The one who told you I was in danger?"

"Lady Stalbridge?"

"Did she say what sort of danger I'm meant to be in?" With each word, she tapped the end of her pencil against the paper, a sign more of nervousness than impatience, he thought. "Might I, for instance, have someone following me?"

He pushed himself more upright. "She didn't specify, no." But now he understood Miss C.'s sudden pallor in the inn. "He's not searching for *you*, if that's what you're thinking—the man who broke the chair."

"How do you know?" she demanded.

Fright masquerading as anger, he told himself. But nevertheless, it prodded uncomfortably at his certainty.

Perhaps she really didn't remember anything about her life before two days ago. Or perhaps her memory was fragmented, and she was struggling and failing to place the jagged pieces back together.

Or perhaps she remembered everything perfectly, right down to a phantom pursuer, and that was why she had been so determined to get away.

He dragged a hand through his hair. "I don't. But it strikes me as unlikely."

"Unlikely that I'm being followed? That I was chased from an alleyway into the street and that's how I hit my head and nearly lost my life?" Her voice was remarkably steady. But her eyes were wide and almost desperate. "Or unlikely that the man who's following me planned to catch up with me at the place where I would have been if not for that mishap with the carriage wheel? Unlikely that he is the sort who breaks chairs—when he'd rather be breaking necks?"

Without conscious thought, he reached across the coach and took her uninjured hand between both of his, trapping the pencil in her grip. "Miss C.," he began,

in his steadiest tone. He had some experience consoling
and reassuring agitated young women. "*All* of those
things are unlikely. Highly unlikely." He would not say
impossible, though privately he thought the scenarios
she had spun smacked of a mind that indulged too frequently in horrid novels. Thanks to five younger sisters,
however, he had learned over the years that to deny
another's fears outright served only to cement them.
"And you are safe. Have I not promised to protect you?"

Emotions warred in her face, relief battling with an
almost innate distrust, a deep temptation to scoff.

"Until I remember," she said.

"I beg your pardon?"

"Back in London, you told me . . ." The pencil
trapped between their joined hands twitched. "You told
me that I would have your protection until I remembered who I was."

Good God. Had he?

No wonder she had been unwilling to tell him anything. No wonder she had reacted with alarm to his
suggestion that drawing would restore her to herself.

"I haven't any intention of abandoning you to the
wolves, Miss C. If I had, I would've done so in London.
I only meant that once your memory returned, you
would no doubt wish to be returned to your family, or
your friends, and would have no further need of my
assistance."

Her chin dipped jerkily in a nod of understanding, an
acknowledgment of error worthy of the queen or someone similar—someone unaccustomed to admitting they

were wrong. "And in the event that I have neither friends nor family?"

For a moment, he said nothing.

"I suppose, my lord, you are thinking of your gentlemanly obligation and weighing whether it can or even ought to be fulfilled for a woman like me. Consider what might become of your spotless reputation." Her voice fairly dripped with disdain.

"I assure you, ma'am, that nothing could be further from my mind at present than my reputation." He sounded insufferably toplofty, even to his own ears, but evidently she expected it of him; she seemed determined to view him in the worst possible light. "I was thinking of the risks—if what you say were somehow true, given that I'm taking you to my home, should I be concerned for my sisters' safety?"

Her whole body recoiled from that question. Tugging her fingers free of his grasp, she turned her gaze toward the wide, empty landscape surrounding them as the carriage rolled on toward Rylemoor Abbey.

Chapter 10

Constantia weighed whether to call out and beg the driver to stop.

They were currently passing through what might as well have been the middle of nowhere, and daylight was beginning to fade. But those were not always disadvantages. Darkness made it easier to disappear, and there would surely be a hedgerow or an outbuilding where she could shelter from the cold and damp. She was still sore and bruised in places, true, but she could walk. If she kept the setting sun to her right, she would be headed south. Eventually she would reach the water. A port town. A fishing boat.

Somewhere, some way she could get free of England entirely, without endangering anyone else.

She could feel Ryland's eyes boring into her with that mixture of astonishment and irritation he did so well. He would never permit her to walk away from the carriage, no matter how worried he claimed to be about his sisters. It wouldn't suit his notion of honor.

"You are right, of course," she said, pushing her shoulders down and turning to face him. She wouldn't cower like a frightened animal. "Ridiculous to think that I might be followed. What could anyone want with me?" She forced a little laugh into her voice. "Artists can be prone to fits of overactive imagination."

He nodded, a trifle wary of her sudden change of mood, if not the sentiment. "Yes. Perfectly understandable. You've suffered a shock, and your mind wants to concoct some interesting explanation for what happened, something that seems worthy of all the pain and disruption the accident caused. With time, however, the simple truth will come back to you. And when it does, I'll be only too happy to make whatever arrangements I can to help you get wherever you belong."

Only too happy . . . That, she didn't doubt. But the truth was, she didn't belong anywhere. She never, never had. Certainly not with Lord Ryland's family, where she might put his innocent sisters in danger. Oh, why hadn't she considered that risk sooner?

To her chagrin, tears sprang to her eyes. Shifting her gaze back to the window, she surreptitiously whisked the moisture away with her bandaged knuckles. "You're too kind," she said, surprising herself with the apparent sincerity in her voice.

"You're overwrought," he said, in that soothing tone she imagined him using with his sisters. "You should try to rest."

She nodded. Yes, she was exhausted and in shock. Leaning her head into the little corner formed by the back of the seat and the frame of the window, she closed her eyes and pretended to sleep. She wished with fresh desperation that she could remember those few moments before the accident. But try as she might, everything between the time of her leaving the meeting of the magazine staff and waking in Lord Ryland's house stubbornly remained a blank—and might always be so. No way of knowing for certain if she had been chased into the street or merely stumbled. No way to determine whether she was already being followed or whether she had a few more days or even weeks of peace.

And so, in spite of the comforting appeal of Ryland's words, in whose warmth she longed to luxuriate for a little longer, she focused instead on the damp chill seeping in around the glass and began to plan.

Once they had stopped for the night, she would set out on her own.

Sometime later, she was roused from thought—or rather, to her astonishment, from sleep—by the slowing of the carriage.

"Almost to the inn," Ryland said, peering outside. The sky was dark. "I wonder whether we shouldn't change horses and press on."

"I suppose that depends," she replied, trying with subtle movements to ease the kink from her neck, "on whether you are more concerned with the distance to be traveled tomorrow or your comfort tonight."

"My comfort?" He made a scoffing noise in his throat, as if he'd never considered such a thing. He looked her up and down. "Yours, certainly. John Coachman's," he added, jerking his gaze back to the window. "No, we'll stay. Tomorrow will have to take care of itself."

She mustered a smile. Tomorrow she would once

more be taking care of herself—as she preferred, of course. Only it had been more than a year since she had faced the peculiar struggles of a woman traveling over long distances alone. She couldn't yet judge how far she would be able to walk in a day, or how far she was from the coast. And then there was the matter of her money, the larger share of which had been entrusted to Lord Ryland. She hadn't yet worked out how to retrieve it without raising alarms.

But she would manage, somehow. Because she always had—and what choice did she have?

The inn was a large and bustling one, well suited to her intention of slipping away undetected. Ryland helped her down from the carriage and into a clean and neat anteroom with a tall counter opposite the door and well-polished benches along two walls hung with flower-patterned paper.

"My lord." A bespectacled woman, her brown hair liberally streaked with gray and arranged in the sort of knot from which softening locks did not dare slip, appeared suddenly behind the counter, as if she had emerged from the woodwork. Only then did Constantia see the outline of the door behind her, carefully papered over to disappear into the wall. "How may I serve you?"

"Two rooms, please," he said. "One for me and one for my sisters' new governess, Miss—"

"Creevey," Constantia supplied hurriedly. If she were right about being followed from London, then *Cooper* might be recognized.

"Very good, sir," the woman said, as if Constantia hadn't spoken. She wrote something in a ledger and handed over two keys. "I'll have a boy bring up your things. Will there be anything else?"

"Miss . . . Creevey," he glanced over his shoulder at her, something like confusion or perhaps speculation lifting one dark brow, "will take supper in her room."

Constantia only narrowly prevented herself from exhaling a sigh of relief. Lord Ryland's sense of propriety—she had almost called it *thoughtfulness*—would make it possible for her to get away that much sooner, and on a full stomach to boot. And if he intended to eat in the dining room, as his lack of instruction regarding his own meal would seem to indicate, that would provide just the window she needed to slip into his room and retrieve her money.

A few moments found her comfortably ensconced in a room on the second floor, blessedly near the servants' stairs, which she hoped would not creak. A girl arrived soon after with a fine supper of roast venison, and Constantia ate heartily, though she was not especially hungry. One never knew how long it might be between meals.

When the girl returned bearing a canister of hot water, Constantia bathed with her new soap and donned her nightdress, though she hadn't any intention of sleeping. She also scattered a few of her things about the room, the sign of a traveler settling in. That way the servants would assume that "Miss Creevey" was intent on a night's slumber, and nothing more.

She even dropped a subtle question regarding the frequency with which public conveyances stopped at the inn. In the morning, when it was discovered she was gone, someone might think to ask the servant, who would say she hadn't noticed anything amiss, but when pressed would recall a seemingly innocuous query about the stage.

At last, heartened by the clatter and commotion rising from the dining room below, she slipped on her mantle in lieu of a dressing gown and her shoes, stepped into the corridor, and took the stairs to the third floor.

After a quiet rap on the door to ensure no one was within, she entered to discover that Lord Ryland had been given a large and well-appointed suite, including a sitting room with a small table for dining and a bedchamber with separate dressing area. Instinctively, a flicker of annoyance, or perhaps jealousy, passed through her. Her money had paid for this luxury, after all—luxury she was not permitted to enjoy.

But he had not requested such accommodations, she reminded herself. The woman below had known his rank and simply assumed. Constantia thought of those faded pink draperies in his bedchamber in London. If one were a necessitous nobleman, it was no doubt difficult to pinch pennies without calling attention to circumstances one would rather not broadcast. Witness the fact that Ryland was at present suffering the noise of a crowded dining room rather than pay servants extra to bring his food here.

He would eat quickly, she decided, eager to retire to this private and pleasant space. She might not have much time. So, crossing the fingers of her bandaged hand for luck, she headed toward the bedchamber.

Like the sitting room, it might well have passed for

unoccupied. The dark green coverlet was unwrinkled; no head had dented the plump pillows. Only in the dressing room did she find evidence of his presence: his greatcoat hung from one peg, the shirt and cravat he'd been wearing from another; his valise sat open on a stool; and the contents of his toiletry kit were spread in orderly fashion about the washstand.

Stepping closer, she touched the outside of the water pitcher. Warm, but not hot. He had not been gone long enough for it to turn cold. She dragged a fingertip over the prickly bristles of his hairbrush, paused to sniff his cologne. He'd changed clothes, taken some pains to make himself presentable, but he had not shaved.

From an artistic standpoint, she rather liked him with the dark shadow of a beard. It made his jaw sharper, his face more . . . interesting.

Though they were hardly necessities, she meant to pack his gift of crayons and paper in her bag. That way she would have the means to draw him from memory once she was safe. Reining in the thought, she turned to the valise.

At first she found nothing but the expected items of clothing: fresh linen, a nightshirt, another pair of stockings. Then her fingers encountered the crinkly paper in which the laudanum bottle was wrapped, used by apothecaries so that patients would know, even in the dark, what they'd got into their hands. She hesitated for a moment, then decided it might prove beneficial and tucked it into the neck of her nightdress, between her breasts.

Further searching found nothing more of use to her

in the valise. Had he taken his purse with him to dine?
It seemed possible, probable even. Nevertheless, she
refused to be thwarted. Turning to the pockets of his
greatcoat, she began to rummage through them. At long
last, the clink of coins told her she had succeeded in
her quest.

Withdrawing the leather pouch, she spilled the coins
onto her bandaged palm. He'd spent carefully, she
would say that much for him. And she did not intend to
leave him without sufficient funds to pay the coachman
or the bill for their lodgings. He had been generous—
generous with *her* money, it was true—but too generous
for her to reward him with humiliation. Counting off a
suitable sum, she dropped those coins back into his
pocket and was in the process of taking the rest when
she heard the click of a door latch.

A servant, mostly likely, come to fetch the dirty water
away. If she were caught here, purse in hand, everyone
would assume she was stealing from her employer. To
preserve his good name, Lord Ryland might have little
choice but to cast her off. She'd be turned out into the
night, all on her own but not as she'd planned, with
nothing and no way to start again. She simply could not
afford to be spotted in his rooms.

But no matter how frantically she scoured the corners
and crevices, neither the dressing room nor the bedchamber offered any place for her to hide.

At least she would not have to wait long for her fate
to be sealed. There was nothing in any other part of
the suite that would require a servant's attention for
more than a moment or two. Footsteps approached the

door to the bedchamber, and she thrust her hands behind her back.

Her pulse pounding in her ears had muffled those footfalls. Otherwise, she might have realized more quickly that they did not belong to a maidservant, or even a footman. No, what she'd heard had been the booted tread of a gentleman.

Lord Ryland appeared in the doorway to the room.

"What are you doing here?" he demanded, his tone not precisely angry, but certainly surprised.

"I, uh—my, my headache has returned. Carriage travel never has agreed with me. I was looking for the laudanum."

He nodded, though one dark eyebrow lifted in a skeptical quirk. "I'm sorry to hear that. But why didn't you ring for a servant, have them find me? If you're feeling unwell, you might better have been resting in your room."

"Oh. Yes, of course. A much better idea. But I-I'm not accustomed to having servants, you see. I prefer to—"

"Do things for yourself," he finished, moving toward her as he spoke, the way one approached a timid animal one didn't wish to frighten. "Yes, I've noticed. Well, did you find it? Or shall I—?"

Eventually only the corner of the bed separated them. Not long until he discovered she'd taken more than the laudanum. And not long after that until he pieced together her intentions. He was rather cleverer than she'd given him credit for being. He would tell her that the risk of setting out alone was too great. He might even try to stop her. She needed a distraction, and she seized on the first that came to mind.

She launched herself forward and kissed him.

Lips and teeth met in an uncomfortable clash. Neither of them closed their eyes.

He didn't kiss like a practiced rake, to be sure.

Not that she had a great deal of experience kissing rakes—kissing anyone. Kisses required a degree of proximity, both physical and emotional, that she made it a rule never to allow.

And to be fair, this might not be his best effort. She *had* startled him. Instinctively, both of his hands had risen as she'd approached. To push her away, she'd thought at first. Or perhaps to catch her, imagining that she'd stumbled.

Now they hovered not quite an inch from her body, one at her waist and the other at her head, almost but not quite cupping her cheek. She could feel the brush of his fingers against the blowsy halo of her hair, the way a cat's whiskers sensed danger.

Why, then, was she tempted to nestle against his palm and purr?

Perhaps because his mouth had begun to soften. Almost imperceptibly, the kiss became something else, not an awkward embrace between strangers or the plundering conquest of a rake, but a tender, eager exploration. His eyes drifted shut, almost unwillingly, like a drowsy child resisting much-needed sleep. Or a proper gentleman succumbing to unwelcome desire. His charcoal-black lashes fanned over his cheeks in spiky shadows.

Her own eyes threatened to follow suit, to close, to surrender to the kiss. But another part of her wanted to go on looking at him forever.

What an effort it had taken to draw the Earl of Ryland as if he were not handsome as sin.

In spite of herself, her eyelids drooped. Other senses surged to take the place of sight. The gentle but insistent pressure of his lips against hers. The spice of his cologne and the sweet sharp tang of claret. The heat of his mouth, his touch, as his hand sank to her hip and drew her closer still.

The whisper of a sigh.

Her sigh.

She leaned into his embrace, pressed her lightly clothed form against his chest, then stiffened at the telltale crinkle of the laudanum bottle.

Good God. What was she thinking?

All he would have to do would be to wrap his arms around her, and he would find the purse.

She broke the kiss, took a step backward, opened her eyes.

"I'm sorry," he said gravely. As if he had done anything other than what she'd asked of him. As if he'd done something far more scandalous than kiss her back.

She shook her head, denying the apology, and almost immediately became aware of the sensation of the bottle sliding down the front of her nightgown, her bosom entirely inadequate to the task of keeping secrets.

Instinctively she brought up a hand to catch it and heard the muted tinkle of coins spilling onto the carpet around her.

Astonishment, disbelief, something very like hurt flared into his dark eyes. "What's this, Miss C—?"

Whether he had intended to use the old alias or the new, she couldn't be certain. She spoke across him before the word took shape.

"Constantia. My name is Constantia."

She blurted it out in part to divert attention from the unfolding disaster of the spilled purse and all it implied.

Also because over the last few days, an unexpected intimacy had grown between her and Lord Ryland, and the continued ruse of lost memory was now an uncomfortable weight she wanted to shed. This way, she could leave with a clear conscience.

But when he repeated *Constantia*, shaping the syllables of her name as if speaking in a foreign tongue, she realized her mistake.

Deception was her familiar, well-worn armor. The alternative was a vulnerability that left her lightheaded, her very spirit scraped raw.

She must have wobbled on her feet, for the next thing she knew, he had caught her by the upper arm and steered her backward to the chair in the dressing room, stepping carefully around the pile of spilled coins.

"You know who you are," he said, stooping so he could look into her face. His dark eyes flitted over her features, his own expression a mixture of confusion, disappointment, and relief. "I suspected as much all along. Yet you were going to"—he glanced toward the money and back again—"to leave without saying anything at all."

"Yes. I—" She paused to gnaw on her lower lip.

"It's safer for you if I do. And you've been kinder than I expected, far kinder than I deserved."

"Kinder than you expected," he echoed, irony hollowing out his voice. "Then you—you remember me too."

Unable to hold his gaze, she nodded. "From the first. But you offered me your protection—"

"Until your memory returned," he finished for her, his voice heavy with something like disbelief.

He sank to the floor, dropping onto his backside with a soft *thud*, then propping one forearm on his raised knee. The pose suggested he expected to be seated thus for some time. "Before you go, Constantia," he said, giving her name a subtle stress, a hint of skepticism, "don't you think I deserve the truth?"

Chapter 11

"People do not always get what they deserve," Constantia reminded him quietly. "But I will tell you what I can."

Because once she had, Ryland would know *what* she was, as well as *who*, and then he would not try to keep her here or insist on introducing her to his sisters. In fact, he would be only too glad to help her get away.

But for the moment, he was looking at her expectantly. Almost eagerly. She pulled her mantle more snugly around her throat, as if mere wool could shield her from the intensity of his dark gaze. Difficult to believe that moments before she had found the nerve to kiss him. That she now knew the feel of his mouth against hers.

Knowledge changed a person, changed the relationship between people.

Everything had changed in the last few moments.

And it was about to change again.

"My mother was the middle daughter of a marquess," she began, dropping her eyes to lap. "He's still alive. But he disowned her long ago. Don't ask his name."

She paused, expecting Ryland to protest. But she was hardly foolish enough to give the name of one peer to another. She understood where loyalty lay. When he did not push for it, she let a shaky breath escape her lungs, part relief, part resignation. She had no excuse not to go on. "At seventeen, she went to London for her first Season and met a man. Not at all the sort of man her father had in mind for her—though," she added with a humorless chuckle, "he did claim to be nobility, in exile from some obscure European principality."

A lie, she was sure, but if such a place had ever existed, no doubt Napoleon had since wiped it from the map.

"He was an artist. She let him make her portrait. Like a fool, she posed without—without any—" She had to pause and swallow past the next word.

"In the nude," Ryland offered quietly.

She jerked up her chin. "You've seen it."

A nod, the faintest movement imaginable. "That first night. You were unconscious, and at first, I didn't recognize you. I went through your things, searching for something that would tell me who you were."

His voice was remarkably free of judgment. She steeled herself against it all the same. "Well, you found it, didn't you? I'm the daughter of the sort of woman who would let a man paint a picture of her naked as the day she was born. Although perhaps that was fitting— he must have made her promises of the sort that only a baby, or a naïve nobleman's daughter, would expect to be kept. She ran away with him. I arrived in due course. And before I had turned three years old, he had abandoned us both."

"Oh, my dear Miss—"

It amused her, somehow, his determination to be proper, to follow the rules of etiquette, to maintain a respectful distance between them.

"Constantia," she corrected. "It's a town on the Black Sea, you know. He claimed to have summered there in his youth, and regaled my mother with tales of its beauty. That's why she chose such an outlandish name. Too distinctive—too recognizable. I hadn't used it for years. And then, in a moment of weakness, I thought I should like to hear it again, so I told it to Lady Stalbridge and the others at the magazine . . ."

That had been almost as grave a mistake as giving it to him.

"But you did not reveal your surname?" he asked. "She seemed convinced the one you gave her was false."

"Have I a real one? I'm—" *A bastard,* she had been going to say. But he would recoil at that, and recoil again when she laughed at him. "I'm the illegitimate daughter of a liar and a fraud. And what claim has my mother's family on me?"

He nodded, though rather absently. She wondered whether he was considering what he might do if one of his sisters found herself in a similarly unfortunate situation. "And after? When your mother had . . . gone?"

"She did not die of a broken heart," Constantia explained stubbornly. *No matter what she said.* "Just an ordinary fever. We lived then in London, in one of those neighborhoods where my mother's family, and yours I'm sure, would never set foot. The woman who attended her at the end was kind enough not to drop me at an orphanage but instead sent me to her sister in Essex, who had sons but wanted a girl around the house. I rubbed along all right with the family, in spite of this." She gestured with her left hand, its dominance a supposedly sinister sign, and then wound a red curl around her first finger. "And this." Her hair had always been the bane of her existence, a mark of her difference, almost impossible to hide. "I was just six years old when I went to them, young enough that my memories began to fade and I forgot . . . forgot those dingy rooms and my mother's stories, my mother's face. Then one day, I was doing my chores—I was nine or so then, at an age when I was eager to please. I stood on a chair to clean the top of the enormous old wardrobe in my foster mother's room—and I found—I found . . ."

"The portrait."

It was her turn to flinch. He understood too much, the Earl of Ryland. She was right to put distance between them.

"Yes," she confessed after a moment. "It was wrapped up in paper and tied with string. My name—my Christian name—was written on the outside, in what I later learned was my mother's hand. At first, I didn't even realize it was in reference to me. In that house, I had only ever been known as Connie, you see. But it stirred something in some corner of my memory. I had to know, so naturally, I unwrapped the package. There was a letter, too, from my mother—perhaps you read the part of it I kept?" His answering nod was sharp, chagrined. "A bit maudlin, but I suppose she wrote it on her deathbed. I was still trying to make sense of it when my foster-mother came in and caught me, my hands full, still standing on that rickety chair. It's a wonder I didn't fall," she recalled with a wry laugh. "I can't believe she didn't have her suspicions about my origins before that day. But the picture was too much for her. Proof of my degenerate nature far more damning than left-handedness and unruly red hair. She sent me packing that very hour."

A sound escaped him them. Pity, or very near it. It plucked at something deep inside her and made an ache in her chest. But of course, children endured worse all the time. She had endured worse.

"She kindly gave me half a crown," she reassured him. "I walked to Cambridge and, from there, posted myself to Sheffield."

"So far! Why Sheffield?"

"I'd read a story where the heroine was said to have 'a spine of Sheffield steel.' I didn't understand it was a metaphor, and I'm quite sure now that it wasn't intended as a compliment, but I was determined to get myself one. Figured it would help me survive."

The bedchamber window showed nothing but the night sky, and the only light came from the lamp in the sitting room. She couldn't easily read Lord Ryland's face, which was in shadow. But she saw his hand twitch, almost as if he wanted to reach for her, to console her.

"I succeeded, you know," she said warningly. "The steel. The spine."

He turned his head, and when the little bit of light struck his profile, she watched wry amusement slide across his features. "Of that, Constantia, I'm certain. What happened next?"

"I found a girls' school, concocted a story almost as unbelievable as the truth, persuaded them to let me take classes in exchange for housework. The other pupils . . . tolerated me, I suppose you could say." She smoothed her hands over her knees, wishing unpleasant memories could be brushed away as easily as wrinkles in wool. "Anyway, I stayed for six years and I learned two things, one of which was that I had inherited my father's artistic gift."

"And the other?"

"That the portrait frame has a hidden compartment, into which my mother had tucked a pair of earbobs. When it became necessary to leave that place, I hocked one and lived off the money until I could hone my skills enough to live by my art."

Even in the dimness, she could see his eyes widen. "I take it there has been more to your career than sketching mocking cartoons for a ladies' magazine."

In spite of herself, a smile tugged at one corner of her mouth. "A bit. But the work Lady Stalbridge had me do was of a piece. I draw and paint to suit my patrons, not myself. It's the rare artist who can afford to do otherwise."

Let him think what he would of the drawings she had made of him. They had paid her rent. She refused to speak of them, or of the watercolor she had entered in the exhibition, the only art she had made in recent memory that was solely hers.

"So, you claim that for"—his eyes traveled over her, assessing, and then he lifted one shoulder—"ten years, more or less, you have been moving from place to place, working under a variety of assumed names, drawing and painting whatever others will pay you to produce, and keeping the real you hidden away."

He finished with another sweep of his dark gaze, recalling her to the fact that she had sneaked into his rooms in her nightgown. He had held her, just for a moment, in his arms, and she had pressed her lips to his. Awareness prickled over her skin and raised gooseflesh.

"I have done what I had to do, told whatever lies would serve, in order to keep myself safe."

If he had any sense at all, he would take those words as a warning.

"Forgive me, but given your . . . unassuming history," he asked, "why should someone mean you harm? Did you paint an unflattering portrait, perhaps?"

She leaped up and stepped toward the bedchamber. "Mock me if you must. I suppose I deserve that." She had meant, after all, to mock *him* and everything he stood for with all those cartoons and sketches.

Though she had never dreamed that he cared.

"No." He, too, had got to his feet, and he came to stand beside her, head tilted so she could not easily avoid his eyes. "I apologize. That remark was unworthy of both of us."

Oddly, she believed him—not just that he was sorry, but that he thought her worthy of some respect, in spite of her parentage and the tale she had told. She dipped her chin in acknowledgment, and to her relief, he took a step back.

"It was the earring," she explained, when her head had stopped swimming from the sudden rush of standing up too quickly, or her too acute awareness of his proximity. "It was more valuable than I expected. And evidently more important. I sold it when I first came to London, and even after all the time that had passed, I think someone must have recognized it and alerted my grandfather. That was when I first became aware of being followed, and when odd little incidents started to occur.

"So I began to move about regularly, changed my name, stayed vigilant. It worked well enough for a while," she insisted. "It's not difficult to hide in the hustle and bustle of Town. Sometimes months would go by with no trouble. Most recently, I enjoyed the better part of a year free from harassment. But now the *Magazine for Misses* has attracted unwelcome attention. Someone has discovered the identity of every contributor, even Mrs. Goode, and intends to expose us. I couldn't stay and find out what might happen to everyone else. I—I ran."

"Into the street. In front of my house." His voice was steady and even—alarmingly so. He sounded almost bored. "Were you being chased?"

"I don't know. That's the only part of my past that truly is a blank."

A pause ensued while he paced twice across the room and back. Evidently it required some effort to take in everything she had told him. "It doesn't quite add up. All this trouble over an earring?"

She shrugged. "An heirloom, I suppose. Although I have wondered . . ."

"Yes?"

"Whether my mother's family knows about the picture. And if so, how far might they go to be rid of the only evidence, the last reminder of her indiscretion?"

But of course, if that were the case, why stop at the portrait? Constantia hadn't realized or remembered until she saw it how remarkably similar in appearance she was to the woman who had brought her into the world. More recently, she had begun to consider how awkward it would be to cross paths with someone to whom her face was eerily familiar.

She knew nothing more of her grandfather's character than that he was a nobleman, and thus powerful. It was terrible to think he might be the sort of man to use his power to make absolutely certain such a meeting could never happen. But once the idea had occurred to her, she could not shake it.

By the light from the sitting room, she saw Lord Ryland's eyes narrow. An expression of disbelief. His gaze did not meet hers.

But then he said, "When I first saw the Unfashionable Plates, I supposed that you didn't like men very much. Now I understand that it is not really a matter of dislike. You do not trust them—and with good reason, it would seem."

She fought the impulse to recoil from the insight within those words.

Then he lifted his dark eyes to her face, their expression as earnest as his voice. "Thank you for trusting me."

It must have been the knock on her head. Because he was right, of course. She didn't trust anyone, especially men. Yet she had trusted him—*reluctantly*, she wanted to defend herself. *When I had no other choice.*

"What now?" he asked after a moment, glancing at the money still scattered at their feet.

"I intend to sell the other earring and use the proceeds to leave England for good."

He dropped onto one knee. "May I suggest an alternative plan?"

Her heart gave a frightful lurch—a reaction, to her chagrin, not made up entirely of dismay. "You can't mean—" she began and then bit off the rest when she realized he had only stooped to gather the spilled coins.

She was in danger of ending up no better than her mother, imagining a gauzy, rose-tinted world of romance, forgetting how the sharp, jagged edges of reality could wound.

"I've seen no indication that we're being followed," he said, perfectly steadily, as if the earth had not ground to a halt, momentarily knocking her off-balance, and then resumed spinning before she had fully recovered. "But I did offer you protection, Miss—Constantia. No, that won't do. *Creevey* is to be, now?"

"Cooper will be fine," she told him. What proof did

she even have that anyone was presently on her heels? Ridiculous, really, for her to imagine that a common surname would be the clue that revealed too much.

"All right, then," he agreed, rising. "Miss Cooper." He gave one of his stiff bows, as if they were being introduced for the first time. "Come to Rylemoor as we planned. Recover fully from your injuries. And in a few weeks, after the Christmas holidays perhaps, you can go to Bristol, where my Aunt Josephine lives, and use this"—here, he tucked the still-hefty purse into her hand—"to sail away from all your troubles. Save the bauble and sell it in some far-off land where no one will be the wiser."

It sounded so perfect, so easy. She wanted quite desperately for all of it to happen just as he said.

But in her whole life, nothing had ever been easy.

"You're certain Rylemoor Abbey is secure?" she demanded, trying to find the flaw in the plan. "Fitted out with wrought iron fences and high stone walls and massive doors to keep the world at bay?"

"After a fashion," he agreed, though there was a certain wryness in his expression. "Most important, there's nothing but bleak moorland for miles about, nothing a stranger in his right mind—or even out of it—would try to cross this time of year."

She had revealed herself to be the daughter of a fallen woman and a rogue; she had confessed to lurking on the outskirts of good society all her life. If the Earl of Ryland were the stodgy moralizer she had drawn him to be, he would have sent her away empty-handed.

If he were a secret scoundrel, as she'd always assumed, he would have tried to seduce her and justified his behavior with her presumably easy virtue. Instead of doing either, he had offered to help her. He had invited her to his home.

She had been waiting, muscles tensed, fully expecting him to betray the trust she'd placed in him. She'd misjudged him terribly.

Perhaps, in future, she ought to place less trust in herself.

Unsure what other gesture of acceptance to make, she curtsied. "Th-thank you. How can I ever hope to repay you?"

At the same time, waving a hand toward the bed, he said, "You should stay here tonight."

Chapter 12

Alistair watched her fingers tighten around the purse until her knuckles turned white. He'd never excelled on the cricket pitch, but he recognized that grip. Why on earth would she be preparing to throw it at him? Unless—

In his mind he heard the echo of her last words. And his. The peculiar way the exchange had collided. As if he had been suggesting that, to repay his generosity, she should sleep in his bed.

Given how the day had started, it wouldn't be an outrageous leap for her to have imagined that he intended to share that bed with her.

Quickly, he raised a hand to stay her. "Alone! I meant, of course, that you should stay here"—he gestured again toward the bed, palm upward, the sort of motion a man made to assure an opponent he was unarmed—"alone, while I pass the night elsewhere. In the room that was given to you, perhaps. That way, if anyone does come looking for you, they'll not find who they expected."

Color gradually returned to her fingers, though she did not drop the purse. "I . . . suppose . . . that makes some sense. I feared that you meant . . ."

"So I gathered." He crossed his arms over his chest. "I realize, Miss Cooper, that my behavior toward you has not always been that of a saint. Or a monk. I accept full blame for this morning's . . . unfortunate incident and have most sincerely attempted to make amends." Her expression might have been carved from granite. "But may I now ask," he continued with unwonted boldness, "what I have done to give you the impression that I am the sort of gentleman who would—who would take advantage—take advantage of—?" He cleared his throat. "That is to say, such a portrait of my character seems inconsistent with the rather, er, staid pictures you have in fact drawn of me. Repeatedly."

He would have been willing to swear that a full minute passed before she blinked. "May not a man be judged by the company he keeps?"

"Ah. You're referring, I suppose, to—"

"Lord Deveraux." Each word rang with disapproval and called to mind the sketch she'd made of the man, complete with devil's horns, to accompany the essay on rakes written by the magazine's advice columnist, "Miss Busy B." Burke—now, Lady Deveraux.

Alistair narrowly bit back a laugh. It was hardly the first time his friendship with Miles had got him into hot water. Though it might, he mused, be the last, since *that devil, Deveraux* had reformed and was now hewing to the straight and narrow—or straighter and narrower, at least.

But if the old Miles had ever happened to find himself stuck with a svelte and spirited redhead, he would certainly have found ways to pass the time that did not induce frustration of one sort or another.

Not that Alistair was without ideas. But unlike Miles, who had only ever been responsible for himself, Alistair had always been too aware that his every choice shaped his sisters' future.

And Alistair's father had seen to it that he had blessedly few choices to begin with.

Be that as it may, Alistair had made one choice all on his own, one he intended to honor: He had chosen to befriend Miles. "Lord Deveraux is my friend and, I hope, always will be. I have no intention of defending him to you, Miss Cooper," he said. "Nor of defending myself. You may make of it what you will." He turned to leave. "I'll wish you good night."

"You . . ." For the first time in their journey, he heard genuine worry in her voice. "You've not changed your mind?"

"About Miles?"

"About . . . me."

In the dim room, her pale skin seemed to glow; the bruise on her cheek might have been no more than a shadow. The ruffles on her white cotton nightdress peeked from between the edges of her dark woolen mantle. She looked younger than he knew she must be, and he thought suddenly of her mother. Had she looked thus when she ran away from home, toward a dream that had become a nightmare?

"I think I was wrong," he said, not really answering her. "You don't trust me after all, do you? But perhaps it is as well. You clearly do not know me either."

She looked as if she would speak. Her lips parted—lips he had kissed, for God's sake—but the only sound that emerged was a shivery sort of sigh.

"Before I go, may I give you a piece of advice?" He paused, waiting for her almost imperceptible nod. "If you're going to throw something at someone"—he jerked his chin toward the leather purse still clutched in her hand—"strike fast. Don't let them see what you're about to do. Don't give them a chance to mount a defense."

Her eyes flared. "You—you thought I meant to throw it at you?"

"Seven sisters, remember?" He managed something close to a grin. "As well as seven years in one of our nation's fine public schools. Sharpens the eye and hones a fellow's reflexes."

She didn't smile. "Your little jokes are rarely amusing, Lord Ryland. And usually poorly timed."

He shrugged. "I wasn't joking. At least, not about the advice."

Then he closed the distance between them, reached for her wrist, and pried the small pouch from her unresisting fingers. Once, twice, he weighed the purse on his palm. Safer, surely, to take it with him. She had deceived him. She was desperate. She would think nothing of stranding him here.

He tossed it onto the bedside table, where it landed with a soft *chink*.

At the sound, she flinched.

"I think I now understand the real purpose of your spectacles," he said.

"To—to take aim?" she ventured, obviously puzzled. "But I told you, I can see well enough without them."

"I'm sure. Plain glass rarely improves one's vision." He paused as understanding washed over her features: He had known all along that she was deceiving him and had still given her help. "Yes, that's right. I had a look at them the day of the accident. I couldn't quite figure out why you wore spectacles if not for poor eyesight. But I've since learned that your eyes reveal more than you must sometimes wish. It must have been useful to have something to hide them behind. Sleep well, Miss Cooper," he told her. After snatching his greatcoat from the peg, he turned and walked back toward the doorway to the sitting room, then paused and glanced over his shoulder. She hadn't moved, though her gaze had dropped to the floor. "I've instructed John Coachman to be ready to depart at dawn. Barring yet another unforeseen disruption, we'll be at Rylemoor shortly before dark."

In the corridor, he listened for the grate of the key in the lock. That sound was followed by the scrape of some large piece of furniture being dragged across the floor—the settee, he supposed—and the bump of it being nestled against the door.

The barricade felt personal, though he knew it likely

wasn't. Her fear and distrust weren't primarily directed at him, and they weren't going to be conquered in two days. Perhaps not in a lifetime—not that he'd ever know.

He had been the sort of boy who'd taken in wild, wounded things and tried—with middling success—to nurse them tame. His friendship with Miles was just another example.

He ought to have remembered the risk of being bitten.

One floor below, in her room, he looked around at the remarkable disorder she'd created in, what, an hour at most? Clothes strewn across the bed, paper on the table. The air smelled of the pear blossom soap she'd purchased in Price's Mercantile.

As did, he now knew, her skin.

He dragged in a shuddering breath, exhaled, and then set about putting the room to rights.

"What a mess," he muttered to himself. Not that he was entirely surprised. It was the sort of chaos he'd learned to expect from artists. "Still, if she intended to be off immediately after retrieving her money, shouldn't she have packed?"

As he neatened the papers, he studied the sketch she'd been making in the carriage: a landscape that must have come entirely from her imagination, as it certainly did not match the dull one that had been scrolling past the windows.

Or perhaps the landscape was not so dull when seen through fresh eyes.

The sketch she had made of the church and churchyard was there, too, and he dared to trace a fingertip over the empty place beside the sexton, where he knew he'd been standing. He wasn't sure whether to be resentful over his deliberate omission or, given her previous treatment of the subject, grateful.

He recalled what she had told him about her art, how she had never really been at liberty to draw what she wished or for herself. At least in some small way, perhaps, he had given her that.

Mostly, though, he wanted something that would tell him whether he was in her thoughts as much as she was in his.

Once the pictures were collected, he carried the paper and box of charcoals over to the bed, tucked it along the side of the valise and tried not to think about the portrait of her mother. Best not to look at it again, even if Constantia's story had made his curiosity twinge.

"Not much point in sending up her clothes now," he debated aloud with himself, recalling the barricaded door. As he folded a pair of petticoats and a dress, laid them on top, and closed the valise with a snap he countered, "But will she still be there if I wait 'til morning?"

He wasn't foolish enough to imagine that the fact she was wearing only a nightgown—and ordinary shoes; her mud-caked ankle boots were lying topsy-turvy on the floor—would be enough to deter her if she was determined to go.

Bending, he snatched up one of the boots and, with a

knife from the discarded supper tray, began to scrape away the mud, collecting it on a crumpled piece of brown wrapping paper from one of her purchases at Price's.

The tap at the door that came a moment later was quiet, unassuming, but even before he could answer, the door swung inward and a mob-capped servant peeked into the opening. "Is everything all right, miss? I thought I heard a man's voi—oh!" The door swung wide as she crumpled into an inelegant curtsy. "It's you, my lord."

"Miss Crawley—er, Creevey—and I elected to exchange rooms."

The maid goggled but was too well trained to ask questions, and Alistair was glad his standing at the inn did not oblige him to offer any further explanation. Her gaze flitted about the room, as if ascertaining that he was indeed alone, and landed finally on him. Her eyes widened further. "I can do that, sir." She nodded toward the boots.

"No. I—" *I need something with which to occupy myself.* "I'm almost finished."

"If you're certain," she said, though her voice was incredulous. She curtsied again, more shallowly this time, as if she were eager to get away—and relate her discovery of a lord turned bootboy to every other servant belonging to the place, he had no doubt.

"See that I'm awakened at five," he told her as he once more bent his head to his task.

"Very good, sir." The door clicked shut and she was gone.

Seated on the edge of the bed, he worked at the boots awhile longer, careful not to mar the leather. It was occupation for his hands but, unfortunately, not his mind.

Constantia had released thoughts and emotions that now crashed through his head without regard to the lanes and fences he'd so carefully built over the years to keep everything in line.

He felt, inexplicably, as if something had been stolen from him. But what? The money was hers, without question. And regardless of how ill-advised it might be for her to slip away into the night, it must be her choice. Even the kiss could not rightly be called stolen.

He'd given it far too willingly.

She kissed with an innocence that seemed somehow at odds with the story she had told. Not that he agreed with those who would claim that she shared her mother's sin—or even that her mother bore the blame for what had happened to her. But there was something in Constantia's unique way of looking at the world that seemed as if it should have made its way to her lips. The same power that made his breath catch when he looked at one of her drawings made him imagine that her kiss could leave a man breathless, if she chose.

Perhaps if she hadn't broken off the kiss quite so soon, or if he hadn't been caught off guard . . .

Perhaps what he'd lost was an opportunity.

But if so, it was an opportunity that he must hope never presented itself again.

No matter how much she intrigued him—oh, and frustrated and exasperated him, too, as in his experience artistic types were wont to do. No matter if he was beginning to suspect that at least some of her annoyance with him might mask another emotion entirely. No matter that hearing part of her story had made him only more eager to pry open all her secrets.

Their paths had been marked out for them long ago, and neither of them could afford to explore other tracks. So, he would do as he'd said, do what he'd always done: ensure that she was safe from predators until her injured wing righted itself, then let her fly free.

While his feet stayed firmly on the ground.

"Firmly on the ground," he scoffed beneath his breath as John Coachman reached out a hand to hoist him onto the top of the coach, where he'd elected to ride the remainder of the journey.

Alistair had risen even before the knock had come to wake him, and when the servant did arrive, he had employed her as an emissary to send up Constantia's neatly packed valise, with instructions that they would depart as soon as she was ready.

Now he was sitting huddled in his greatcoat, watching dawn begin to streak the sky, and wondering if she would show up.

The leap of his heart when she emerged from the inn told him that he'd been wise to take extra precautions.

She pushed the edge of her hood back just enough to

give him a glimpse of her red-gold curls and looked up at him quizzically.

"Thought it would be best to have a second lookout," he told her. And it wasn't an untruth; there was even a pistol by his feet, though he'd never been what anyone would call a crack shot.

Her nod of understanding held a bit of uncertainty, but she accepted the hostler's assistance into the carriage. In another moment, they were off. And once the sun had risen, he did, indeed, feel a bit safer for being able to see far and wide.

A great deal safer for not having to share the cozy interior with her.

And a great deal colder too.

At most stops, she did not leave the coach, and when she did, she was back again more swiftly than previous travels with a party of young ladies, namely his sisters, had led him to believe was possible.

Late afternoon, they alighted for dinner at a modest-looking inn.

"You will dine with me?" he asked, offering an arm to escort her inside.

She shivered when her hand brushed the wind-chilled wool of his coat. "If you wish it."

He did, though he knew it was not wise.

While waiting for her tea, Constantia removed her gloves, and he glimpsed the telltale marks of her craft. "You've been sketching again."

"It passes the time."

He did not ask her subject.

"You spent a restful night, I hope?"

"Entirely," he lied.

"I'm glad to hear it. You certainly ceded the more comfortable room to me." In spite of that fact, there were shadows beneath her eyes. Sleep, it seemed, had not come quickly for either of them.

The food arrived then, relieving them of the burden of conversation. When they had finished, he donned his hat and gloves and buttoned his coat securely over a woolen muffler he'd borrowed from the coachman.

"I'm sorry you have had a chilly ride," she said—ironically, the warmest sentiment she had uttered all day. "Without . . . incident, I hope?"

He knew precisely what she meant.

He considered whether she might be amused by a recounting of his reaction to his first—and only—slug from the coachman's flask. Whatever it contained, he felt certain she could use it to thin paint.

But he remembered what she had said the night before about his failed attempts at humor.

"Entirely," he said instead. Again.

He had no intention of mentioning the solitary rider who had kept pace with them just long enough to catch even the coachman's notice—and to make that ordinarily taciturn fellow recall a rather hair-raising tale about a three-fingered highwayman—before shearing off northward and being lost to sight.

Alistair had never before been prone to flights of fancy, had strenuously avoided them in fact, and he didn't intend for that to change now.

Once they reached his home, he would order things so that he and Constantia saw very little of one another, as it should be. They would put this strange, intimate interlude behind them.

As night fell, he spotted the approach to Rylemoor, marked by a wrought iron gate suspended between two stone pillars. He hoped that bit of fancywork would put her mind at ease, though he'd never employed a gatekeeper. Those were wages he couldn't afford to waste, not when there was nothing and no one from which the house needed to be guarded. Bleak and treacherous moorland stretched in every direction, with nothing more than outcroppings of stones or a few scrub trees for an intruder to hide behind. For an abbey, and a religious community bent on isolation from the world, it was the perfect spot.

But he had often wondered whether the long-ago king who'd presented this particular earldom to Alistair's ancestor had intended the gesture as reward or punishment.

The house itself was hardly more inviting. Over everything loomed the dilapidated west wing, made up by and large of the former church, which he would dearly love to raze. Unfortunately, even tearing down required funds.

They rolled to a stop on the graveled courtyard, surrounded on three sides by weathered stone walls that blocked what little daylight remained. He had not expected his sisters to be waiting in the cold to greet him, arriving as he was in unexpected fashion and later than he'd hoped. But evidently even the servants had been caught out. Alistair swung down and opened the carriage door himself.

"Welcome, Miss Cooper," he said with a flourish that was only a little self-mocking, "to Rylemoor Abbey."

Chapter 13

All Constantia's efforts not to form expectations about Rylemoor Abbey had been in vain. And now that she saw it, all her expectations were—no, not *disappointed*. That word was wholly inadequate.

Exploded, then.

She had seen abbeys before, of course. Some still in use. Some crumbled into interesting ruins that people traveled far to see and sketch.

Rylemoor was neither. And both.

Lights, draperies, and other evidence of habitation in the two lower wings disguised the building's great age. The former church, however, had long since surrendered to the wildness of the moors around it, battered by centuries of wind and rain since its lead roof had been stripped away in the time of Henry VIII.

To one side, something approaching coziness beckoned. To the other, a skeleton of stone that loomed in awful splendor and fired her artistic imagination. It was everything that the little stone church in the village was not.

She was drifting in that direction without conscious thought when Lord Ryland touched her elbow and directed her the other way. "I know better than to forbid you from exploring the west wing, like some ogre of old," he said with a small smile. "But be advised, it's not in safe condition. I certainly don't recommend it after dark. And besides, my sisters will be eager to meet you."

She stumbled against the crushed stone of the courtyard. "How can you be certain?"

"Because . . ." His voice trailed off and he shook his head. "You'll see."

The tall carved door was surrounded by elaborate stonework softened by time, and as they approached it swung inward. A man well past his middle years, the butler presumably, bowed. "My lord. We did not realize—"

Ryland waved off the explanation. "Not to worry, Wellend. Our arrival was unpredictable. I was delayed in Town by . . . circumstances beyond my control. This is Miss Cooper."

She curtsied, a little uneasily. She might as well have been wearing a placard around her neck bearing the word *circumstances*. "Good evening, Mr.—Wellend, was it?" The butler inclined his head.

"Are my sisters abed, Wellend?"

"Not yet, sir. I believe you'll find them in the family sitting room."

"Excellent. Please have Mrs. Swetley make ready the chamber near the old schoolroom for Miss Cooper."

"Very good, my lord." With another bow, the butler left them, betraying no hint of surprise.

"I think you'll find the light in the schoolroom well suited to your purposes, Miss Cooper," Lord Ryland explained. Constantia only nodded, fully absorbed by the task of taking in her surroundings.

She knew enough about architecture to recognize the Tudor influences on the entry hall in which they stood: rough-hewn beams, walnut paneling, arched windows. At one end of the room stood a fireplace tall enough to roast a stag. But the fire was low and gave off too little heat to stave off the room's stony chill. Three centuries ago, there would have been tapestries to soften and warm the room, but now the walls were bare.

"This way to the family parlor." He gestured toward a short passageway, and at the end of it a winding staircase, the treads polished and worn by generations.

"Oh. I, um . . ." She glanced down at her travel-stained and wrinkled dress. "I hadn't thought to meet your sisters quite so soon." Not that she had a fresh, un-wrinkled dress into which she might change. But at least *she* might be fresher.

"Nonsense. Once they get wind of your arrival, no one in this house will be permitted a moment's rest until you've been introduced."

She couldn't imagine why anyone would be so excited to meet her, or why, given that she was an entirely unexpected guest, it would be difficult to keep her presence under wraps a bit longer. She gathered from Lord Ryland's instructions to the butler that she was to be placed in some corner of the abbey little used by the family.

But she followed as she was led, rather than risk being left alone in the entry hall, watching the fire sputter and eventually die.

The stairs ended at a small alcove, which opened into what must be the family sitting room, with a cozy fire blazing in the hearth and comfortable furniture collected over several generations. On those furnishings were seated four young women, ranging in age from about fifteen to one- or two-and-twenty, employed in various tasks: letter writing, embroidery, and a contentious game of chess. Constantia stood for a moment, taking in the scene over the earl's shoulder, until he cleared his throat and drew their attention.

"Alistair!" they cried out almost as one, and two of them—one of the chess players and the one at the writing desk—leaped up and came toward them.

"We were wondering what had become of you," said the other chess player, who nonetheless had returned her attention to studying the board. "We expected you yesterday, on the mail coach."

"Instead, it brought us a letter from Aunt Josephine," said one of those who had approached to hug her brother. She made a sour expression to indicate that the substitution had not met with her approval.

"I wish you'd been half an hour earlier, at least," said the one beside her. "I was forced to play Georgie instead, and she's not very good."

"Is that so?" The aforementioned Georgie—Lady Georgiana, that was—stood up from the table so abruptly that she jarred the board and several pieces toppled over. "Then I quit."

That earned a shrug from her opponent. "You were going to lose anyway."

"Harry!" exclaimed the young woman still seated with her embroidery. And then all four of them began to jabber at one another. They all had their brother's dark hair and similar enough features that Constantia hadn't a prayer of sorting out which sister was which, or even who was speaking to whom. This was the cacophony that staid Lord Ryland had professed to miss?

"We have a guest," he said to his sisters, speaking so low that Constantia was certain he could not have been heard.

But something about the deeper timbre of his voice cut neatly through his sisters' chatter. They turned, almost as one, and Constantia felt four pairs of dark eyes settle on her.

"This," he said, stepping to one side so that they could see her better, "is Miss Cooper. An accident befell her in Town and I offered her my assistance in the form of employment. She is engaged to offer all of you instruction—"

Four faces met that announcement with varying degrees of suspicion and wariness.

"In drawing," he finished.

At that, silence settled over the room as quickly as the noise had first erupted. The sisters looked from one to the other, as if deciding collectively on their response.

"Drawing?" repeated the letter writer, an edge of disbelief to her voice.

"Yes. And whatever else in that line she feels appropriate. Watercolors, perhaps. Or pastels."

"Art?" That was one who had been chastised and addressed as Harry. Lady Harriet, then. The one whom Lord Ryland had described as possessing not just an artistic inclination, but a gift. "You—you are going to allow us to have instruction in art?"

"It occurred to me that a ladylike accomplishment or two might rid me of you faster," their brother teased.

But Lady Harriet's expression was solemn. "Truly?"

The earnestness of the question wiped the smile from Lord Ryland's face. "Truly."

And then Harriet's arms were around her brother and the three remaining sisters were approaching Constantia with outstretched hands and more sharply whetted curiosity. "However did you manage to persuade him, Miss Cooper?" asked the one who'd been losing at chess.

"I—" she began, and then shook her hand. "Your brother is a generous man. My art was the only currency with which I might repay him." She was suddenly aware of the weight of her reticule and the purse within, and her mind flooded with the memory of last night, the twinge of regret she'd felt when he had left, and the large, comfortable bed she had slept in, alone.

That answer only partly appeased them. She watched a speculative glance fly between the two she thought might be the eldest, though they were all so close in age, it was difficult to tell.

"I am Edwina," said the one who had been embroidering.

The one who preferred country life, Constantia recalled, and thus stayed at Rylemoor. What a gloomy existence for a young woman! Though her expression was mild and obviously her manners had not been affected by the solitude.

"This is Frederica," Edwina went on, indicating the letter writer, "and Georgiana, and Harriet, the youngest."

"And Danny will be here in a week," added Frederica.

Harriet piped up. "*With* Aunt Josephine. *And* they're staying for *six weeks*."

"Our aunt means to stay, too?" their brother asked, the very evenness of the question betraying his surprise. "I expected her to send Danny alone while she went to her friends at Bath, as she usually does, and then return for our sister at the end of her visit."

"It's all in the letter," said Frederica, going to the desk and returning with a folded missive she handed to him. "The entertainments in Bath have grown insipid and she prefers to spend the time with her family." It was not quite mimicry, but close enough that Constantia had to bite back a smile.

No one else looked amused.

"Well," he said after a moment. "Christmas is a time for family, is it not?"

"You're not going to send Miss Cooper away now?" Harriet demanded.

"Certainly not," Georgiana answered stoutly for him.

Lord Ryland's "no" was considerably more measured. Alarm flickered through Constantia. Was her position here as tenuous as that? The aunt might be a dragon, but surely the earl was not powerless in his own home.

"Miss Cooper will no doubt prefer to keep to the schoolroom," he went on, "and take her meals alone, as your other teachers have done."

Alone. Isolated. Constantia thought of the hours and rooms they'd shared, and might have shared, on their journey and understood she did not really have a choice.

She also had the distinct impression that Frederica—or perhaps that was Georgiana? They'd all shifted about a little and those two were remarkably similar in appearance, even for sisters—was inclined to protest her brother's edict.

"That is, indeed, as I would prefer it," Constantia insisted. She was, after all, accustomed to solitude. "And as is proper, of course."

"Miss Blackstone ate dinner with the family on occasion," either Georgiana or Frederica reminded him—whichever had not been on the point of speaking before.

"That's true," Lord Ryland agreed. But he extended no offer.

"You must be tired after your journey," Edwina said kindly after an awkward silence. "And my sisters will not give you a moment's peace here." She picked up a candlestick. "I'll show you to your room if you like."

"I would like that very much indeed."

She curtsied and followed Edwina out the door. The remaining sisters immediately began to speak—asking questions of their brother, she supposed—but they were discreet enough to keep their voices too low for her to hear any details.

"The family apartments are all here in the center hall," she explained. "Where the monks used to live, closest to the church. The public rooms and the schoolroom are all in the east wing."

They retraced the path Constantia had traveled earlier, down the narrow spiral staircase and across the entry hall, which was now nearly dark. Then up another staircase, straight this time, two floors. "The drawing room and library are just here," Edwina indicated with a wave of her hand when they paused at the first landing. "But it will be easier for you to learn your way about once it's daylight."

One floor up, the stairwell ended at a door that opened onto a large, low-ceilinged room, with a row of smaller windows along one side. The space was filled with serviceable tables and benches. She could imagine a team of monkish scribes bent over them. When—if— the sun shone, it would be a passable studio. Better, certainly, than any she had had in many years.

"Your room is back there." Edwin gestured with a nod toward a door on the room's far side. "Wellend will have had your things brought up, and I'll see to it that Mrs. Swetley sends hot water."

Constantia wondered at the likelihood of hot anything, given the distance it would have to travel to reach her. But she nodded her thanks all the same. "You're very kind."

"I hope you will be comfortable here, Miss Cooper. Please tell me if there's anything I can do to make you more so. As the eldest Haythorne sister still living at home, I fancy myself mistress here at Rylemoor—until my brother marries, of course."

"Of course."

"You can't imagine what a surprise your arrival has been. A blessing, really. I thought we had done with teachers and masters and the like, after—well, anyway. And a teacher of art? Harry—Harriet—especially is pleased, I know."

"I hope my instruction does not disappoint."

Edwina looked surprised at that. "I cannot imagine it would. You must be an accomplished artist. My brother would not have brought you so far if you were not."

It was on the tip of Constantia's tongue to point out that an ability to do a thing did not necessarily guarantee a facility for teaching that thing to others. And also to mention that her brother's opinion of her art—both good and bad—may have been, well, *colored* by certain factors.

But she contented herself with dipping her head, a gesture of acknowledgment if not honest agreement that she feared she had picked up from Lord Ryland himself.

Edwina set the candlestick on the nearest table; its flame wavered warningly in some draft. "I'll leave you to your rest, then, Miss Cooper."

"Thank you. But won't you need the light?" Not that she was eager to be left in the dark.

Edwina's answering smile was gentle. "I know my way."

And then she was gone and Constantia was alone—in the room, and possibly the entire wing of the house. The silence, to which she had imagined herself accustomed, was awful. After a moment spent studying the odd shadows cast around the room by the flickering light, she crossed to the bedroom. It was larger than she had expected, with a bed, a washstand, a small clothes press, and a table and chair. A good many governesses, she felt certain, managed with far less.

An oil lamp sat on a small shelf above the washstand. She lit it and placed the candlestick on the table, beside her paper and box of charcoals. And then she realized that their presence there meant someone must have unpacked her things.

Reaching for the clothes press, she jerked open the door and found her things already arranged, the muddy-hemmed dress from yesterday brushed clean, and the one she'd been wearing on the day of her fall taken away, no doubt for mending. On the bottom of the cupboard, beside her shoes, sat the valise. She snatched it up, her heart thumping too hard to be much reassured by the familiar weight of it. Dropping back into the chair, she fumbled with the clasp and rummaged in its dark depths, prying up the false bottom with her nails.

Her fingertips brushed the edge of the picture frame. Carefully withdrawing it from the bag, she laid it atop her sketch pad and drew a steadying breath. The servant who had unpacked the valise had not found it. No one had seen it.

Except, of course, for Lord Ryland.

Alistair.

In four days of increasing intimacy between them, up to and including the revelation of secrets she'd never told anyone, his given name was information that had never fallen her way. She thought perhaps she still ought not to have it. But now that it was in her possession, it could not be taken from her.

She traced the clasp on the frame with trembling fingers but did not open it. Had it been a mistake to tell him about her mother? Certainly, she could not be surprised at his aloofness in the hours since, or his decision to tuck her away so far from everyone he held dear, from the warmth and chatter of his family. He had not cut her loose, for which she could only be grateful.

But that did not mean he would ever again hold her close.

Another gust of wind rattled the schoolroom windowpanes, breaking the silence. She shivered and returned the portrait of her mother to its hiding place.

No sense in wondering why he had brought her here, or why he had agreed to her mad scheme in the first place. She would focus on the delight and enthusiasm in his sisters' eyes, particularly Harriet's, at the prospect of being taught to draw. With a little hum of satisfaction, she opened her sketchbook, took out the landscape she'd been amusing herself with over the last day and a half, and pinned it to the wall above the table.

Only then was she struck by a realization. Hadn't he assured her she would find sufficient models here to use for his sisters' instruction in shape and perspective?

There was still a great deal of the house to be explored, of course. But she hadn't glimpsed a single work of art, not a painting or sculpture or tapestry, anywhere she'd looked.

Chapter 14

Alistair's library at Rylemoor was considerably more impressive than the one in Town, with bookshelves lining three walls, a mahogany desk, and a Turkish carpet covering the stone floor.

Not that anyone ever journeyed all the way into Devonshire to be impressed by a library. In point of fact, no one came here at all.

Nevertheless, some previous Earl of Ryland had furnished the room in what was then a modern style, eschewing the monastic austerity of much of the rest of the abbey. It adjoined the drawing room, similarly furnished, and the two rooms together could have entertained a houseful of guests, if Alistair were either circumstanced or inclined to entertain.

Truth be told, he preferred the shabbier comforts of the family sitting room. But there was work to be done, work that required concentration and privacy, and the library fairly rang with silence. Even though his sisters were just above him in the schoolroom turned studio, no doubt boisterous in their attempts to learn whatever it was that Constantia—Miss Cooper—had elected to teach them, he heard nothing of it through the thick floors and walls.

Not that he escaped the effects of her presence entirely. One or more of them reported over dinner every day what progress was being made or some witty remark that had fallen from their teacher's lips.

Lips he had kissed. Lips that had kissed him.

With a groan he dropped his head into his hand and rubbed his eyes until he saw spots. Nothing wiped away the memory, though.

Just as nothing erased the numbers in the ledgers piled at his elbow.

It seemed, in spite of all his efforts, matters at Ryle-moor had only grown worse. The estate's lands were mostly moor, as the name implied, rather than fertile farmland. His few tenants cut and sold peat and struggled to pay their rents. He had extended their leases anyway—those poor souls had nowhere else to go, and what they might have contributed to his coffers would not have made a dent in his debts.

Or rather, his father's debts, in the form of spend-thrift habits, investments gone sour, and a mortgage on everything as far as the eye could see.

When Alistair had inherited those debts, along with the title, he'd made it his mission to right the wrongs his father had perpetrated and keep the estate running as best he could.

The abbey required constant repairs, only the most desperate of which it received. It needed a staff at least twice the size of the one he could afford. Even with all of his cost-saving measures, he was staring down a pile of bills he couldn't pay: interest due on loans, taxes owed to the Crown.

And then there was the matter of dowries.

Seven of them, to be exact.

In his will, his father had written down sizable numbers, made outlandish promises he expected his son to keep. But he had never actually set aside any funds.

Bernie's husband, Lord Brinks, had need of the money—new curricles and cattle were not cheap—but when Alistair had begged leave to defer payment, Brinks had professed himself too much in love to wait and married her anyway. Then he'd made up for the loss by withholding his new wife's pin money until she produced an heir, who still had not arrived.

Charlie's husband, Mr. Powell, who did *not* have need of money and also claimed to be head over heels in love with his bride, addressed the matter of the unpaid dowry differently: by having his solicitor send a polite reminder of the balance due every quarter.

Eddie had fallen in love with Samuel Forster, the village curate, who could surely never afford to marry her if she brought nothing but her gentle nature to the match. Danny had sold herself into servitude with Aunt Josephine and might never have the opportunity even to meet an eligible man.

If all that weren't bad enough, he had Freddie, Georgie, and Harry yet to manage. The elder two had begged for a London Season. Pretty dresses. Balls. He had taken them to Town this year expressly to introduce them to good society. And to keep his eye on them.

And because, even with all the expensive temptations on their doorstep, Haythorne House was smaller and less costly to run.

Still, he'd had to deny them more than he would've liked. And in the end, taken aback either by their headstrong natures or their lack of dowry, or both, every promising suitor had melted away.

The only thing worse than having seven dowries to pay was having seven unhappy sisters, most of whom were only going to grow more miserable as the years went on.

With a muttered oath, he slammed shut a ledger and shoved it aside. His best efforts would never be enough. Everyone would be better off if Rylemoor Abbey sank into a bog . . . and took him with it. Perhaps whatever distant relative who presently stood to inherit the title had a mint.

He shoved away from the desk, stood, and strode to the window. Wind was whistling through the cracked lead around the diamond-shaped panes. He would have liked to have built up the fire to drive back the icy fingers of air. Instead, he tugged his coat more snugly around him and reached up to draw the drapery. As he did so, a flash of bright copper down below in the courtyard caught his eye.

Constantia was sitting on what appeared to be a three-legged milk stool, her sketchbook propped on one knee. The wind had pushed down the hood of her green wool cloak and was now whipping her hair around like tongues of flame.

He wasn't surprised to see her. She'd been seated thus every afternoon. Though he couldn't make out her drawing at this distance, she was obviously working on a sketch of the abbey in the hours after her lessons were done.

While he stood watching, she rose and walked toward the crumbling west wing, closer and closer, until she had to crane her neck backward to look up at what remained of the bell tower, a jagged peak piercing the gray sky.

Alistair found it, well . . . not soothing, exactly, to watch her sketch. *Compelling* would be the better, more accurate, word. What had begun in the carriage, where there had been little else to attach his interest, had become a habit. Each day, he found it more difficult to tear his eyes away.

Over the course of a week, her gait had lost its stiffness. Though her wrist was still bandaged, the plaster on her cheek was long gone, and the scrape and bruise it had covered were already beginning to fade.

How long would she find it necessary to stay?

That question sent his gaze to the distant horizon, as bleak and empty as ever. Had she told him a story about pursuers to garner his sympathy? He could well imagine dangers lurked out there for her, as they did for far too many women. But a mysterious hunter, sent by some nameless marquess who wanted to rid the world of any evidence of his daughter and the mistake she had made? Alistair looked back at Constantia. It seemed more than a little far-fetched, but one expected as much from creative sorts.

Or perhaps the marquess hadn't yet learned that family portraits were all but impossible to destroy.

Alistair had persuaded himself that bringing her here was the safest thing to do. Safer for her, as she recovered from her injuries and determined the future course of her life. Safer for him, because Rylemoor Abbey was big enough that he could keep his distance from her.

And filled with reminders of why it was essential for him to do so.

Fortunately, the architecture of the east wing was too utilitarian to be of artistic interest. She had never once looked in his direction. She had no idea he watched her, day after day. His sigh, loud in the hushed library, fogged the glass.

When her head whipped around as if in response to the sound, he leaped back from the window.

But she couldn't have heard him, of course. Unlikely even that she had seen him. He dared to peek around the edge of the curtain. She tilted her chin as if listening to something far off, then tucked her sketch pad against her breast and scurried inside.

Alistair could just make out his puzzled frown in his faint reflection on the glass. Something obviously had startled her. She had darted from the courtyard like a doe flushed from a copse. But what had she heard?

He was on the point of abandoning his fruitless speculations when a familiar chaise and four lumbered into view: Aunt Josephine. And a day early, at that.

Constantia had been wise to run.

He found himself watching with a sort of horrified curiosity to see whether Wellend had noticed the arrival. The lack of a proper, deferential greeting would result in endless complaints.

Then again, if no one assisted his aunt from the carriage or opened the door to the house, would she turn around and go home?

He had momentarily forgotten about Danny, who was employed by their aunt to do precisely those sorts of menial tasks, along with reading aloud, answering correspondence, and taking her yippy little dog for walks.

No sign of the dog, at least. Aunt Josephine was marching across the courtyard now, not even pretending to require her companion's arm. Then, abruptly, she stopped. She snapped open her lorgnette, gestured with it at some obstacle in her path—though God knew there was ample room to go around whatever it might be. Danny hurried forward, bent, and retrieved the item at which their aunt had been pointing: Constantia's stool.

Aunt Josephine would no doubt give him an earful over dinner about lax servants and unsightly litter. But for now, and in spite of himself, he snickered. Constantia did have a way of upending plans.

He really ought to go down and welcome his aunt, though in point of fact, she had invited herself. She was his father's sister, as unlike the man as it was possible to be. As such, she should have been Alistair's ally in the war against the trouble his father's foolishness had caused.

But her help always came with a heaping side of judgment. She'd offered employment as a lady's companion to one of his sisters—she'd wanted Edwina, but Danielle, recognizing her next younger sister's misery at the prospect, had fallen on her sword. For nearly a year Danny had been bristling under the weight of constant comparison to docile, domestic-minded Eddie.

His aunt had also, more than once, recommended he hire a man of business who could restore some semblance of order to the estate's account books, *as from the look of things, Ryland, it seems you've inherited your father's incapacity for figures.*

Stubbornly, Alistair sat down on his chair. Dinner was in an hour. That would be soon enough to greet her.

And he would spend the time between now and dinner checking his sums. Perhaps his aunt was right. Perhaps he'd made some mistake in his arithmetic . . .

"Alistair?"

He wasn't sure how much time had passed since he'd sat down again. He only knew that his fingers ached from the grip on his pencil, and his head ached from the conclusion he'd reached again and again. No, not his head—his heart.

What choice did he have but to ask Aunt Josephine for help?

But all that melted away when he looked up from the ledger at the sound of his name and saw Danny hurrying toward him, arms outstretched. "She's not mistreating you?" he asked, enfolding her in an embrace and resting his cheek against the top of her head. Was it his imagination, or was she a little thinner?

She pulled back just enough to look up into his face, her dark eyes dancing merrily. "You must know I'd never allow that."

Eddie would not have stood up for herself. Freddie or Georgie would have been sent home inside of a fortnight. But Danny? Well, Danny had a way of putting people in their places, without ever seeming to have done so.

"Oh, I've missed you." He hugged her close again, at the same time steering her away from the desk. He couldn't risk her seeing the ledgers. He never wanted any of them to worry.

Danny clasped his hand and led him toward a pair of brocade-covered chairs in front of the empty hearth. "What's this about a drawing master? Harry was so excited I could hardly make heads or tails of anything she said."

"Oh. Yes. I brought someone from London."

Her brow wrinkled. "Are you sure that's wise, given Papa's . . . struggles?"

Danny was the closest to Alistair in age, and the youngest of the eight of them to have any real memories of their father. Eddie recalled what others had told her of him more than the man himself, and the three youngest had been too young when he died to remember anything at all.

She knew their father had dabbled in painting, and she probably remembered seeing his work around the abbey before Alistair had ordered it all taken down.

She knew, but she didn't . . . *know*. Not everything Alistair did.

He'd had a week of listening to his youngest sisters prattling away about the pictures they'd drawn, watching the sparks of creativity flare in their eyes. A week of sharing his home with the most maddeningly unpredictable woman he'd ever met. A week of wanting, with every fiber of his being, to throw old cautions to the wind. "In fact, I'm sure it's *not* wise. But it . . . it couldn't be helped."

That earned him another skeptical frown. "You make it sound as if some starving artist flagged down your carriage and demanded to be taken to Rylemoor Abbey and employed to teach your sisters."

He managed to laugh. "I would say you've been reading the wrong sorts of books, but I know Aunt Josephine would never allow that. Oh, Danny." He reached out to pat their still-joined hands. "Is it awful in Bristol?"

"Bristol's fine," she answered, deliberately evading the question she must know he'd meant to ask. "But I'm glad to be home."

Those words pushed him to his feet. Releasing her hand, he took two unsteady steps back toward the desk and his gaze fell on the ledgers. Then he raised his eyes—not toward heaven, but toward the schoolroom turned studio. Did Miss Cooper mind dining alone? Freddie had wheedled every day to have her to join them at the table, but he hadn't given in.

He couldn't give in to his own selfish desires. Couldn't let Rylemoor crumble around him. Couldn't doom his sisters to lonely, miserable lives.

He knew, perhaps had known for some time, what he must do to put things right.

"Come," he said, holding out an arm to his sister and offering her a reassuring smile. "We don't want to risk Aunt Josephine's wrath by being late to dinner."

They entered the dining room one floor below to find all the others already assembled, and Aunt Josephine seated at the foot of the table in Edwina's usual spot. Her iron gray hair was arranged in a tight chignon, and she turned to inspect Alistair through her lorgnette—an entirely unnecessary affectation, he was sure. Aunt Josephine might look frail, but there was nothing weak about her, not even her eyesight.

"Did our early arrival prevent you from changing for dinner?"

"No, Aunt," he said around a fixed smile as he bent to kiss the air near her cheek. "We do not stand much on ceremony here in the country."

Meanwhile, Danny rushed to their youngest sister's side. "Harry, there you are! I didn't see you earlier."

"I despise those nicknames," Aunt Josephine muttered.

Harry paid her aunt no mind at all. "I was upstairs, admiring Miss Cooper's latest sketches of the abbey."

Danny's dark brows climbed her forehead. "*Miss* Cooper? I had not realized your drawing master was a"—she turned and shot a speculative glance toward Alistair—"mistress."

Freddie giggled, and Alistair turned a quelling look on each of them.

"I for one do not approve," said Aunt Josephine, "of

young ladies being taught by men. But I must say, Ryland, I am surprised you have gone to the trouble and expense of hiring a drawing master. How can you afford it?"

"The truth is . . ." He had made his way to the head of the table, intending to take his seat. But for what he had to say next, he decided, it would be better to stand. "I cannot. Things are . . . difficult. Which is why I must ask you this favor."

He paused to glance around at each of his sisters, who were staring at him with varying degrees of wide eyes and slack jaws. They all realized things must be bad if he was contemplating placing himself in their aunt's debt. Some of them might even have understood he was doing it for them.

But not one of them had any notion of how far he was going to have to go to set things right.

He cleared his throat, took a sip of wine, and carefully returned the glass to the table. "Aunt Josephine, I wish you to find me a wife."

Chapter 15

The next morning, after a solitary breakfast of tea and toast, Constantia set out to make the improvised studio ready for the day's instruction. At every table, she stopped and studied the results of yesterday's efforts. The assignment had been to draw a chair—specifically, the straight-backed wooden chair from her bedchamber, which she had dragged out and positioned at the front of the schoolroom. Dull as ditchwater, perhaps, but more challenging than most beginning artists were willing to acknowledge, because of the varying angles involved.

Edwina had drawn it almost as it appeared in life. Somewhat bereft of detail, but precise. Careful. Unassuming. Like the young woman herself.

Frederica's and Georgiana's she expected to find similar to one another, for the two girls were themselves difficult to tell apart, close in age and temperament, as well as appearance. But here, Constantia was surprised. Frederica had drawn the chair—not well, but there was nonetheless something interesting in the flattened perspective she had employed. An error, some teachers would have called it. Constantia wasn't so sure. One day, the world might be ready to call that unusual collection of shapes and lines art. But not yet.

Georgiana, who had rolled her eyes and yawned through the lesson on light and shadow, had sketched a rather childish daisy in place of the chair. Constantia leaned over and jotted on the edge of the paper: *I asked for an ordinary chair. How clever of you to give me a seat for a fairy instead.*

Last of all came Harriet, whose rendition was extraordinary for someone untrained. Far more interesting than the chair itself. The rough wood leaped from the page. Constantia could have sworn she would risk a splinter if she touched it.

And there, she thought, scanning over the whole room, were the Haythorne sisters in essence: A rule-follower. A rule-breaker. A troublemaker. And an artist—as Alistair had predicted.

But it was up to her to tease out the greater potential in each of them, with whatever limited tools she could find and in whatever time she had left.

Absently she wound her hair into a knot and secured it with a pencil. Her injured wrist still ached a bit, especially at the end of the day, but it was no longer useless. As she stood staring across the room without really seeing it, weighing the subject of the next lesson, she heard voices and the clamber of footsteps in the stairwell that heralded the arrival of her pupils, fully half an hour ahead of their time.

"You're here early," she said, as the door to the schoolroom swung open.

To her surprise, Georgiana was the first to enter. "Oh, miss, you're not going to believe it."

"Take your seats," she urged when they persisted in clustering together at the back. It took a full minute for her to realize there were five dark-haired young women now, instead of four. But of course, the carriage yesterday must have brought the last of the unmarried sisters home.

"This is Danny," said Edwina, bringing her forward. She was nearer to Constantia's age than the rest, a year or two younger than Alistair perhaps, with the same dark brown hair, almost black, and eyes extraordinarily like her brother's.

"Lady Danielle," Constantia said and curtsied.

"Only Aunt Josephine insists on our proper names," Frederica told her, not for the first time.

"And right now especially," said Georgiana, propping one hip on the corner of an empty table, "you do not want to encourage any comparison to our Aunt Josephine."

"I don't see how this is her fault, Georgie," insisted Edwina. "*He* asked."

"But to give her of all people the power over such a choice. She'll *try* to make him miserable, I just know it."

"Danny, can't you talk sense into him?"

"Stop it! Just stop it!" That was Harry, who had all but thrown herself into her usual seat and was covering her ears. "Can't we have an hour to think about something else?"

"Lady Harriet is right," Constantia said, glancing from face to face as each young woman slid into a spot.

"I would be remiss in my duties if we wasted a lesson. But you also need to be in the proper frame of mind to create. So, at the risk of encouraging gossip, I'll ask the question you all seem to be dying to answer: Did—did something happen last night?"

Five voices answered her at once, and the phrases she could catch refused to sort themselves into sense. She must have misunderstood.

"Forgive me, but it sounded—it sounded as if you said something about someone getting married . . ."

They all would have spoken at once again, but Edwina held up a hand. Once something like silence fell, she explained, "Our brother has asked our aunt to find him a wife."

Constantia sucked in a sharp breath and sat down abruptly on her chair.

Not, of course, that Lord Ryland's decision to marry had any bearing on her life. In fact, she could hardly think of any matter that concerned her less.

It was only this strange . . . fluttering in her chest, like . . . like butterflies.

If butterflies had fangs.

And claws.

Fortunately, the sisters were too distracted to notice anything odd about her behavior. Harry crossed her arms and scowled at Eddie. Freddie added, in a sardonic voice, "A *rich* wife. You forgot the most important part."

"Some Bristol merchant's docile and doe-eyed daughter who has assiduously pursued the sorts of accomplishments her family imagines will make her welcome in the *ton*," sneered Georgiana, "but whose most pleasing attribute is an ample . . ." She made a gesture that insinuated she was referring to a woman's bosom but finished with ". . . purse."

"Georgie!" Edwina scolded. "You're speaking of the future Lady Ryland, who will be our sister! And I also think it's highly improper of you to suggest that our brother may have"—her cheeks pinked—"prurient motives for making a match."

"I fail to see how that would be worse than the pecuniary motives to which he himself confessed last night."

"Do none of you understand what this means?" Danny's question was quiet, but her voice possessed the same knifelike quality as her brother's and sliced cleanly through her sisters' chatter. Everyone turned and looked at her. "Do none of you recall how Bernie and Charlie married first and foremost out of esteem and affection?"

"Love," Edwina corrected.

"Yes," Danielle conceded. "Love. And has he balked even once at your understanding with Mr. Forster?" Edwina shook her head. "Because he wants you—all of us—to be happy. Could any of you have foreseen"— she looked almost frantically about the room, taking in the scattered sketches—"having someone here to teach art, given what—"

She broke off without finishing that thought, though Constantia found herself on the edge of her chair, wishing to know what she'd been about to say.

"That only makes his decision more inexplicable to me," declared Frederica. "To allow Aunt Josephine, of all people, to choose his bride, and based on the size of her dowry? That's not like Alistair at all."

"It's a sacrifice," said Edwina, in a tone that made clear a willingness to sacrifice was very much in her brother's nature. "For us."

"I think we all suspected that the estate finances were not perfectly in order," Danielle said. Four dark heads bobbed in agreement. "But for him to do this, things must be desperate indeed."

Constantia knew it was unlikely that in that particular moment, they were wondering about her presence at Rylemoor Abbey. They'd probably forgotten about her entirely.

But she could not help but think of the circumstances that had brought her here. She thought of the crumbling spire of the abbey church and recalled how Alistair had told her he hadn't the ready funds to hire a coach, how his cheeks had flushed at the confession. She hadn't any notion what had produced this state of affairs, but she was ashamed she had ever thought him irresponsible. He was bowed down with his own worries, but he had insisted on caring for her nonetheless.

She had no reason to go on increasing his troubles or intruding on his hospitality. He had his family around him, and he—why, he was to be married, to someone who could help make his problems go away.

Certainly, she had no call to be jealous.

Rising, she clapped her hands twice to draw her students' attention. "Thank you for satisfying my curiosity, but now it is time to begin our les—"

"We can't let him do this," insisted Harriet, her anguished eyes raking over her elder sisters. "We have to put a stop to it."

Frederica nodded, and Georgiana said, "You're right, of course." She had been slouching slightly in her seat, but now she raised her eyes to Constantia, who could not read their expression. "But how?"

Edwina glanced at Danielle. "And what will become of us if we succeed?"

Tabetha, Lady Stalbridge, held the saucer in one hand and lifted the cup to her lips, blowing across the surface with enough energy that her breath ruffled the papers spread before her.

"I happen to know your tea is *not* hot," said a male voice behind her. She turned to see her stepson Oliver, Viscount Manwaring, standing with one shoulder propped against the doorjamb. His chestnut brown curls were unruly, as always, and his eyes looked tired. She suspected he had made a late, and rather wild, night of it, as he often did.

Smiling up at him, she returned the cup to the saucer. "And how would you know that?"

"It's my house, Mamabet." Which was true, though he rarely made a point of it; they had shared the house for many years after his father died, and now, even after her remarriage, she stayed with Oliver whenever she came to London.

He pushed away from the door and into the morning room. "And my housekeeper just informed me she served your breakfast an hour ago. So," he said, pulling out a chair across from her and dropping into it, "what has you so distracted this morning? Another love letter from Stalbridge?"

She sent him a mock scolding glance. "Those arrive by the afternoon post, as you well know."

After twenty years in a loveless marriage, she had been reunited with and married her childhood sweetheart a year ago, and now each of them dreaded any moment they had to spend apart. But Kit, the Earl of Stalbridge, was dedicated to the estate in Hertfordshire he had unexpectedly inherited, and equally supportive of Tabetha's decision to found the *Magazine for Misses*, which often demanded her presence in Town.

"I was reading the reviews of last night's premiere of *The Poison Pen*." Ransom Blackadder's latest vicious satire, this one on theater critics, had been said to have as its particular target Julia Addison, known to readers of the magazine as Miss on Scene. Tabetha had of course attended the performance, apprehensive of the damage the play might do to the magazine and everyone associated with it. Now she sifted through the newspapers and broadsides scattered across the tabletop. "They have remarkably little to say about the play itself."

"It is rare one goes to the theater and finds the action on stage the most compelling part of the evening." Oliver picked up an untouched piece of toast from her plate, took a bite, chewed twice, and grimaced. "Perhaps more performances ought to involve shocking revelations and attempted murder."

Even with his mouth full, she could hear the irony

in his voice. The shocking revelations threatened by *The Poison Pen* would have cost both Oliver and Tabetha dearly, but he would have paid the greater price. Eventually, they would have led to society's discovery that he was the famed Mrs. Goode.

In the end, though, the performance had shocked its audience for far different reasons, including an attempted murder onstage. Thanks to some quick-wittedness on the part of a few, and a heroic sacrifice on the part of the playwright, the identities of Mrs. Goode and the *Magazine for Misses* writers remained a secret.

"I gather," he continued, washing down the cold toast with a slurp of cold tea from her cup, "Ransom Blackadder means to marry Miss on Scene?"

"Miss Addison and Lord Dunstane are betrothed, yes. And after the wedding, I expect they will return to Scotland."

"You are fretting, then, about the loss of your theatrical reviewer?"

"Actually, I was thinking of my artist."

"Miss C.?"

"Yes. She got up and left in the middle of our last meeting, the day we all got those terrible letters. She seemed particularly unsettled at the prospect of our exposure."

He waved a hand over the collection of papers, each with an account of what had transpired at Covent Garden—a dozen at least. "Unless she's locked in a cellar or an attic somewhere, she must have heard the news that the letter writer was exposed instead and we're all safe."

"For now," Tabetha conceded. "But the very evening she left, I had another letter, this one from a . . . well, I shall simply call him a mutual acquaintance, indicating that an accident had befallen her and she was in need of assistance. Under the circumstances, I had little choice but to reply that I was not at that time in a position to help. And since then—nearly a fortnight—I've heard nothing more."

"You trust this mutual acquaintance?" He sounded annoyed at the secrecy those words implied. Oliver dearly loved to gossip.

"Indeed I do." Forgetting it was cold, Tabetha picked up her cup again, brought it to her lips, and then returned it to the table untasted. "But I have reason to think Miss Cooper does not. She doesn't appear to place much faith in anyone, really—I'm quite sure she alone, of all the magazine staff, gave me a false name. I've often wondered why."

"Trouble at home, perhaps. A family who would be displeased to find their daughter had taken an aesthetic turn." Oliver knew whereof he spoke; his father had frequently berated him for dressing and acting in ways he considered *detrimental to the name of Manwaring*. The discovery that his son and heir had written a housekeeping manual in the guise of a lady would have been the last straw.

"Mm," she answered noncommittally. She would not minimize her stepson's difficulties, of course, for they had been great indeed. But she could not shake the feeling that Miss Cooper—or whatever her name might be—faced something even worse.

Oliver rang for hot coffee and picked up a newspaper, turned to something other than the theatrical reviews, and began to read. Tabetha pretended to do the same. A quarter of an hour later, Oliver let the upper half of his paper fall and peered over it at her. "I can hear the wheels turning in that head of yours. Still fretting about Miss C.?"

"I'll have to go to print with no Unfashionable Plates in the next issue. People will wonder."

"Let them." He folded the paper and laid it aside as the housekeeper came in, thanked her for the coffee, and made a project of adding milk and sugar before taking a series of scalding gulps that must have drained the whole cup. "Ahh. Now I can think again. So why don't you tell me what's really bothering you, Mamabet?"

She hesitated, but only for a moment. With one forgivable exception—his authorship of *Mrs. Goode's Guide to Homekeeping*—they had never kept secrets from one another. "Should I give up the *Magazine for Misses*?"

A frown of surprise wrinkled his brow. "Your dream? Your mission to help young ladies think independently, as you wish you had been helped? Why would you do such a thing?"

"Because," she replied, gesturing toward a review bearing the tortured headline "Miss on Scene's Near Miss," "every month, the work I undertake to help the many puts a few people I hold dear, you included, at risk."

Were their contributions discovered, the young ladies might be ostracized by their families, cut off from good society. Even someone as professedly carefree about such matters as Oliver would hardly benefit from being known as the man behind the most highly regarded voice on matters domestic *and* the most popular ladies' magazine.

"Some risks are worth the rewards." He shot her a mock-stern look. "Rewards which, until very recently, included seeing you happier than you've been in years. Though perhaps I ought to give some credit to Stalbridge?"

"Some," she agreed with an impish smile. "Much as I love being here with you, I do consider the time away from my husband one of the disadvantages of the present situation."

"Fair enough. Though you must find some consolation in the fact that the *Magazine for Misses* has helped more than one young lady find true love."

"That's another matter—the fact that half my writers are no longer *misses*. It feels . . . disingenuous, I suppose."

"I daresay you could find replacements without too much trouble. You might even find someone else to run the damn thing, if you chose. Or to share the responsibility with you. Better that than letting it wither on the vine, to say nothing of killing it outright."

"Are you offering, Oliver?" She directed her attention

to a speck of dust on the tablecloth rather than meet his eye.

He laughed. "I don't mind giving you the benefit of Mrs. Goode's imprimatur, or her occasional wit and wisdom. But I fear anything more would cut dreadfully into my social calendar."

"I wonder if it mightn't benefit from a little trimming?" she suggested, studying the dark circles beneath his eyes.

"Mamabet . . ."

She recognized the warning note in his voice. "All right, all right. So then, I'll need an editor, an advice columnist, and a theatrical reviewer." She ticked off each position on one fingertip as she spoke. "Where will I find them all?"

"Don't forget an artist."

"Oh, no. Not yet. Miss C. may return."

Oliver looked skeptical but said nothing.

Privately, Tabetha hoped that Lord Ryland had offered Constantia his assistance, and that the young woman had taken it. Her mocking cartoons of him were no doubt a point of contention between them. But rough patches could be got through.

Tabetha knew of no one so steady and reliable as Ryland, and no one more in need of someone trustworthy than Constantia. She had always struck Tabetha as a frightened wild thing, snapping at anyone who came too near.

Perhaps a gentle hand, belonging to the right person, might soothe her at last?

Chapter 16

By late morning, Constantia had given up any pretense of teaching her students anything about art that day. The lesson on the importance of leaving empty space in a composition would have to wait until the sisters were capable of focusing on something other than foiling their brother's marriage plans. At midday she shooed them out of the studio and listened to them plotting as they filed down the stairs.

As silence fell, she began to roam around the room collecting their sketches from the day before. When she reached the last table, she stretched out a hand for the drawing and froze. On the back of the sheet of paper containing the picture of the chair, Harriet had drawn something else. Something entirely new and yet devastatingly familiar.

Constantia had just slid onto the bench to study it more closely when she heard a peremptory rap on the schoolroom door. Swiftly setting the other sisters' work on top of Harriet's, she turned toward the sound. But before she could speak or move to open the door, it swung inward to reveal a perfect stranger: an elderly woman, slight of stature, wearing a high-necked, wine-colored gown and a frown.

Constantia scrambled to her feet. This could only be the infamous Aunt Josephine.

"I am Lady Posenby," the woman said in a chilly voice. "And you must be the drawing master."

She exhibited no desire for an introduction, so Constantia merely inclined her head and curtsied.

"I question the wisdom of encouraging my nieces' inclinations in this area." She pointed with a folded lorgnette toward the stack of drawings on the table beside Constantia. "But they are clever enough girls, so I trust they are making progress?"

"We have only just begun," Constantia explained as the woman strode closer and began to inspect the pictures. "However, I am satisfied with what they have produced so far."

"What a lot of waffle. I see nothing remarkable here," she declared.

Was it Constantia's imagination, or did she sound pleased by the discovery?

Lady Posenby raised her lorgnette halfway to her eyes to peer at the comment Constantia had written on Georgiana's picture. "You mustn't allow them to run roughshod over your rules," she said, then added, not quite under her breath, "though certainly flowers seem a more fitting subject for young ladies than rickety old chairs." Then she reached Harriet's work. The lorgnette rose higher. "What's this?"

"It, um, it appears to be a cartoon, ma'am."

"Was this part of your instruction?" she demanded, whirling on Constantia. "To ridicule Ryland in the style of that awful magazine?"

For her part, Constantia hadn't decided whether the cartoon was making more fun of Alistair or Aunt Josephine. But neither of them had fared well under Harriet's pencil.

"Certainly not, ma'am. I believe Lady Harriet must have been doodling during the lesson."

"Well, you ought not to permit it," she said, crumpling the paper into a tight ball. "Just as Ryland ought not to permit his sisters to read that trash. The *Magazine for Mischief*, or whatever it calls itself."

Constantia wanted to say a great many things in reply. But she settled for boldly correcting her ladyship: "It's the *Magazine for Misses*, ma'am."

"Read it, have you?" She turned the lorgnette on Constantia and looked her up and down. "I can't say as I'm surprised. You artistic types aren't much for the rules of polite society."

Constantia bristled instinctively at the tone, though the words themselves were unexceptionable. The rules of polite society were, after all, the ones by which her mother had been as good as sentenced to death. Should anyone be surprised to find she had little patience for them?

"If you were looking for your nieces, they work here in the mornings. When the light is best." She drew her spine straighter as she spoke, until she stood head and shoulders taller than Lady Posenby.

"It was you I wished to see." And she looked displeased at having to crane her neck to do so.

Constantia made no effort to hide either her suspicion or her surprise. "Why?"

"You are familiar with those cartoons of my nephew, I take it?" Constantia managed to nod. "Well, now he requires a wife. His fortunes may be strained at the moment, but he's still the Earl of Ryland. It ought to be no great feat to find a wealthy merchant's daughter who will thrill at the prospect of being addressed as 'my lady.' But"—she gave the ball of paper a threatening shake before tossing it onto the floor—"the nonsense spewing from that magazine has made the task considerably more difficult than it ought to have been. That artist has made him ridiculous in the eyes of every young lady in Britain—and Ireland, too, for all I know."

As she spoke, Lady Posenby directed her gaze out the window, as if scouring the landscape for potential magazine readers lurking in the bleak moorland. Constantia could only be grateful she was not scouring her face, for she feared the emotions at war there would reveal too much.

Did the *Magazine for Misses* truly have such reach? Did her sketches truly have such power?

At the risk of betraying herself, Constantia said, "What does all that have to do with me?"

She'd wanted to prick Lord Ryland with her drawings, it was true. Though she had certainly never dreamed that by doing so, she could damage his marital prospects. But if what Lady Posenby said was genuine, it seemed she had, however inadvertently.

And she found she could not be sorry for it. Not now that she knew him better, knew the scent of his cologne and the taste of his kiss. The announcement that he intended to take a wife had produced an unexpected sting of jealousy in her breast. Some wicked part of her did not regret making his path more difficult.

Not, of course, that he ever could or would marry *her*—or that she wanted to marry anyone.

"Ryland seems to have judged you a competent artist." She sounded skeptical but resigned. "Therefore, I wish to hire you to make a small portrait of him. Flattering, but not obsequiously so. He is handsome enough without exaggerating, do you not think?"

Constantia nodded, aware that Lady Posenby was not looking at her and thus might not even see the gesture but unable to make herself speak.

"I want something to reassure prospective brides about his true character. Help them see how wrong those silly cartoons are."

Constantia's heart began to thump in an alarmingly erratic rhythm. "Forgive me, ma'am. But why not, er, display Lord Ryland himself?"

Lady Posenby gave a soft *harrumph* of displeasure. "He says he's completely indifferent to my choice and will come to Bristol once I have matters arranged, and not before."

No wonder his sisters were unhappy—he did indeed seem to be taking every imaginable step to ensure he would be miserable.

"I see. And, um, where will the young ladies be viewing this picture? Do you have in mind a portrait for your home, or a miniature you can carry with you at all times?"

The grande dame whipped her head about with surprising speed, as if she suspected some mockery in those questions. And her suspicions were not far off— the situation was absurd, and Constantia was doing everything she could not to laugh.

Or perhaps that stinging sensation at the back of her throat was tears.

I draw and paint to suit my patrons, not myself, she had told him.

This picture must be no different.

Lady Posenby replied to her query with more questions. "Which size do you think would better show his features to advantage? Where do your skills lie?"

Constantia weighed her answer. She hadn't the tools or supplies necessary for completing a miniature, the fine brushes or the ivory on which to paint. And even if she had, miniatures were delicate work. Her hands were already trembling at the prospect of painting Alistair's picture, and she did not know whether she could stop them.

"A larger portrait, I think," she said after a moment, though she hadn't the oils or canvas for that either. But she could make do with paper and pastels, if she must. She would not allow herself to imagine the young ladies looking up at it and tittering amongst themselves, or one of them positioning herself just so in order to be able to fancy she had caught his eye.

"Excellent," said Lady Posenby. "I shall inspect your progress in a fortnight's time."

Constantia nodded. But her ladyship, who obviously expected obedience, had not waited for confirmation and was already out the door.

When she was alone again, Constantia bent, picked up Harriet's crumpled drawing, and straightened it out on the nearest table. The likeness to one of Miss C.'s cartoons was extraordinary. She would have to speak to the girl about the perils of imitation.

And satire.

A painting of Lord Ryland could be Constantia's chance to make amends for every hurtful sketch she'd dashed off in a fit of pique. A chance, even, to make something of a name for herself as a portraitist, if Lady Posenby was pleased with her efforts.

And she had fairly itched to draw him again, had she not?

If completing a portrait of the man she now knew him to be would also be a kind of punishment, well, it was only what she deserved.

When the clock in the schoolroom chimed two, Constantia rose from the table where she had been pretending to work, smoothed her skirts with damp palms, and went downstairs. Carefully she followed the directions she had been given, down one flight and along a short corridor, then across the empty drawing room to a tall pair of oak doors carved with the faces of the twelve apostles, their features still surprisingly sharp in spite of the doors' obvious age. Raising her hand, she rapped her knuckles firmly in the narrow panel between Matthew and Mark.

"Come."

The reply was muffled by the thickness of the wood. If she wished, she could claim she had not heard it at all.

But she would not be a coward.

The breadth of Alistair's shoulders greeted her as she entered the library. He was standing looking out a window with his hands folded behind him. Nearby stood a massive mahogany desk, its gleaming surface entirely bare.

"Forgive the intrusion, my lord. Lady Danielle told me I might find you here."

He spun, obviously startled to discover the identity of his visitor. "I was expecting—"

"Someone else?"

He glanced once over his shoulder toward the window, then shook his head and strode toward her. "Not at all. I am at leisure." He gestured toward a pair of chairs. "Come, sit down." She perched uneasily on the edge of one seat, expecting him to take the other. But he remained standing, his hands still crossed behind his back. "My sisters have been cooperative pupils, I hope?"

"Oh, indeed, my lord." At that, something wrinkled his brow—disbelief, displeasure? She relaxed her spine and added, more honestly, "To varying degrees."

That earned a smile. "That's more like what I expected to hear. But is that what's brought you here this afternoon? They gave me to understand—and I have, er, noted myself—that you generally employ this time with your own work."

Had he been watching the progress of her drawing of Rylemoor Abbey, waiting by the window for her to appear? The thought made her at once nervous and pleased.

"You are not bothered by my doing so, my lord? I would not like to overstep."

One brow lifted in a skeptical arch. "Really? That would be a change." His gentle teasing—no doubt the same fashion in which he teased his sisters—made her chest ache. Then he sank onto the opposite chair, the better to scrutinize her more closely. "Is everything all right, Constantia? You do not seem yourself."

"All is well," she said, feigning brightness. "It is only that your aunt—"

"Good Lord." His laugh had an edge. "Do not tell me she approached you with her mad idea of having my portrait made?"

"She did." She plucked at the fraying edge of the bandage around her wrist. It was no longer strictly necessary; she might better take it off than risk dragging it across a sketch and smudging the pencil. "And I have agreed to do it."

"Oh." He was on his feet again and in half a moment had placed the desk between them. "Well, given the ample practice you have with the subject, it should pose no challenge to you to make my picture."

"But a portrait of the sort your aunt has commissioned is something rather different. It will require sittings, I'm afraid. At least a few."

His shoulders rose and fell on a deep but silent breath. "I see. Well, that will be no very great matter.

I'll just pop round to the schoolroom a time or two, shall I?"

She had already considered what might become of whatever remained of her wits if she had to sit alone with him in the schoolroom, just a few feet away from her bed. "The light there is only suitable in the mornings, I'm afraid, and that is when I teach your sisters."

"Ah." He swept a hand in front of him. "Here, then?"

She glanced around the library, which felt heavy and dark in spite of high ceilings and a row of tall windows facing west. No one, not even Alistair, could truly be comfortable in such a room. Discomfort produced awkward portraits, and this one would be uncomfortable enough already. "Perhaps we would do better to seek a less . . . formal space?"

"Less stuffy, you mean," he said, crossing his arms over his chest. But there was a smile in his voice now, albeit a reluctant one. He ventured out from behind the desk again and propped one hip against its bulk. "So what did you have in mind?"

"I don't pretend to know the house well." She thought of the few parts of the abbey she had visited. "The family sitting room, perhaps?"

Quickly he shook his head. "Not unless you fancy working with an audience."

"No," she agreed. "No, that wouldn't be ideal."

"So, if I understand you correctly, you'd like to find, somewhere within the confines of this nearly six-hundred-year-old building, a comfortable place, with better than adequate natural light, where we won't be disturbed?"

She gnawed at the inside of her bottom lip and nodded.

Silence fell as they both paused to think—well, she presumed he was thinking. Other than a steady drum-beat of the phrases *I* can *do this, I* must *do this*, her mind was an utter blank.

Eventually he pushed himself to standing and approached her chair. His features were carefully schooled to blandness, but there was something glim-mering in the depths of his dark eyes that might have been anger. Or pain. Or perhaps both.

"I know a spot. Come with me."

With the wave of a hand, he ushered her from the library, across the drawing room, and down a different set of stairs. Out of habit, she started to cross the entry hall before realizing he had turned in the opposite direc-tion. Toward the west wing.

His stride grew longer, though not, she felt almost certain, out of eagerness. Determination, perhaps. In spite of her long legs, she had to trot to keep up. They walked along a passageway that was open to the court-yard on one side, a sort of arched colonnade. It was not difficult to imagine monks marching two by two from their cells to the abbey church.

At the end of the passageway stood another heavy oak door, this one studded with iron nails and shut with a rusted padlock. From his waistcoat pocket, Alistair produced a key of equal antiquity and opened it. With the aid of a shove from his shoulder, the door scraped across the stone. Though they were as good as standing in the open on this cold and damp day, the air that swept out of the door was somehow colder and damper still.

"Is it safe?" she asked, taking a last upward glance at the crumbling church tower.

"That depends entirely on how far you go." He went in first and waited for her to follow. "You'll need to watch your step."

Heeding those words of caution, she kept close on his heels. Even in the dimness, she could make out wispy cobwebs and patches of green growth on the walls and at their feet. No one appeared to have passed this way in quite some time.

They walked through what must have been ante-rooms to the chapel proper. Offices, perhaps, or the sacristy. Here and there, fallen stones had tumbled into the pathway or crumbled almost into dust. When they reached yet another staircase, spiral and narrow, he led the way up.

It opened onto a large square room whose original purpose she could not begin to divine. Large windows, their glazing mostly intact, overlooked the grounds to the west and the north, an awe-inspiring expanse of wilderness. But it was not that which took her breath.

All around the room stood canvases, some half-finished, others blank. Some leaned against white-washed walls grown dingy with age, while others stood propped on easels or lay across a large table. In one corner sat a glass-front cabinet filled with bottles she instinctively knew contained pigments. In another corner she spied a collection of cloth-covered bundles tied with twine, dozens of rectangles and ovals of varying sizes—shapes that bore all the hallmarks of Ryle-moor Abbey's missing artwork.

"I don't—" she began, but stopped herself. For the next word would have been a lie. She did understand.

"My father's studio," he said, looking at her and not the room. "Will it suit?"

There had been hints, of course. She would not have been at all surprised to learn that his father dabbled in art, a pastime of which Alistair clearly disapproved. Harriet's gift had come from somewhere, after all. But this . . .

She spun slowly in a circle, trying to take it all in. This wasn't dabbling.

"Yes," she answered quietly. "If you're sure."

"Of course," he said, though his face could hardly have been less so. "Meet me here tomorrow at two, then, and we'll begin."

"How will I get in?" she asked, thinking of the pad-locked door and wondering whether the intent had been to keep others locked out or keep the memory of his father locked in.

He reached for her hand and pressed the key into her palm. The metal was warm from his touch. "Take this. I have another."

Then he turned to go, obviously intending to leave her to look around the space and assess its contents. She had taken only a step or two toward the cabinet when he reappeared in the doorway. "What shall I wear for my portrait?"

She thought of how his battered greatcoat coat set off the breadth of his shoulders, and the way he'd looked when rain had dampened his hair and made it curl. Swallowing past a sudden sharpness in her throat, she said, "Something that you believe will show you to advantage for your future bride."

Again that unnameable emotion flashed in his dark eyes, but he nodded and left without another word.

In the center of the room sat a chaise longue covered in worn rust-colored velvet, its scalloped arm framed in gilded wood. She made her way across the floor and sank onto it, no longer convinced her knees would hold her. A small cloud of dust rose from the fabric. She tasted its bitterness on her tongue and wondered how long her mouth had been gaping. A shaft of late-afternoon sunlight pierced the omnipresent clouds, making the dust motes sparkle and transforming the chaise to a chariot of flame.

The artist in her felt as if the gates of heaven had just been thrown wide. In her wildest dreams she could not have imagined an opportunity to work in a studio like this, and certainly not here.

But when she recalled the anguish in Alistair's dark eyes and considered how the late earl might have contributed to the present state of affairs at Rylemoor Abbey, she wondered whether he hadn't instead opened the portal to his personal hell.

Either way, what might it mean that he had chosen to do such a thing for her?

Chapter 17

Alistair swore when he looked into the mirror, then clawed at the misshapen knot of his cravat. He'd tied and untied the damn thing half a dozen times already, and what little remained of Mrs. Swetley's starch was on the point of giving up the ghost. "Good God, man. What's the matter with you?" he muttered sternly at his reflection. "You don't care about this picture, remember?"

But he did care, too much, for the artist.

He closed his eyes, tied another knot without watching himself or without checking his success afterward, and finally pulled on his most elegant, most carefully tailored coat of blue superfine. Miles had selected it last spring. He'd paid for it, too, after insisting that Alistair couldn't possibly squire Freddie and Georgie about Town in the drab sort of thing he usually wore. Alistair tried not to think about what any of his sisters would say if they happened to see him as he crossed the house.

Why had he taken Constantia to his father's studio? He never acted on whims, and that had been a whim of the worst sort.

Or had it?

Truth be told, he'd been thinking of it since the day they'd arrived.

He couldn't help but think of it whenever he was at Rylemoor, of course. Couldn't help but think of his father. Memories of him were like a smudge in the corner of his vision that he couldn't blink away.

But as much as he would like to tear down the entire west wing, to bury that room and its contents and its history in the rubble, he had hated the thought of Constantia toiling away in the schoolroom with a box of cheap crayons when he knew a proper art studio was just a stone's throw away.

He scoffed to himself as he trotted down the steps. As if anything his father had ever done could be described as *proper*.

The entry hall was empty as he crossed it. As were the cloisters, though given where they led, this was hardly surprising. In spite of the bite of the late-November air, he paused when he reached the door at their end. The padlock hung open. Constantia must already be inside. Picking his way across the stones, he made his way to the stairs and went up, then hesitated two or three steps from the top. A mixture of dread and eagerness stewed in his gut.

There was a word for men who took pleasure in torturing others. Was there a word for a man who was willing to torture himself? For the pleasure of a woman who regarded him with distrust and even contempt?

Fool.

For just a moment, as he stood on the threshold of the

studio, he wondered whether he'd mistaken his way and ended up somewhere else. The light streaming through the west-facing windows was almost the only familiar thing left about the room.

He wasn't surprised to discover that she had re-arranged a few things. He hadn't expected her to clean, however. To brush away cobwebs and polish jars of pigment until they shone like gems. He'd always thought of her as a bit . . . well, scattered. Disorderly. Weren't all artists? But in her case, perhaps his judgment had been skewed by the accident, the jumbled contents of her valise, the muddied shoes, the worn and wrinkled dresses.

Here, certainly, she had instilled order. She had sorted and stacked the canvases, tucking the spoiled ones neatly away in a corner. She had even covered that wretched orange chaise with a sheet.

The transformation was almost enough to make him forget the awful history of the room.

He dragged in a shuddering sort of breath, and with it a lungful of air spiced with the sharp tang of mineral spirits. His sputtering cough alerted her to his presence.

"Ah, Lord Ryland. I was just beginning to wonder." She stepped from behind the open door of the cabinet, her dress covered with a pinny apron made of coarse osnaburg, which he suspected her of having borrowed from the scullery. Her wrist was no longer bandaged. "I apologize for the smell, but I found some brushes that needed to be cleaned."

"That may be a lost cause." Surely whatever sort of

animal hair they were made of had deteriorated over time.

"It may," she agreed. "But I thought it would be worth a try to salvage them. They were excellent quality, once."

Of course they were. My father insisted on the best.

She had looked him up and down as she spoke, so he stretched out one arm to his side. "Do I meet with your approval?"

Her mouth popped open and he caught a glimpse of the pink tip of her tongue pressed against her teeth. He could almost read the retort on it. But then she pressed her lips together instead and gave an enigmatic smile. "My approval is hardly relevant, my lord. Won't you sit down?" She gestured toward the covered chaise.

He took a circuitous route toward the center of the room, past the now-empty table. "You must have worked for hours after I left yesterday."

"Mm. Yes." She was looking for something now, first peeking into the depths of the cabinet and then feeling in the pockets of her apron. "I wanted to be prepared. And drat it all, what have I done with my pencil? Oh."

With a self-deprecating little laugh, her fingertips went to the knot of hair piled on the top of her head, and she tugged free the implement that must have been strained with the task of holding all of those curls in place. Locks of fire tumbled over her shoulders and down her back.

He stood there for a moment, mesmerized at the sight, weak-willed as a moth when it spied a flame.

"Sit, please." She twitched her fingers at him, motioning him toward the chaise again. In the afternoon light, her hazel eyes were bright, a sort of golden brown flecked with green. "Make yourself comfortable. I'd like to get a number of sketches today, different angles and expressions. They will make it easier for me to finish the details of the portrait without requiring you to sit for hours. And most of all, they will help ensure that the final product is true."

"I don't think my aunt is aiming for truth." He eased onto the edge of the cushion. He'd always imagined it would be more comfortable—such an ugly thing ought to have some redeeming quality. "She wants . . . an advertisement, of sorts. Something that will make eligible misses—or really, their doting papas—open up their purses and buy what's pictured." She turned her face away so that her hair hid her expression from him, but he heard some small noise of disapproval. "But I forget, you do not like my little jokes."

"I—I did not believe you to be joking." She paused to fiddle with something he could not see. "You cannot imagine how I regret my part in making this portrait necessary."

Was she so reluctant to spend this time with him, then? She might have refused his aunt's request.

But he was absurdly glad she had not.

"Is that what she told you? That your cartoons are the reason I have not yet found a wife?"

She made some noncommittal sound that he took for confirmation.

Silently cursing Aunt Josephine, he rose and took a

step toward her. "Don't believe it. The truth is, my romantic woes date from my inheritance of this crumbling abbey and, with it, a mountain of debt. Of course, that did happen in the same year I grew six inches taller and, according to my dear sister Bernie, became 'an awkward, insufferable prig'—the man Miss C. captured so well. So perhaps my flaws have worked in tandem to make me unlovable."

"You are not—" Her head whipped about, and a few strands of her hair swept across his face. Pear blossoms again. "You are not sitting down, my lord," she said, pointing with her pencil toward the chaise.

Reluctantly, he acceded to her wishes and returned to his seat. The chaise creaked beneath him as he turned his body first one way, then another, and finally draped one arm over the curved side. "How shall I—?"

"Doesn't matter. Today, I simply intend to make a few rough sketches of your face." With the pencil she traced an oval in the air around her own head. "Eyes, nose, mouth."

Had any words ever been calculated to make a man more self-conscious?

But at least her intent study of him gave him license to study her in turn. She had pulled over a chair and now sat across from him with her sketch pad propped on her knee. While she worked, a charming little frown of concentration wrinkled the space between her fair eyebrows. Occasionally, she paused and rested the unsharpened end of the pencil against her lips.

Mentally, he traced the constellation of freckles across her nose, then spied a pair of them near her collarbone, and another at the very edge of her bodice. Dear God, that was a dangerous discovery to make.

She wasn't classically beautiful—that red hair, those freckles, the pertly upturned nose, the slightly crooked smile. Her tall, almost angular frame. And yet, when he looked at her, it was like looking at one of those Grecian sculptures, all the more extraordinary for its supposed imperfections.

And like a schoolboy at the museum, he fairly burned to run his hands over every inch of cool, smooth marble—perhaps because he knew it was strictly forbidden.

"You may talk if you wish," she said. "It won't disturb me."

If she knew the present direction of his thoughts, she would not make such a claim.

"What shall I talk about?" he asked.

"Oh, anything." As she spoke, her pencil flew across the paper, and he wondered which bit of him she was capturing with those bold, unhesitating strokes. "What qualities do you hope for in the woman you wed?"

"Other than a vast fortune?"

The pencil stopped and she lifted her eyes from the paper to frown at him. "Other than that."

Unable to bear her scrutiny, he directed his own gaze toward the windows.

"Hold there, please. You have a strong profile," she said. He heard the pencil move again.

"Do I?"

He fought the urge to reach up and inspect the angle of his own jaw. For God's sake, didn't he know it well enough already? He'd scraped it with a razor just that morning. Or perhaps her remark had been a euphemistic reference to his nose, which he'd always considered overlarge for his face . . .

"She must be kind to my sisters," he blurted out, desperate to change the direction of his thoughts, and perhaps hers as well. "A suitable chaperone for them in Town—which, as you have no doubt discovered, will require patience, determination, and a certain degree of cunning."

Constantia chuckled softly at that, and he only narrowly resisted turning his head to look at her, to see the way her laugh lit up her face.

"I should like her to be an excellent household manager," he went on. "Neat. Well-organized. Firm but kind with the servants. A good hostess."

She made a little hum to show she was listening. For a few moments after that, there was no sound but that of the tip of her pencil sweeping across the paper. Then silence. His neck was starting to feel stiff.

"That's quite a list," she said. "Rather . . . business-like, though. Is there nothing you want for yourself, to promote your own happiness?"

"Shouldn't a well-run home be enough to make a man happy?" he countered.

She didn't answer.

After another quiet moment, he said, "Very well. I should like her to be intelligent. Well-read. Capable of carrying on interesting conversation."

"My goodness. You do not ask for much. Pretty, too, I suppose?"

"Not . . . unappealing," he conceded.

That earned him another laugh. "So, pretty." A few more sweeps of the pencil, then, "Turn this way now, please. Thank you." As he shifted to face her, she moved her hand to a different spot on the paper. "Anything else?"

"Well, I suppose it would be remiss of a man in my position not to think of finding a wife who was willing and eager to bear him sons."

He thought her cheeks pinked at that. Her head was tipped downward, though, so he couldn't be sure. It *had* been an outrageous thing for him to say.

But if she had been bothered by it, it didn't distract her from her work. She began yet again in another corner of the paper. He imagined a sheet covered with disembodied eyebrows, noses, and ears and screwed shut his eyes to drive away the thought.

"Eyes open, please," she instructed in a mild, impersonal voice, such as a physician might use while conducting an examination. "And your bride-to-be . . . have you given any thought to what the young lady might like? What is it you hope she'll see in this portrait of you?"

Another horrible vision rose in his mind of haggard women at the marketplace, examining a cartload of gaping-mouthed, glass-eyed fish, ever wary of being cheated, giving this one a poke and that one a sniff.

But better that, perhaps, than marrying a girl who'd fallen for a flattering picture and then watching the stars fade from her eyes once she saw . . . all this.

"I haven't thought about it, no." *And frankly, I'd rather not.* What one wanted and what one got were almost always very different things. "She'll see whatever you choose to show her, I suppose."

The pencil paused in mid-stroke as she lifted her gaze to him. "That's giving me a great deal of power, my lord."

Abruptly, he stood. "Yes, well. See that you don't abuse it. Again." He jerked his chin toward her sketchbook. "You must have enough to be getting on with. I can't spend all afternoon sitting about."

"No, of course not. I understand. And yes"—she lifted the sketchbook as if to show him, but at this distance he could make out nothing but a series of stark and faint lines—"I have enough here to begin my work." She rose from the chair and stepped aside so he could pass. "But you will need to come again, say the day after tomorrow, to pose for the portrait itself. And at least a time or two after that."

"Very well." And before he could do or say any more rash things, he hurried away.

Constantia knew she'd struck a nerve. She was only surprised it had taken so long. Heaven knew she'd been probing hard enough.

Those little almost-witticisms of his, they weren't chinks in his armor. They were defensive barbs, designed to keep others at a more comfortable arm's length. She wanted to make him lose that calm, composed, always proper demeanor. In a string of dubious decisions, it might be the least wise thing she had ever done.

But, oh, she was determined to see him crack.

For the portrait, of course. Because it wasn't art if it wasn't true—and hang Lady Posenby's wishes in the matter. Constantia had agreed to ply her skills reluctantly. Regretfully. But since she had agreed, why not at least paint the real man? Alistair, not some caricature of an unfortunate earl in search of a wife.

A clever, capable, interesting, eye-catching, *eager* wife.

She nearly snapped her pencil in half.

She had others now. Not just the stub she'd had to wheedle from a disgruntled publican in some nameless village. But those others were back in the schoolroom and she had work to do here.

After dragging her chair over to the table, she spread out her unfinished sketches—hardly more than suggestions—chose one, and began to fill in the details. The determined shadow of whiskers along the turn of his freshly shaven jaw. The perfect symmetry of his cheekbones, made more interesting by the way the hawkish bridge of his aristocratic nose divided his face. The lock of dark hair that persisted in falling over one brow.

And those eyes . . . a shade somewhere between the rich brown of coffee and the unfathomable blackness of ink. The way they sparkled when he spoke of his sisters—even their misdeeds. *Especially* their misdeeds.

The way they narrowed with worry when he thought no one would see.

The way they had looked at her. Through her. Aggravation and pity and something she desperately longed to believe was desire.

Bending her head to her paper, she set about filling in the details of each fragment. Sunlight began to fade from the room, but rather than fetching a lamp, she only worked faster, coaxing light and life from each sketch.

At last she finished the final one. With a sigh of something like relief, she gathered the pages and rose from her hard wooden seat, tipping her head and stretching her back. She was exhausted, and the chaise beckoned.

Pictures in hand, she sat down where he'd been, then reclined, wishing she'd thought to bring a pillow. Head against the arm, she held the sketches above her in one hand and tried, in spite of the increasing gloom, to judge her success.

His eyes bored into hers, just a hint of wildness in their depths. That flash of . . . something he'd shown just before striding from the room. It made her pulse tick faster and sent a rush of warmth through her core.

She tilted her head one way, the picture another. Her free hand, which had been resting at the base of her throat, slid lower, almost of its own volition, caressing the hollow at the base of her throat. After another moment, her fingertips plucked one peaked nipple as they passed. Lower . . . lower. Closing her eyes, she pressed the heel of her hand against the aching spot at the joining of her thighs. It wasn't enough.

It would have to be enough.

The chaise creaked as her spine arched upward. No one ever came here. No one would see if she . . .

Her thready gasp pierced the silence as her fingertips sought and found her damp, needy quim. Not a ladylike word, but what did it matter? She wasn't a lady, certainly not the sort who fell in love with a portrait and begged her doting papa to buy her an earl. She was merely the artist.

And if she kept one sketch to herself—for herself—no one need ever know.

Chapter 18

Two days later, Alistair once more donned his blue coat and returned to what he had come to think of as the scene of the crime. Not *his* crime, to be clear.

At least, not yet.

He'd spent part of the morning in the library with Edwina, going over the household accounts. If he'd needed another reminder of why he'd asked his aunt to find him a wife of means, his sister had supplied it—not only with proof of how she had scrimped and saved, but also in her soft-voiced retelling of the curate's, *her* curate's, efforts to help those on the estate who were in far worse straits.

If Alistair's thoughts had tended to wander into forbidden territory now and again since leaving London, that meeting had been a spur to his conscience.

He was the Earl of Ryland. He had certain obligations, which he intended to fulfill.

Constantia must remain off-limits.

"Is all well with you, my lord?" she asked when he stepped into the studio.

She was clad much as she had been the day before, the heavy apron pinned over her light woolen dress. Her hair was once more down around her shoulders, but this time, it was tied back from her face with a length of cream-colored ribbon. She looked ready for work.

An easel sat ready with a blank canvas upon it. Nearby stood the wooden chair with another canvas propped on its seat. On that canvas, she had pinned some of the sketches she'd made two days before. Points of reference as she worked, he supposed.

"Why would you ask?" He approached, but not near enough to view the sketches of himself clearly.

Mischief twinkled in her eyes as they grazed over his face. "I do not think that scowl is one you would wish to have immortalized in oils."

His efforts to clear his visage only succeeded in making a muscle leap in his jaw. "Surely you could use one of those faces for your purposes?" He nodded toward the collection of sketches.

"That is the general idea, yes. It lessens the need for you to sit in one pose or maintain one expression for hours. Do you wish to see?" With a fluid wave, she motioned him closer.

Reluctantly he examined the dozen or so renditions—some partial, even a single feature, as he'd imagined, but not as unsettling as he'd feared; others in profile, which drew rather more attention than he liked to his nose. Just three captured his entire face, and of those three, one in particular drew his eye. The strokes of which it was composed were starker, somehow, and there was a hint of wildness in his gaze.

It cut him to the quick to learn that she saw him thus.

It was not a picture—not a version of himself—he wanted anyone to see.

"I had not realized there was so much of my father in my face." He knew his voice was rough, but he hadn't a prayer of softening it.

Constantia seemed to recognize that this was dangerous ground. With a light touch to his shoulder, she motioned him toward the chaise. "I daresay there is a bit of him in all his children," she said in a brusque, businesslike voice. "Lady Harriet's love of drawing, for example."

"Pray God that's all they share," he barked. But he seated himself on the chaise as she wished, angling his shoulders and turning his face toward the light. "Like so?"

"Look here, if you please." She held up her pencil at the level of her nose, giving him something to focus on that thankfully was not her penetrating eyes. "Yes, that will do."

While she applied herself to her work, his thoughts churned so loudly through his head that she could surely hear them. They drowned out the soft *scritch-scritch* of her pencil sweeping across the paper.

"You've seen some of his paintings, I know," he blurted out when he could stand it no longer. "You must have done, when you straightened up this room."

The movement of the pencil slowed but did not stop. "Yes."

Despite the obvious reluctance embedded in her reply, the way she stretched the word to avoid having to say more, he couldn't keep himself from asking, "You are a skilled artist. What is your expert assessment of his work?"

For a long moment, she said nothing. All of her attention appeared to be focused on some detail of her sketch as she frowned at the canvas, erased some errant line, and lightly drew another in its place.

At long last, she laid the pencil on the ledge of the easel, but still she did not look at him. "Some of the paintings were . . . extraordinary," she said, in a voice that confessed she would rather have found them otherwise but refused to lie. "Like nothing I've ever seen before. There's a—an unusual quality to the brushstrokes. A boldness. He had a way of capturing light . . ."

Even having steeled himself for praise of his father, he hadn't expected the wistful, almost covetous, look in her eyes. As if the man's abilities were something to be envied. But he knew just what she meant.

"His work used to hang in every room of this house," he told her. Ordering it taken down had been one of his first acts as Earl of Ryland. He could not bear to look at it, so he'd had it wrapped up and stowed away. He ought to have had it destroyed.

"Given his choice of colors and subjects, I can certainly understand how being surrounded by it might be overwhelming." She glanced toward him but did not hold his gaze. "But to leave the walls bare? Surely there must have been other artwork that could have taken its place. Something must have been there before."

"Family portraits, Dutch and Italian masters, medieval tapestries, that sort of thing?" he suggested with false airiness. She nodded. "When the creative impulse struck, he was known to paint over them, give them away, use them to wipe his boots, even toss them in the fire." And if he had not, Alistair would have been driven to sell them, to put a price on those invaluable pieces, to pay down the man's debts.

He saw her stiffen with shock, heard her sharp intake of breath.

In a slightly mocking voice, he reminded her, "He was bold, just as you said."

"I might better have said *selfish*," she countered, clearly horrified by the thought of such destruction and desecration.

"Oh, that too. You told me once that it was a rare artist who was not subject to the whims of a patron. Well, my father was such an artist. He painted only for himself."

Alistair pushed to standing and began to pace in front of the chaise, heedless of how the motion drew Constantia's eye. "Regardless of the fact that his wife was often in poor health or that he had a houseful of young daughters, he would invite his artist friends to stay for a month, or two, or six, to paint, to indulge their . . . passions." He sent a baneful glance around the studio. "Things here rarely looked so neat."

"Creation can be messy, chaotic," she reminded him, and he was not sure whether she was defending herself or making excuses for his father.

"Yes," he agreed, having already made such arguments to himself. "But sometimes it is also decadent. Dissolute. Mad. It would have mattered less, this selfish, self-destructive bent, if he hadn't also been an earl. But he had a nobleman's responsibilities and obligations." He wandered now toward the window and stared out across the barren moor. "When he came into the title, the earldom included thousands of acres of farmland in Wiltshire and Somerset, the source of generations of prosperity for not just my family but the hundreds of families who lived on it." Swiftly he turned back to see her still watching him. "Upon learning that the land was not entailed, and having no interest in agriculture, he sold it for a pittance, probably to buy paints"—he waved an arm toward the cabinet—"or canvases"—the other arm shot out toward the half-finished paintings she had stacked in one corner—"or to fund one of his lavish parties. My mother died of a fever following Harriet's birth. I was away at school. She breathed her last, all alone, while he sat here, not a hundred yards away. Six months later, he fell down the stairs and broke his neck." Then, suddenly drained, he made his way back to the chaise and sank onto it, propped his elbows on his knees, and dropped his head into his hands. "All of my life has been spent cleaning up after him."

He did not realize she had stepped from behind the

easel and approached until he saw the tips of her shoes peeking from beneath her skirts, not quite toe-to-toe with him.

"I'm sorry," she whispered. "Sorry to learn that your father was such a man. Sorry you have been weighed down with the burden of making things right. Sorry most of all that my art was the cause of your having to relive such pain. Reopening this studio, making those sketches . . ." She flicked her fingers backward, in the direction of the easel. "None of this would have been necessary if not for the drawings I did in London."

"Miss C.'s cartoons, you mean?" He lifted his shoulders, part shrug, part wry laugh. "I won't say I liked them, but you weren't wrong about me. I've had to be dull, prosaic, stern to countermand everything he did, everything for which he stood. Though I have wondered from time to time . . ." He lifted his face to hers. "How did I happen to fall under the point of your pen?"

A flicker of unease passed across her features, masquerading as a tight smile. "I rented a room from a modiste who calls herself Madame D'Arblay." The name tickled some remote corner of his mind, but he couldn't stir a memory to the forefront. "Your sisters placed a rather substantial order with her shop early last spring. You came to speak with the modiste one afternoon, and I happened to overhear . . ."

His recollection of the day burst from wherever it had been hiding. "Oh, God." He dropped his head forward again. "I quibbled over the bill, did I not?"

"And the styles your sisters had chosen, yes. I had

been searching for a subject for the next edition of
'What Miss C. Saw' and it suited my purposes perfectly
to cast you in the role of hypocritical peer, miserly with
your sisters and puritanical in your tastes—except, of
course, for your taste in friends."

"Miles again?" Alistair could only laugh. He lifted his
head and flung himself backward on the chaise, tipping
his head against the arm. "As if my lack of funds and
execrable taste in clothes weren't damning enough."

"I'm sorry," she said again, now with a slightly incredulous tinge to her voice.

Perhaps she wondered if he weren't mad too.

"Don't be. You amused my sisters, Miles, and half
the *ton* with those cartoons." He dropped his voice as
if imparting a great secret. "Sometimes even me." And
then he laughed again at the sheer ridiculousness of the
turn his life had taken.

"Amused?" She looked affronted. "I intended them
as a biting satire on the duplicity of the nobility. Noblemen especially. But perhaps my efforts were lost on
such a facile audience. Perhaps we should return to the
portrait." As she spoke, she lifted one hand and reached
for him.

Instinctively, he shot out his hand to stop her. She
was, no doubt, simply intending to smooth his now-
unkempt hair. But if she touched him, she who had
glimpsed his soul even before he'd laid it bare, he knew
he would not be able to walk away.

He failed, however, to consider what would happen
if *he* touched *her*.

He had intended merely to brush her away, to ward her off. Instead he caught her hand in his, his fingers curling lightly around her wrist, his thumb nestling in the curve of her palm. He made no effort to hold her.

She made no attempt to pull away.

"I'm no rake," he insisted in a harsh whisper. "I never have been."

"I know it. I think I always have."

"Yet I want you"—ever so slightly, he tightened his grip, and she shivered as he drew the pad of his thumb twice across the tender heart of her hand—"even though I shouldn't."

Her pupils flared and she took a step closer, into the space between his spread knees. "Yes."

A single word. Acknowledgment and agreement all at once.

"But," she continued when the next words wouldn't come to him, "you're afraid that if you give in to what's between us, if you indulge your desires"—she raised her other hand to spear her fingers through his hair, then slid her palm over his stubbled jaw—"you'll be no better than your father."

Yes. That was exactly what he thought—what he knew to be true.

And still he lifted his other hand to her waist and dragged her down into his darkness, beside him on the chaise where no doubt a hundred other conquests had been made.

"I can't marry you," he whispered against her throat.

"I know that too." A soft groan escaped her as his

lips sought and found the delightful pair of freckles above her collarbone. "Please. Don't stop."

He had, God help him, no intention of stopping. She sighed with apparent satisfaction when he eased her back onto the raised end of the chaise and rose above her to claim her mouth in a searing kiss.

When had he become the sort of man who seduced the woman he'd sworn to protect? Even Miles in his rakish heyday would have drawn the line at that.

But such philosophical inquiries would have to wait until a time when all his blood was not directed somewhere other than his brain.

Between them her hands moved to slide beneath his coat and curl around his ribs. But he did not immediately accept her invitation to snug their bodies together. Instead, he levered himself onto one knee and one arm, while with the other he smoothed the tangle of red hair away from her eyes so that he could look deep into their gold- and green-flecked depths.

"You've been driving me mad for a fortnight, Constantia. No, months," he corrected. No point in dishonesty now. Her cartoons had irritated and fascinated him in equal turns, and when he had finally seen her in person last spring? Well—suffice it to say, he had never forgotten.

She stared up at him from beneath eyelids already drowsy with desire. But her lips quirked in a crooked smile, not at all chagrined by his chiding. "And I suppose you mean to show me how it feels?"

He cupped her cheek, traced his fingers over her parted lips, bit back a growl when her tongue darted out to taste him. He let his hand slide lower, over her chin, down to her throat, where he could feel her pulse race. "I'm not sure I have the patience for that."

He felt rather than heard her sigh. "Please?"

It was tacit admission of a truth they both knew. They had an hour—or a handful of them, if they were weak—to explore what might have been between them, if he were not duty bound to marry another and she were not a wild thing determined to fly free.

They had to make the afternoon last.

Chapter 19

Ruthlessly, Alistair tamped down his need, pulling his body away from hers just a fraction of an inch. "If you're sure."

Constantia's eyelids dropped closed as a shudder of longing passed through her slender frame, and she nodded her surrender.

"First things first," he said, rocking back onto his heel, with his bent knee pressed into the cushion of the chaise between her thighs. "Help me take off this coat." It was elegantly cut, more tight-fitting than he was accustomed to wearing, and nothing he could afford to spoil.

Her smile returned as her hands skated from his waist, over his rib cage, and up his chest. "If I must." Despite the layers of silk and cotton still between them, her touch left a trail of heat. Slipping her fingers beneath the collar of his coat, she slid it over his shoulders and down his arms with surprising ease. "A pity," she murmured as it landed on the floor with a soft *fwump*. "You look well in it." Mischief twinkled in her eyes.

"Though I confess I am eager to see what lies beneath." Her fingers went to his cravat.

"Ah," he said, catching them in a firm grip and bringing them to his lips for a kiss. "All in good time. But since you've been making it your business to study my figure for months"—he raked his gaze down her body as she lay supine before him—"I think it's only fair now that I get to study yours."

Pink rushed into her cheeks and toward her hairline as a breathy "Oh!" escaped her lips.

With a tug on her hands he urged her back to an upright position and ducked his head for a kiss, soft at first and then firmer as she leaned toward him and let him wrap her arms around his neck. So much could be conveyed with the press and parting of lips: desire and hunger and a connection that went deeper still, pinning together two lost souls who had been running away from something all their lives and anchoring them to this place, this hour.

When he traced the seam of her lips with his tongue, she opened to him readily and he sank into the sweet, wet heat of her mouth. And she, wary but never timid, explored him with equal fervor, their tongues soon sliding over one another in a sensuous dance until the kiss grew so deep it was impossible to know where his breath left off and hers began.

He plucked loose the pins holding the bib of her apron in place and dropped them to the floor. Breaking the kiss, he studied the gentle swell of her bosom and watched his fingertips trace along the edge of her bodice. With a tug he discovered an unexpected smattering of freckles hidden just beneath the narrow hem. Possessiveness surged through him, catching him off guard with its force. He wanted to be the only man ever to have seen them, the only man who ever would.

Lowering his head, he traced them with his tongue, like the path marked out on a treasure map, and felt her chest rise and fall with increasingly ragged breaths. At the same time, he let his free hand follow her figure from just above her knee, over the curve of her hip to her narrow waist, finally stopping to cup her breast and tease her nipple with his thumb. Then, pressing a kiss to the pulse fluttering at the base of her throat, he reached behind her to untie the apron and unfasten her dress.

It was the same one she had been wearing the day of the accident, and the evening he had helped her undress in the makeshift inn. That night had given him proof of what he'd already suspected: She wore no corset. As it had then, the bodice now gaped slightly to reveal only her shift. Unlike that night, he no longer needed to fight the temptation to trail his fingertips slowly over each vertebra—unless withholding his touch would further ratchet up her sensual need?

But in the end, he hadn't the strength to deny either of them what they wanted.

He reveled in the softness of her skin, the delicate strength of her spine. Sheffield steel, had she said? Of that, he hadn't a doubt. But she was still pliant beneath the warm stroke of his fingers.

When he sat more upright, she followed, both drawn by his arms and chasing his embrace. "Stand up," he told her in a voice gravelly with lust. She stumbled but didn't hesitate, and with a sweep of his hands her dress and shift and petticoats slithered down her arms and over her hips to puddle at her feet. She stood before him, bare but for her stockings, the Grecian statue of his fantasy.

And yet more than any fantasy, for her lean form was soft and warm and touched here and there with a peach-pink blush, her diamond-hard nipples a shade darker yet, and her mound covered with auburn curls. His swallow was audible in the reverent stillness of the room.

She made no motion to cover herself or hide from his greedy gaze. "You like to be looked at?" he asked.

"I like what I see in your eyes."

Regardless of the picture Miss C. had made of him, he was neither a closet sensualist nor a man who denied himself all physical pleasure. But at present he felt as unsure as a randy schoolboy reaching for his first woman with trembling hands. Anchoring one at each of her hips, he brought her close enough to kiss her belly button, then set his mouth to her breast.

"Aah!" Her hands rose to grip his head, his hair, steadying herself, holding him there—as if he had any desire to pull away. Every time he glanced upward, she was watching him, eyes bright with wonder, as he licked and sucked her small, pert nipple until it was the color of wine. *Yes, that's right! Store away this memory,* he thought, shifting his ministrations to the other breast. *Someday, when you're alone, think of me thus.*

As she grew weak with need, he found the strength to stand. She gripped his shoulders to steady herself as he unknotted his cravat and unbuttoned his waist-coat, kissing her thoroughly all the while. Then, with gentle pressure at her waist, he turned her back toward the settee. Snatching away the rough linen sheet—she deserved nothing less than velvet against her skin—he urged her back to the chaise. While she sank down, he swiftly divested himself of everything but his breeches, knowing that once he gave in to his desire to match her nakedness, this golden hour would too soon be over.

Sunset colors of pink and violet streamed through the windows, bathing them in magical light and restoring the studio to what it had once been: a holy place.

Blasphemy it might be, but he was determined to worship her.

He knelt, the stone floor softened by the pile of their discarded clothes, and let his eyes drink in every inch of her. Her body followed the languid curves of the chaise, one hand draped along the curved arm and one knee raised, her legs falling ever so slightly apart.

"Constantia," he breathed, lightly painting her with his touch from her collarbone to her knees. "A beautiful name for a beautiful woman." He wanted to follow his fingers with his tongue, but not more than he wanted to see her reaction as his fingertips danced over the delicate skin of her inner thigh, rising slowly higher until they brushed along the seam of her sex. Her silky petals were already dewed with desire, inviting him to probe deeper. When his thumb nudged her clitoris, she gasped.

"Alistair!"

Hearing his name on her lips—not *Ryland*, not *my*

lord—was almost his undoing. He rewarded her with two quick circles of his thumb. She rasped out his name again and splotches of color appeared on her throat and chest. Slipping a finger into her hot, tight channel, then two, he urged her toward bliss, reveling as her pupils flared and her nails dug into his biceps and her hips lifted in a frantic rhythm, chasing his touch. Triumph surged through him as he watched her shatter.

He might have tried to tell himself it was enough if he hadn't heard her murmur of disappointment as he slid his fingers from her body. Leaning forward, he nuzzled her ear and whispered, "More?"

Her coppery curls tickled his nose as she nodded. "Everything."

That breathy word shot straight to his cock. It took him less than a moment to shuck off his breeches and kneel between her spread knees. Even the creaky old chaise did not protest. Her hands slid over his chest to his shoulders and looped behind his neck, drawing him closer.

The arm supporting his weight shook with barely leashed desire as with the other hand he fitted himself to her entrance. With a strength he had not been sure he possessed, he restrained his aching need to thrust into her wet heat. Slowly, advancing with firm but gentle nudges, he eased his hips forward until their bodies were fully joined.

"All right?" he asked, searching her gaze for any hint of discomfort.

For answer, she hooked one of her stocking-covered feet around his calf while the other leg slid to the floor, splaying her hips and giving him greater access. Even as lust spurred him onward to completion, something very like regret made his heart twinge.

She was wrong for him in all the ways that really mattered—at least, when it came to fulfilling his duty—but he also knew as surely as he had ever known anything that he would never feel this terrifying yet blissful sense of being perfectly vulnerable, perfectly matched, perfectly *seen* with anyone else.

So he held off as long as he could, until his breath sawed in and out of his chest and perspiration beaded on his brow. Until she pleaded with him in wordless moans, and the fingers twined in his hair began to tug. Until the clenching of her sex became an irresistible beacon to his own climax, which tore from his body with a shout.

He pressed his forehead to hers and they lay together in a sweaty, satisfied tangle. After several minutes, he found the will to take most of his own weight onto his arms. "I must be crushing you."

She laughed, a deliciously throaty sound. "Not quite."

Still, she shifted almost restlessly beneath him. Though he knew their interlude must soon come to an end, it was with great reluctance that he heaved himself upright and let her slip free.

Whatever he had imagined had been her motivation for rising from the cozy chaise, he could not have been more surprised to see her dart to the easel, still absolutely naked, and begin to draw. "I want to remember," she said, almost to herself.

Oddly flattered, he stretched like a cat in the fading

sunlight and propped one arm behind his head. "Don't think this is quite what Aunt Josephine had in mind," he teased.

"No." Her answering smile was somehow both wicked and sad. "This one is just for me."

Not being an artist himself, he would have to content himself with storing away a mental image of her in that moment, her soft, wild hair tumbling over her bare shoulders and her face aglow from within.

As he lay watching her, he thought of the portrait of her mother, of beginnings and endings, of art and mystery and stories told and untold. Perhaps it was in Constantia's nature to try to create symmetry out of chaos.

He closed his eyes and let the whisper of her pencil lull him into something like peace.

Chapter 20

Some days later—Constantia refused to allow herself to count how many—she was sitting in her bedroom before lessons began. On the otherwise bare table before her lay the leather case that contained her mother's portrait.

She hadn't seen Alistair since the afternoon in the studio. She had sent word to him with Edwina that there would be no need for another sitting. If he chose to read more into those words than their plain meaning, well, that couldn't be helped. In any case, he had not sought her out, for which small mercy she told herself she was glad.

She preferred solitude and self-reliance—hadn't she been on her own for almost twenty years?

With a shuddering breath, she lifted her hands from her lap, unfastened the clasp on the portrait, and unfolded the letter that lay within. As she always did, she traced a fingertip over the ragged top edge of the paper, where she had torn away the date and the words *My darling Constantia* and consigned them to the fire.

I intended to begin by wishing that you might never know the pangs of separation I presently feel, realizing I must say goodbye to you too soon. But in order to escape sorrow, one must also avoid all the passions in life, for it is only the pain and fear of loss that makes parting so hard. So instead, I will wish for you a life of joys, both small and great, and say only that I am sorry I will not be there to see my wish come true. Remember me fondly and know always that I loved you, just as—

The loops of her mother's handwriting ran off the edge of the page. There had once been a second page to the letter, but Constantia had burned that, too, rather than risk it falling into the wrong hands.

But she had never forgotten what it said.

I loved you, just as I loved your father, and we were loved by your father in return. When I am gone, never fear. He will return to take care of you.

Your loving Mama,
M. K. F.

Something like a laugh huffed from Constantia's chest. How very like her mother to believe in such errant nonsense. *Joys* and *care* and worst of all, *love.*

She hadn't intended to look at the picture, but of course, it had been painted to draw the eye. Her mother had indeed been a beautiful woman, her soft, lush figure a reflection of her upbringing in a far different world than the one that had made Constantia so lean and hard.

This time, however, it was her mother's eyes that she found particularly compelling, their expression a potent mix of mischief and desire. And sorrow? She could not decide whether the painter—her father—had caught a glimpse of sadness, or whether her own misery had clouded her vision and made her see something that was not really there.

Oh, knowing what she did, how could she have let herself fall prey to her mother's delusion? How could she have given herself, body and soul, to a man who would never be hers?

In order to escape sorrow, one must also avoid all the passions in life.

Well, she hadn't avoided them, had she? She had stepped willingly into the fire. She had danced in the flames and basked in his warmth like some mythical salamander.

And even if it left her heart a cinder, she would not regret that golden afternoon.

Hearing footsteps on the stairs, she folded away the letter, closed the portrait case, and returned it to the depths of her valise. When she stepped into the doorway to the schoolroom she met Georgiana, who was the first to enter.

"Miss," she said rather cheekily, "you look tired."

She *was* tired. Exhausted, in fact. Night after night, she had stayed late in the studio, painting by candlelight, though it was far from ideal. And then she had risen early in the morning to do the same before lessons began. Two days earlier, and well before the promised fortnight, Lady Posenby had sought her out in the schoolroom to enquire after her progress. She had been surprised and pleased to learn that Constantia was nearly done.

But Constantia had grown accustomed to working to a deadline, thanks to the magazine. She was determined to finish this commission quickly and without running the risk of another sitting, another hour alone with Alistair.

She must be—she *would* be—content with her memories and sketches of him, and nothing more.

"Then perhaps we ought to work today on sketching people," she told Georgiana. Laying her hands on either side of her face, she tugged her cheeks downward, comically contorting her expression. "Lined, aged faces are always the most interesting to draw."

Behind Georgiana, Frederica and Danielle laughed and made silly faces at one another. "Oh, yes, let's!"

None of them but Harriet was ready, artistically speaking, for the challenges posed by drawing human features. But she could certainly introduce the topic, tie it to her previous lessons on angles and space and light, and offer a few practical, preliminary steps.

"Where is Lady Edwina this morning?" she asked as she opened her own sketchbook to a blank page and propped it against a stack of books so that the others could see as she drew.

"She told Mrs. Swetley a child in the village had been struck with fever and the family required assistance," said Danielle. "She set out just after dawn. Alone."

At that, Frederica and Georgiana exchanged knowing glances, but nothing more was said.

An early-morning assignation with her curate, perhaps? But Edwina—as prim and proper as any cartoon of her brother Miss C. had ever made—hardly seemed the type.

Then again, Edwina and Mr. Forster had been waiting a long time to marry. In spite of his religious vocation and her gentle and quiet nature, they were only human and presumably subject to all the ordinary human frailties, including desire.

A quarter of an hour later, as Constantia was explaining how to properly proportion a face and how best to approach the obvious difficulties of the nose, a servant appeared in the doorway with a message for her from Lady Posenby, who evidently had elected not to climb the stairs this time to deliver it herself.

"She wishes to say, miss, that she would like to present the portrait of Lord Ryland to the family at a small celebration on Thursday."

Tomorrow.

There was no question, nothing really to be answered, but all the same, Constantia said, "You may tell her ladyship that the painting will be done."

It would be a bit of a stretch, requiring another long night in the studio, but she was glad to have the occupation. It kept her mind from wandering to other things, even when the subject of the portrait was Alistair himself.

She had trained herself to focus on lines and angles and brushstrokes when she painted, just as she had been trying to explain to the girls.

"Now, as I was saying . . ." She turned her attention again to her pupils, who were looking eagerly at one another, and then pointed at her sketchbook. "The portraitist must exert great control over his pencil as well as his brush, attending to the smallest detail in order to avoid making a flaw where there wasn't one, or emphasizing an existing flaw better left omitted."

No one was listening. The four sisters had all begun chattering animatedly to one another the moment the servant had left the room.

"A party? Here?"

"Not like Aunt Josephine to—"

"Seems to me an awful lot of fuss over a picture of Alistair."

Constantia rapped her pencil against the table to call for quiet, which fell only when Danielle gave an emphatic "Shush!"

"You'll come, won't you, miss?" That was Frederica, and the question caught Constantia off guard.

"Your aunt's message was not meant to be an invitation, I'm sure," she explained. "Merely a polite way of informing me"—Danielle coughed at the suggestion her aunt was capable of politeness—"when she expects the portrait to be done."

"But you're the artist," Harriet countered in an insistent tone. "The guest of honor."

Constantia scoffed but Georgiana said, "Why else would anyone throw a party to look at our brother?"

Heat prickled Constantia's cheeks as she recalled just
how hungrily she had studied every detail of the man's
body. "I believe you're forgetting that the entire purpose of the portrait is—"

"To show him off to girls with wealthy papas. Yes,
yes." Georgiana somehow sounded both bored by the
explanation and aghast at the prospect.

"I was going to say 'to highlight your brother's many
appealing qualities,'" Constantia finished, raising one
brow.

Harriet tried and failed to stifle a giggle. "*Many appealing qualities*?" she repeated, sounding incredulous.
"Can you really do all that? For Alistair? I can't wait to
see it. Oh, miss, you must come!"

Constantia felt her resolve weakening, but she managed to shake her head. "I have nothing to wear appropriate for a celebration, small or otherwise, in the home
of the Earl of Ryland."

For a moment, that restored a thoughtful hush to
the room. Then Danielle said, "I have a dress you can
borrow. It's two seasons old, but I doubt that will
matter."

It was at once an extraordinarily generous gesture
and a reminder of Constantia's place. She dipped into a
shallow, stiff curtsy. "Thank you."

She hadn't intended to accept the offer, but Georgiana and Frederica immediately seized upon it and
chimed in with, "We can arrange your hair."

"And I'll loan you my pumice stone," said Harriet,
with a sheepish smile. Ink- and charcoal-stained fingertips were an affliction they shared.

Constantia parted her lips, on the point of giving in to the pleas—and her own wishes—when Edwina burst into the room. Her normally neat coiffure was disordered and damp. Breathless, she collapsed onto the farthest chair.

"Eddie!" Danielle gasped. "What happened?"

Edwina gave a feeble wave to indicate that answering questions was presently beyond her.

Constantia stepped into her room and poured clean water from the pitcher on the washstand into a tumbler. Parting the sea of sisters, she offered it to Edwina. "Drink this."

While Edwina alternated between sips of water and deep, shaky breaths, the others all had a chance to examine her appearance. Her hems were muddy, which was only to be expected if she'd had a long walk. But her skirts were also torn in two places, and the palms of her gloves were scuffed and stained with something that might have been blood.

Constantia recognized all the indications that Edwina had fallen, or been pushed, onto her hands and knees.

"Tell us what happened," Danielle urged again when her sister's breathing had slowed a little.

"I—I was returning from the village and decided to take the shortcut across the moor, rather than be late for our lesson." She sent Constantia an apologetic glance that pierced her to the quick. "I was almost halfway here when a t-tall man stepped out from behind a cairn and spoke to me. His voice was strange. *He* was strange. I started to tell him that I had nothing for him, that my basket was empty, when he reached out and grabbed me by the arm." A collective cry rose from her audience. "My hood fell back and he looked right into my face. Oh! I shall never forget that scowl. He said something more, but by that time I was too frantic to catch the words. My basket was in my other hand, so I swung it at his head and that startled him enough that he let me go. I fled, but I stumbled, twice," she said, plucking at the rents in her skirt, "and fell down. I raced all the way home."

"Did he follow?" demanded Danielle.

Edwina shook her head. "I don't think so." She paused to gulp down the final swallow of water that remained; the tumbler shook in her hand. "I knew you'd all be here, so I came right up. I didn't want to alarm the servants, and with Alistair gone, I didn't know what else to do—"

"Alistair—I mean, Lord Ryland—is away from home?" Constantia repeated.

Her slip seemed to have gone unnoticed. "He told us at dinner a few days ago that he had to meet with a solicitor in Exeter. He left the next morning," explained Harriet.

Frederica added, "He's due back tomorrow."

That explained why Lady Posenby had chosen Thursday evening for the unveiling of her portrait.

Had he left Rylemoor to avoid seeing Constantia?

None of that mattered, of course, not in the face of what had happened to Edwina. She was peeling off her gloves and making motions for her sisters to return to their seats. "Please," she said. "I'm all right." Her fingers trembled as she reached up to untie her cloak. "I'd rather not talk about it anymore. Can't we just return to the lesson?"

Reluctantly, her sisters obliged. As Constantia turned toward the table at the front of the room, she glanced instinctively out the windows, as if she expected to see the monster who had attacked Edwina lurking somewhere just outside. But a drizzly rain had shrouded everything in mist.

When she faced the class, she saw that Edwina had risen to remove her cloak and watched as she laid it over an unused chair. Previously only the checked lining of the garment, flung back from her shoulders, had been visible.

But now that Constantia could see what the cloak was made of, her pulse began to throb in her temples and all the strength left her legs.

Gray-green wool, remarkably similar to the mantle she had purchased at Price's Mercantile. In fact, if she hadn't just seen her own mantle hanging in her bedroom when she'd gone to fetch the water, she might have thought they were one and the same.

Had the hulking stranger on the moor in fact been looking for her?

For days, she had been presented with signs that it was time for her to leave Rylemoor: The bruise on her cheek had all but vanished, her wrist was better, Mrs. Swetley had laundered and mended all her gowns. And of course the most obvious sign that she'd overstayed was her foolish infatuation with the Earl of Ryland himself.

She had ignored every one of those signs.

But this? This was different. She glanced back at Edwina, whose cheeks were still flushed red from the exertion of fleeing a would-be predator.

Constantia was putting others at risk, just as she'd feared.

Tomorrow, once she had presented Lady Posenby with the finished portrait and been paid for it, she must be gone.

Chapter 21

After a cold, damp, and fruitless trip to Exeter to listen to a bespectacled man with graying skin and ink-stained cuffs confirm what Alistair already knew, the very last thing he wanted on his return was a party.

Particularly not one planned by his Aunt Josephine.

If he had to spend his evening among people, he would have preferred the noisy comforts of the family sitting room and losing a game of chess to Harry.

If he had to look at that damned portrait and be reminded of a future he'd rather not face, he would have preferred to do it with Constantia at his side.

"Absolutely not!" he scolded himself as he slipped into one of his oldest, most comfortable coats, after hesitating a moment too long over the blue one. Someone had ironed out the wrinkles and sponged away the dust. It looked just as if that afternoon had never happened.

Constantia's message had been clear enough.

No more visits to the studio. No more indulging his desires.

No more dreaming of what might have been.

He tried to take some comfort in the fact that his aunt

was too much of a stickler to have invited a person as humble as the artist tonight. Seeing *her* would only weaken his resolve.

The drawing room, whose elegant, rarely used furniture had still been draped in holland cloth when he left, was now ablaze with the light of wax candles he couldn't afford—but which, he presumed, his future wife would be able to.

He glanced around at the assembled guests: four sisters—only Danielle had not yet appeared; one aunt, her trusty lorgnette already in hand; the elderly rector and his wife, whose presence at Rylemoor was a rarity, since that gentleman preferred the comforts of his other parish; and, to his even greater surprise, Forster, the long-suffering curate, whom Aunt Josephine surely thought of as unworthy of the attention. Alistair only hoped Eddie hadn't sold her soul to wrangle his invitation.

As he approached the center of the room, he spied an easel. The small, unframed painting upon it was turned at present toward the wall, awaiting the moment of dramatic revelation.

He pressed two fingers to the center of his forehead, attempting to hold back an incipient headache.

Freddie appeared at his elbow, wearing one of the low-cut, costly gowns from Madame D'Arblay's shop. The throbbing between his temples grew.

"Are you unwell, brother?" she asked, though her expression was one of barely suppressed amusement, rather than concern.

"Tired," he replied. "I did not expect to be hosting a party tonight."

"I think, technically speaking, Aunt Josephine considers herself the hostess. Which may call into question the appropriateness of the term *party* for this particular event."

Alistair's lips curved in spite of himself. "What would you call it, then?"

"Oh, I'm withholding my answer until I see your portrait."

Unbidden came an image of everyone's faces if the picture turned out to be the one Constantia had playfully sketched of him after . . . well, *after*. Heat crept up from beneath his collar.

"I think you *are* unwell," Freddie insisted, peering at him. "I'm going to fetch you a glass of wine."

She stepped away to be replaced by Edwina's intended. "How did you find Exeter?" Forster asked.

"Dismal," Alistair snapped, then inwardly chided himself for his rudeness. He genuinely liked Forster and believed the fellow would make Eddie happy. If all went according to Aunt Josephine's plan, the two of them would not have long to wait, now. "Sorry," he said in a chastened tone. "Legal business always makes me grumpy."

Forster gave a knowing nod, then seemed to realize his error and shifted to shaking his head. "No, never pleasant. Though I daresay this must have been a bit better than most—planning for your nuptials, eh? Drafting marriage settlements and the like?"

Alistair pressed his lips into something he hoped

would pass for a smile. "Yes, something like that. Still raining?" he asked, a transparent attempt to turn the conversation.

Weather in Devon was always a fruitful subject because it was changeable and, on the moors at least, frequently dramatic.

"Oh, aye," the curate confirmed. "With the air this heavy, I wouldn't be surprised if we had a storm."

The strength and duration of this possible storm then had to be discussed, with hopes expressed that neither person nor property would be greatly harmed if it came to pass. That took up the several moments required for Freddie to return with his wine. His sister and the curate then took up the topic, while he once more scanned the room.

At the sight of his aunt bearing down upon the easel, he brought the glass to his lips and drained half its contents in a single gulp. He couldn't decide what he hated most about the evening: viewing the portrait itself or having to face the moment in such a public fashion.

Not that he doubted it would be an interesting picture. Too interesting, he feared. After all, he knew better than most the artist's abilities and had seen the way she had looked at him.

No, it was the prospect of the portrait being put to its intended use. The idea of his face and his title being dangled in front of young ladies, like a flashy lure to fool a fish. The prospect, in other words, that all his aunt's plans would succeed.

Once the picture was revealed, it would be not a beginning but an end. An end to any pretext for intimacy with Constantia. An end to the strange and eventful and unexpected journey that had brought her here. An end to a dream that for one brief hour he had let himself wish could be real.

The room seemed to hold its breath as Aunt Josephine reached for the painting. "I present to you—"

Alistair screwed shut his eyes.

A collective gasp made his heart stutter in his chest, but still he refused to look. He couldn't imagine what could have inspired such a reaction. *Had* Constantia been so mischievous as to have switched out the formal portrait for the, uh, considerably more informal one she'd been working on when he'd left?

Or had she perhaps painted him with a pair of devil's horns, as she'd once depicted Miles?

Or—?

Freddie nudged his elbow, almost upsetting his glass. "Look!"

Daring to crack open one eyelid, he discovered that the reason for the uproar had not been the painting, which was still turned toward the wall.

Instead, every eye in the room was focused on the doorway, the arched shape of which perfectly framed Constantia.

"If I may, your ladyship," she said, and the small crowd parted as she strode, head held high, toward the easel.

She was wearing a gown of ivory silk overlaid with gold net that sparked fire with every step she took. Alistair no longer regretted the expense of the candles. Her hair was piled high on her head, rich waves of honey carefully coiled and pinned, with a few soft curls around her face.

He recognized the dress as belonging to Danny, one she had worn during her first and only London Season. And the artistry of the coiffure could probably be credited to Georgie or Freddie, or both, as he knew that the lack of a ladies' maid last spring had driven them to excel at such things. But the posture, the crooked smile, the piercing eyes . . . those were entirely, utterly Constantia.

She looked beautiful, breathtakingly so—but not more beautiful than she had been to him when she had been wearing nothing at all.

He took half a step toward her before Freddie laid a hand on his arm. Constantia had reached the portrait and now grasped the picture by the edge of the wooden stretcher that held the canvas taut. With a gracious tip of her head to Aunt Josephine, she turned the portrait around to face the gathered guests.

But to look at it, Alistair would have had to tear his eyes away from Constantia.

Eventually, however, he became aware of other things in the room. Conversation swelled more loudly than one would expect for a party of a dozen people. Over it all, he could hear Aunt Josephine complaining about something, though that was hardly unusual. Danny, who had entered the drawing room behind Constantia, wore an irritated expression and hurried right to Harry's side. Harry looked unhappier still.

"Well," said Freddie, still near his elbow, "that should do the trick."

"Trick?" he echoed absently, his attention now captured by Danny appearing to comfort their youngest sister. "What trick?"

When Freddie made no answer, he crossed the room to join Danny in her efforts. Before he reached them, he heard Harry say in a choked voice, "You said you thought she was on our side. You said she—" She broke off when Danny laid a hand over hers, signaling for quiet at their brother's approach.

"What's wrong?" he asked.

Harry's mouth popped open, but Danny spoke over her with determined calm. "Nothing. Really. We all knew Miss Cooper was a talented artist. And with a portrait like that, you and Aunt Josephine will surely get what you wanted."

He had to look at the picture then, as he was quite certain he and Aunt Josephine had never seen eye to eye on anything. Because what he wanted was Constantia.

With a squeeze for Harry's shoulder and a nod to Danny, he turned at last to face his portrait. Constantia stood to the right of the easel and Aunt Josephine to the left. Or rather, Aunt Josephine was positioned to argue and Constantia was regarding her with detached amusement.

As for the portrait itself, well . . . it was not, as he'd again begun to fear, the picture of him reclining nude on the chaise. It was also not, he felt quite certain, the sort of thing his aunt had had in mind.

Most noblemen's portraits were serious and unsmiling. The subject's powerful eye tended to bore into the viewer's and send a prickle of discomfort down one's spine.

In contrast, Constantia had painted him not quite in profile, his eyes focused on something, or someone, in the middle distance, the lips quirked in half a smile, as if he'd just told a truly terrible joke and knew his listener was fighting not to laugh. His hair was tousled, his cravat was slightly askew, and he was wearing not the elegant blue superfine, but his ancient, battered greatcoat.

"When I said I didn't want flattery," his aunt was saying, "I certainly did not mean for you to make him look like a farmer."

"I think he looks . . . dashing," insisted the rector's wife, who, despite her age, punctuated that statement with a girlish titter.

"Charismatic," corrected her husband. "The sort of fellow you'd like to get to know."

Harry, who had just joined the little group standing closest to the picture, nodded. "Yes, exactly," she said. And she didn't sound happy about it at all.

Was this how Constantia saw him? Was this what she'd meant when she'd spoken of painting something true?

He needed to speak to her, to ask her—

At just that moment, the rector enjoined her in earnest conversation. On the other side of the room, and much to his surprise, Georgie began agreeing vocally with their aunt's assessment of the portrait: "Oh, indeed. Quite shocking. I would not recommend hanging such a thing in your house, Aunt Josephine. I wouldn't show it to a soul."

That was odd. A moment earlier, Freddie had sounded as if she thought the portrait would be successful in attracting a bride, and it was unusual for the two sisters to disagree about anything of substance. She and Georgie were less than a year apart in age and had always been like two peas in a pod.

And then there was Harry's unhappy-sounding assessment and the scowl on Danny's face . . .

Had they been hoping Constantia would make a portrait so awful, it would ensure his matrimonial efforts would fail? But that would mean they didn't want him to—

No, that couldn't be. If he didn't marry, they would all have nothing.

He'd ask Eddie. She was unfailingly honest. And as luck would have it, she was headed toward him now, arm in arm with her curate.

Before Alistair could speak, Forster did. "Ryland, there's something we should discuss."

It could have been their plans to assist the most unfortunate residents in the village. But Alistair had the awful feeling it was their marriage plans instead. Awful not because he opposed them. Eddie's happiness—all his sisters' happiness—had always been his first concern. But awful because, if they were finally ready to proceed, it must mean they assumed he was about to succeed. About to bring home a wealthy wife.

Thanks to Constantia's portrait.

"One moment," he said to Forster, turning away even

as he spoke. "Danny?" He found her nearly where he'd left her, now standing alone. "What did you mean when you said *a portrait like that*? What did Harry mean when she said she thought Constantia was on your side?"

A frown wrinkled between her dark eyebrows; clearly she did not wish to answer. But after a moment, she breathed in sharply through her nose and said, "I had thought Miss Cooper might do you an injustice."

"She would never—"

His sister spoke across him. "Because I rather thought she fancied you herself. And I—we—had persuaded ourselves you fancied her in turn."

"Whatever gave you that idea?" he asked, even as he feared the unsteadiness of his voice must be giving away his feelings.

"Your pointed refusal to be in company with her first suggested the notion to Freddie and Georgie. I myself have observed both your and her expressions whenever the other is spoken of. And most important, you had always refused the idea of a drawing master until now. Harry told me she knew it could not be for her sake, so it must be for Miss Cooper's—or for your own."

In short, having five sharp-eyed sisters had been his undoing—but also, perhaps, his salvation?

"So," he said, "you did want the portrait to be a failure, to thwart Aunt Josephine's plans."

Danny's dark eyes were incredulous, pleading. "I don't care about the portrait. Or anything else. We wanted—want—you to be happy."

Happy? Easy enough to say. But poverty would be much harder to bear.

He had to talk to Constantia. Had to ask her—

Had to know . . .

He glanced toward the rector, but she had already moved on from that conversation. His eyes darted from group to group, and then to the corners of the room. She was nowhere to be found.

"Excuse me." Abruptly he stepped past Danny and headed for the door. Aunt Josephine called after him, but he pretended not to hear. Nothing mattered but getting to Constantia before she left Rylemoor for good.

He raced through the house, his eyes searching everywhere he passed, just in case he was wrong. Charging up a spiral staircase faster than a marauding knight, he burst through the door. "Constantia?"

In the schoolroom, all was dark. But might she be in the governess's quarters just beyond? He thought he saw a flicker of light. As he hurried across the floor, his thigh collided with the corner of a table and he swore, none too softly. The oath echoed in the schoolroom's silence. No one emerged from the adjoining bedchamber, either to chide him or to see that he was all right. Still, he pressed on and pushed open the door without pausing to knock.

Except for furnishings and a single candle left burning, the room was empty. The wardrobe door was ajar—no sign of her things within. And across the neatly made bed lay the golden gown she'd been wearing. He swore again and had turned to continue his search elsewhere when something caught his eye.

A piece of paper had been pinned to the wall above the table. A drawing. He took it down and held it up to his eyes, trying to make it out. He recognized the jagged spire of the church and the long, low lines of the house. But the sketch was unfinished.

He clutched the picture in his hand, heedless of wrinkling the paper. Surely, she wouldn't go without—

The studio.

He knew the odds of finding her there were long. The storm predicted by the curate had begun to rattle the windows. She would not have wanted any delay in setting out.

Nevertheless, he dashed back across the schoolroom, down the stairs, and through the abbey to the cloisters. Wind whipped icy rain into his face. On the door to the west wing, the padlock hung open.

She might have come and gone, he cautioned his racing heart. But if she had left for good, wouldn't she have closed the lock behind her?

It was a slight hope, but he clung to it as he picked his way through the rubble and across the moss-slick stones to the stairs.

In sharp contrast to the blazing candelabras in the drawing room, the equally large studio was lit by a single lamp, whose glow barely penetrated the gloom. Her valise sat open on the table. She was gathering up various fragments of papers, sketches, supplies, sorting them into piles. Though his approach had been muffled by the howl of the storm, when he paused on the threshold, she looked up.

She didn't seem surprised to see him. Neither did she exactly seem pleased.

"I thought certain your guests would distract you a little longer."

"You can't leave now," he said, closing the distance between them. "You can't leave things"—he gestured with the sketch of the abbey crumpled in his clenched fist—"unfinished."

She glanced from him to the paper and back again. "Some pictures are like that. Sometimes you begin a work with a grand plan in your mind. Other times it seems to grow beneath your hand with a will of its own. And then, just when you're sure you've got it, the perfect rendering of everything in your head . . . or your heart . . . you"—her shoulders rose and fell, as if she wasn't sure of the right word—"you stumble. Perhaps you're interrupted. Or a crucial line refuses to lay right, no matter how you try. The spark fizzles. You set it aside, vowing to finish it another day." Mournfully, she shook her head. "But that day never comes."

Then she turned away and began placing things in her bag. "You haven't said—how do you like your portrait?"

"Is that how you see me?"

Even in profile, he could see the wicked smile that lifted the corners of her mouth. "This is how I see you," she said, sliding another piece of paper toward him. He knew without looking that it was the nude sketch she had made on that fateful afternoon, after they had given in to their desires. "But I didn't want to give your aunt an apoplexy."

"I don't want it," he told her, pushing it back across the table to her. It would only resurrect uncomfortable memories, things better forgotten.

She put a few more items in her valise and then closed it, leaving the sketch where it lay. "A picture like that should stay with its subject, rather than risk having it fall into the wrong hands."

"You can't go," he insisted again, pleading now. "There's a terrible storm brewing."

"I know. That's a good thing. It will mean fewer people out and about."

Was she still afraid she was being followed? "This is madness. We had a plan."

"*You* had a plan," she countered, plucking up her mantle from a nearby chair and draping it over her shoulders and the simple woolen dress she now wore. "Correction, you *have* a plan—and it cannot include me."

Desperate, he stepped between her and the door. "But I—I love you."

He could see how valiantly she fought to keep all expression from her face. But hope swelled in his chest when her eyes flared, catching the meager light.

"Do you know why I went to Exeter?" he asked.

One brow arced. "Other than to avoid seeing me?" He could not help but wince at that—she wasn't entirely wrong. "To speak with a solicitor," she amended her answer. "Or so I was told."

"To see if there was some other way for me to—to—" It was too much to put into words. He gestured again with the hand holding the crumpled sketch, toward the east wing of the abbey and his family.

"And was there?"

Hope sputtered, like a guttering candle. Reluctantly he shook his head. "But still, I could—"

"You could not. More important, you would not. Because to do any such thing would jeopardize the future of Rylemoor and your dear sisters. It would be selfish—and, unlike your father, you are not a selfish man."

Then she hoisted up the bag with both hands—though she still favored her injured wrist, he saw—and prepared to go around him. She was close enough now that he could see the tears glittering in her eyes when she looked up into his.

"Do you know why I painted you in profile? Because I could not bear to think of some girl standing in front of that picture, fancying you were looking at her—looking at her the way you once looked at me." It was, he thought, her way of confessing that she loved him too. "Goodbye, Alistair."

Then she stepped past him and out the door.

Every fiber of his being screamed at him to stop her. But her fierce independence was one of the things he loved most.

He let her go.

Chapter 22

When Constantia reached the bottom of the stairs, she realized how much more intense the storm had grown. The wind wailed eerily through the anterooms; Alistair must have left the door leading from the cloisters open. But if so, it did not let in any light. All around her was in utter blackness. She wished for the lamp she had left burning upstairs, though she knew it would not have lasted long against these wintry blasts.

Leaving Rylemoor was by far the most difficult choice she had ever made, and the prospect of stepping out into the storm made her all the more reluctant. But if she hesitated, she would lose her nerve. If she hesitated, she would only be making herself, Alistair, and the entire Haythorne family more miserable in the end.

So, she hitched her valise higher on her hip, dragged in a determined breath, and took a step toward the door.

The darkness was disorienting. For a moment, she feared she had turned the wrong way and was walking deeper into the abbey, where the building's decay posed greater dangers. She groped blindly until her gloved hand encountered cold, damp stone. A wall. The wall that divided the anterooms from the ruined church. If she walked along it, keeping it to her right, it would lead her to the door.

She had taken only a few shuffling steps when she became aware of another sound, barely audible beneath the storm. Scuffling noises. A deeper chill, one not caused by the weather, shuddered through her. *Rats.*

But rats wouldn't make that much noise, would they? Some larger animal, then. Something that had been driven to take shelter from the storm. She reminded herself that, whatever sort of creature it was, it was no doubt more reluctant to encounter her in the dark than she was to encounter it.

She found herself probing every step with her toe before setting down her foot, thinking not just of that frightened animal somewhere in the darkness but also the fallen stones and slick spots along her way. If she stumbled and fell, hit her head . . . if Alistair found her injured and carried her to warmth and shelter . . . she knew she would never find the strength to leave again.

Not much farther now. She thought she could detect a slight lessening of the gloom ahead of her, in the arched shape of the doorway. Soon she would be out in the open. In the rain and wind and darkness. Surrounded by treacherous moor.

Nothing a stranger in his right mind—or even out of it—would try to cross this time of year.

No, no, she scolded her fear, driving back the memory of Alistair's voice and replacing it with her own. *I have a plan.* Across the courtyard to the drive. Follow the drive back to the main road. Main road to the village.

As long as she stayed on the beaten path, she was unlikely to stumble into a bog.

Perhaps the wild creature who had taken shelter in the abbey had the right idea. It was making its way deeper into the building, away from the door. She strained to listen, to pick out the sounds of its approach beneath the noise of the storm. Its shuffling, tentative steps seemed to mirror her own.

And then, from very near, a muffled *thump*. As if whatever it was had struck a stone with its foot.

Did animals stub their toes?

Well, if so, they surely didn't mutter oaths afterward.

Constantia's scream strangled in her throat when the creature—a man—reached out and grabbed her. He was speaking to her, she thought, but the blood pounding between her ears made such a roar that she couldn't pick out the words. His grip was implacable, trapping the arm in which she held her valise so she could not use it as a weapon. Her other wrist was still too weak for her to defend herself with it. And if she tried to kick him, she was as likely to strike stone and break her foot instead.

He was saying the same thing over and over in a gravelly voice, and it sounded very much like "At last, at last." After all these years of hiding and running, to be found out here? To lose the battle for her freedom in the one place she so desperately did not want to leave? No, she had to fight, had to get away from this craggy-faced mountain of a man, had to—why could she see his features now? Was the storm lessening? Where did the light come from?

Then, like a vision, Alistair appeared, lamp in one hand and jagged stone in the other, arms raised high, his expression fierce and bloodthirsty, ready to knock her assailant's brains from his head.

Relief poured into her. She was safe. He had saved her. Again. And that knowledge gave her the strength to cry out, "Wait!"

A half second too late, perhaps. But Alistair hesitated, and the shift in momentum made the blow more glancing than it otherwise would have been. Her assailant's eyes grew wide with surprise just before he tumbled to the floor, nearly pulling her down with him.

Alistair snatched her up before she hit the ground and gathered her to his chest. The lamp fell from his hand, struck stone, and guttered, leaving them in darkness again. "Constantia!" His hands raced over her head, her back. The valise slipped from her numb fingers and landed beside her with a *thud*. "Are you harmed? Did he hurt you? Good God! Why did you tell me to wait?" he murmured against her hair, and she could feel his mouth tremble. "When I saw the fear in your face, I wanted to kill him."

"I know. I know you did. But first, I want answers. I want to know who he is." She tipped her head back to look up, though Alistair's features were nothing more than a pale blur against the dark. "I want to know why."

A groan from the floor near their feet made it clear that the man was not dead. "We may not have much time before he rouses," Alistair said, setting her back on her heels. "Can you fetch a candle?" She heard the whisper of cloth. "I'll tie his hands."

Once more, she felt along the damp wall to the staircase and hurried up. Thanks to the windows, the darkness in the studio was not absolute. With icy, fumbling fingers she found and lit a candle, and by its unsteady glow, she returned to Alistair, who was kneeling beside their prisoner and had secured the man's wrists with his cravat.

"I don't know how long that will last," he said, looking up at her. "We need help." She thought of the handful of servants, mostly young women, and the elderly butler, Mr. Wellend. "Go to the drawing room. Fetch Forster."

"The curate?"

"Hurry."

She did as she had been bid, though her head was filled with doubts. Though she'd only met him that evening, and briefly, he had struck her as rather too gentle and studious to provide much assistance in such a matter. He was young, yes, but . . . well, rather doughy.

When she burst into the drawing room, her eyes were momentarily dazzled by the blaze of light. Her mind struggled to make sense of the discovery that almost everyone was still assembled, chatting and drinking and admiring the portrait of Alistair, oblivious to what had occurred.

"Mr. Forster," she blurted out, heedless of the rector's wife's gasp or Lady Posenby's gimlet-eyed stare. "Please come. We need your help. Lord Ryland has apprehended an intruder, and the man is built like a mountain."

Edwina, who had been seated near the fire, stood up. "Not the man who accosted me on the moor yesterday?"

"What?"

Doughy, had she thought? Forster's face was carved from granite—so too the fists curled at his side.

"I'll explain on the way," Constantia promised.

He turned toward Edwina. "Did he hurt you?"

"I'm fine," she insisted, stepping closer to him as if to prove the point.

"Please," said Constantia. "We haven't much time."

After glancing over his beloved to assure himself she was still in one piece, he gave a sharp nod of satisfaction, then turned to Constantia and said, "Lead the way."

Back again they raced, down the stairs, across entry hall, and out to the cloisters, while Constantia breathlessly told him of Edwina's frightening encounter and her own too-frequent alarms.

"What does the fellow want?" he demanded as together they pushed the heavy oak door wide.

"That's what I'm hoping to discover," she said as they entered to find the prisoner sitting upright, eyes closed, with his head tipped against the wall.

Alistair was standing a few feet away, sheltering the candle from the draft. Constantia hurried to him. "He hasn't said anything," he told her. "Except your name."

A chill passed through her, one that had nothing to do with the storm and the cold stone pressing in upon them. She wished she still had Alistair's arms around her, but of course, that had happened before only because of the panic of the moment, both his and hers. She must not expect his embrace again. Certainly not in front of the curate. "What do we do now?"

Forster, who was not a big man, nonetheless reached down and grabbed the fellow by the scruff of the neck, clearly intending to drag him to his feet. "I say we make him explain himself. And then, we make him pay for what he's done."

The normally quiet man's vehemence and sudden taste for vengeance drove Alistair's brows up his forehead. "He approached Edwina on the moor yesterday," she explained, "and gave her an awful fright." The brows dove downward at that. "She also wears a green cloak, did you know? I realized immediately he must actually have been after me."

"That's why you were so determined to leave tonight," Alistair said. "To draw him away from here." She couldn't disagree.

But, oh, she didn't want to go.

Even after they heard everything the mysterious man had to say, however, what really would have changed?

Alistair was an earl. He had responsibilities. There could be no place for a nameless, as-good-as-penniless artist in his life.

Together, Alistair and Mr. Forster raised their prisoner from the floor and pushed him toward the door, directing his wobbly steps along the cloisters and into the entry hall. She followed along, valise in hand. "Where to now?" asked Mr. Forster, and Alistair looked at her.

"The drawing room?" she said, thinking only of the

blaze of candlelight. She wanted desperately to be free of the darkness and fear surrounding this stranger.

Surprise flickered across Alistair's expression, but he nodded and nudged the man in the direction of the east wing stairs.

When the four of them appeared in the drawing room, Constantia in front and the trio of men, one bound, behind her, heads swiveled and mouths popped open. Her stomach dropped as if she had just swallowed a mouthful of lead. She had not considered how it would feel to have whatever the stranger might say revealed before a dozen pairs of curious eyes.

Lady Posenby snapped her lorgnette. "Is this the man, Lady Edwina?" she asked as the curate shoved him into a chair that looked entirely too spindly to bear his weight. She recalled the story of the broken chair in the pub—had this truly been the man involved? The others crowded about.

Slumped and squinting against the light, he appeared far less fearsome than he had in the dark. It became apparent that at least some of his bulk was a heavy, fur-lined coat and stout boots. He had the haggard complexion of a man who had been on a long, difficult journey. Constantia judged him to be about fifty years of age, with sandy hair that had begun to gray and needed to be trimmed.

When he looked at her with his bright blue eyes, she saw . . . relief.

"Who are you?" she demanded. "Why are you here?"

He opened his mouth to speak, then squinted as if his head ached, which under the circumstances seemed unlikely to be an act. "*Trinken* . . ." he rasped. "Please, somefink to trink?"

They all seemed to be dumbfounded by the request, such that for a moment, no one moved. At last Edwina rose, went to the tea table, poured a cup, and brought it to him. "Careful, Eddie." Mr. Forster spoke low, in a wary tone, as she held the cup to the man's lips and helped him to drink.

"*Danke*," he said, looking up at Edwina with grateful eyes once he had drained the cup. "I frighten you," he said to her. "Outside, *ja? Entschuldigung*. I mean no harm."

Edwina drew in a sharp breath. "Why, then? Why did you do it?"

"You." He nodded toward Constantia. "Her."

"I believe he mistook you for me," Constantia explained. "Our cloaks are very similar in color." She turned to the mysterious man. "But then, why me?"

"You . . . lost. So many years. But I . . . find."

"Can't you speak proper English?" Lady Posenby demanded. "At this rate, we shall be sitting here all night waiting for answers. *You* must have some explanation." She looked sharply at Constantia.

"Miss Cooper has been concerned for some time that someone was following her," Alistair said, stepping in to explain. "It spurred her decision to leave London, in fact. And this fellow lurking about"—he jerked his head toward the stranger—"would appear to be the proof she was right. But I agree with you on one thing. These one-word answers won't get us far."

Harriet had been wending her way around the edge of the circle and came to stand beside her brother. "I believe I can help. *Sprechen sie Deutsch?*" she asked the man.

Relief surged into his face. "*Deutsch! Ja!*" And followed those giddy exclamations with a stream of words that made Harriet blink.

"*Langsam, bitte*," she said to him, and from the gesture she made as she spoke, Constantia gathered she had asked him to slow down.

He obliged, or tried to. Harriet had to stop him frequently to ask for clarification.

"Well?" Lady Posenby snapped.

"Wait," Alistair said, before his youngest sister could speak. "We should consider that whatever this man has to say may be full of untruths. It may also concern matters of a deeply personal nature—"

A combination of gratitude and relief made Constantia's shoulders sag. But of course, having heard most of her story already, he understood how reluctant she would be to share it with the rest of them.

Several members of the assembled company immediately took his meaning. "We should be only too glad to go and grant you privacy," said the rector, "but I fear the storm prevents us from safely traveling home anytime soon."

"If you will follow me, sir, ma'am," said Edwina with one of her usual gracious smiles, "I will be only too happy to see that you are made comfortable for the night." And then, a bit more sharply, she added, "Freddie, Georgie," and jerked her chin to indicate that they were to follow too.

They protested vociferously, but eventually did as they'd been bid.

Forster moved as if intending to go with the rector and his wife, but Alistair motioned for him to stay. "I may yet have need of your help."

Alistair's gaze then swiveled to his aunt, a none too gentle hint that, as Constantia's situation concerned her not at all, she certainly had no cause to stay.

But Lady Posenby was the sort of woman who believed everything was her concern. She lifted her chin and met her nephew's eye with a haughty stare, then motioned Danielle to her side with a snap of her fingers, as one might bring a dog to heel. Constantia saw a muscle in Alistair's jaw twitch.

At last, he looked at her, lifting one shoulder and tipping his head as if to say, *I've done my best. The rest is up to you.* She turned to Harriet and nodded for her to continue.

"He says that he has been watching you," Harriet translated. "No, watching *over* you for years. He—he claims you are a daughter of the Royal House of Friedensfeld, and that he can prove it, if we will but untie his hands."

A chorus of scoffing noises rose.

"The drawing master? Royal? Ridiculous," declared Lady Posenby.

"A nice trick," said Forster. "Asking to be untied. He must think us fools."

Alistair looked again at Constantia. "Well?"

She hesitated. How could she trust a stranger? Trust

this man who had been the cause of so many waking nightmares and sleepless nights?

"Ask him, please, about this proof he claims to have," she told Harriet. "Find out what it is."

"A piece of jewelry," Harriet translated a moment later. "And a . . . well, I'm not sure. A paper of some kind?"

"The jewelry . . . is it an earring?" Constantia asked, tugging on her bare earlobe.

The man, who apparently understood the gesture if not the English words she had spoken, nodded eagerly. "*Sie waren ein Geschenk*—uh, uh, a geeft."

"Show me."

With obvious reluctance, Alistair stepped forward to untie his wrists. Mr. Forster came, too, positioning himself next to them and laying a warning hand on the man's shoulders. "Don't try anything foolish."

The man rubbed his wrists and looked affronted at the suggestion. "*Ich bin Herr Dieter Schenk*," he said, jerking a thumb toward his chest once the feeling had returned to his hands. "*Abgesandte zum . . .*"

Constantia turned desperate eyes to Harriet, who wore an uncertain frown. "His name is Mr. Schenk. Beyond that, I'm not sure."

With a racing heart, she watched as Mr. Schenk reached into his breast pocket and withdrew a folded parchment bearing an elaborate seal and something still hidden in his fist. Then he opened his hand to reveal an earring identical to the one she'd sold so long ago.

"He says . . . that you were lost to them for many

years, but the appearance of this, this—oh, I'm sorry, I don't know! Crown jewel? But that hardly seems right, for how could you have come by any such thing? Anyway, because of . . . whatever it was, he was sent to London to find you, but you . . . you hid. He says he knew you had not gone far, because he could identify you by your drawings, the ones you made for . . ." Harry's eyes rounded to saucers. "Miss Cooper?"

"*Nein!*" Mr. Schenk protested. "*Nicht* Cooper. Bah! *Das ist eine Beleidigung.*" And he waved the paper vigorously in their faces.

"Settle yourself," said Mr. Forster, tightening his grip on the man's shoulder.

Mr. Schenk might easily have thrown off his hand, but instead his broad shoulders sagged, and he sent a desperate look to Harriet, Alistair, and Constantia. "*Bitte?*"

"What's he on about now?" asked Lady Posenby, who, despite her determination to stay, was watching the proceedings with an expression that said she'd seen better performances on the London stage.

"I'm not . . . sure," murmured Constantia, even as she rose and went toward the door, where she had dropped her valise when they had entered. Kneeling beside it, she rummaged in its depths and withdrew the leather case. "But I think it must have something to do with my mother and father."

She approached Mr. Schenk with the case held out before her, as if it were a cannonball she feared to drop. Opening the clasp, she hooked a finger in a crevice of the frame and withdrew the matching earring. Those standing nearest gasped.

But Mr. Schenk had eyes only for the picture. "*Sie sehen wie Ihre Mutter aus.*"

Harriet whispered the wholly unnecessary translation: "You look like your mother."

"It's true my name is not Cooper," Constantia explained, looking around the small group of wide-eyed faces as she clutched the portrait to her chest. "My mother was an Englishwoman, and my father—I never knew. An itinerant artist. When I was a young woman, I discovered that I inherited some portion of his skill. The last few months, I have been drawing cartoons for *Mrs. Goode's Magazine for Misses.*"

"Miss C.," breathed Harry, a shade too reverently for Constantia's taste. Lady Posenby clucked.

"How this man came to concoct such a fabulous tale about my origins, or where he acquired what looks like my mother's earring, I cannot say—"

"*Keine Märchen,*" Mr. Schenk insisted, rattling the paper again. "No fable."

"Perhaps," suggested Alistair gently, "we ought to read it."

"*Ich lese, ja!*" With a grin, Mr. Schenk broke the seal, unfolded the paper, and began to read aloud—in German. Constantia's head ached from trying to pick out meaning from the unfamiliar sounds. She heard her own name, its syllables delightfully strange on Mr. Schenk's tongue, and preceded by a word that sounded a great deal like—but no. That could never be.

"Did he—?" Harriet ventured. "Did he say *princess*? *Auf Englisch, bitte?*" she pleaded with Mr. Schenk, who grinned again.

"*Ja, ja. Moment.*" He dragged one stout finger down the page, then jabbed the paper and looked up at Constantia. "*Auch auf Englisch. Für Ihre Mutter, natürlich.*"

"The document also contains an English translation," Harriet explained. "For your mother's benefit."

"In that case, may I?" Lady Posenby stepped forward and snatched the paper from his hand. "I'd rather not listen to this fellow mangle every other word." Without any assistance from her lorgnette, and in a voice that grew more incredulous with every sentence, she read out,

A Proclamation of Prince Christoph, of the Royal House of Friedensfeld

Made this seventeenth day of February, seventeen hundred eighty-four.
I, Christoph von Friedensfeld, do hereby make known my marriage, lawful in the eyes of God, to the Lady Marianne Kent and announce the birth of a daughter, heiress of my body, to be known henceforth as the princess Constantia . . .

There was more, but the buzzing in Constantia's ears would let her hear none of it. If Alistair hadn't helped her to a chair, she might have fainted. "It isn't true," she insisted to him. "It can't be."

He slipped the parchment from his aunt's slackened grasp and inspected the seal, then looked at her with marveling eyes. "I think it might be."

Chapter 23

A lost princess?

Alistair did not find it as difficult to believe as perhaps he ought.

His heart still ached for the girl she had been, deprived of her family, fighting to keep even her name a secret, because it was one of the few things she had known to be truly and only hers. But now all of that had changed.

She wasn't lost anymore.

He longed to wrap his arms around her, just as he had done earlier that night. But the very strength of his longing was a warning.

These revelations were for her alone. He'd already heard more than he should.

"Come," he said to the others, careful not to look at her. "I think we can agree that Herr Schenk presents no danger. We should leave them to work through the details of translating Miss—" A series of surnames swirled in his head, none of them real or right. Changing course, he finished lamely, "Uh, this private family matter."

He picked up a sturdy brass candelabra, strode toward the doors that divided the drawing room from the library, and threw them open. "You'll find paper, pens, whatever you might need in here." He paused to slide one slender volume on German history from the shelf, intending to offer it to his sister, and then at the last minute, tucked it into his pocket instead. "Danny, help our aunt to bed. She must be exhausted. Come, Forster. I'll have a servant show you to your room."

Aunt Josephine sputtered but went when Danny touched her arm. Forster hesitated.

As if to reassure both men of his honor, Schenk laid his arm across his chest in the manner of one taking an oath and bowed, clicking his heels together as he did so.

Alistair bowed in turn and left without another word.

After handing Forster off to a somewhat bewildered housemaid, Alistair's restless feet took him not toward his own bed, or even back to the library, but in the direction of the west wing. Before he had even made a conscious choice of destination, he found himself in the studio.

The walls still seemed to echo with their conversation of earlier that night.

You are not a selfish man.

Oh, but he was. How he had wanted to be able to give her all the things she had never had. But of course what she'd really wanted, really needed, was exactly what some other man was giving her now: a history. And a future. Far from here, and from him.

Slowly, he walked around the room. He'd always hated this place and everything it represented. But now, tangled up in those memories of his father and his past were memories of her. Of the art she had made. Of the passion they had shared.

On the table, he found the drawing of him reclining nude on the chaise. He wanted to touch the flame of the candle to it, to turn it to ash, but he made himself study it instead.

This one is just for me, she had told him as she'd sketched it.

Then she had left the picture behind.

This is how I see you, she had said earlier tonight.

Stripped bare. Dark eyes that should have been soft and sated but instead burned with lust. As if, in spite of having had her just moments earlier, he'd never needed her more.

She had never needed him less.

Snatching it from the table, he strode from the room. He carried the light with him, but the darkness followed. When he shut the door between the church and the cloisters and snapped the iron padlock, it clanged with awful finality.

As if summoned by Harriet's third noisy yawn in as many minutes, Danielle and Edwina appeared in the doorway of the library. "It's time for bed," Danielle announced.

Constantia glanced around the room and squinted at the clock on the mantel but couldn't make it out. How many hours had it taken for her and Harriet and Herr Schenk—together with the aid of pen and paper, a

great deal of patience, and Harriet's German primer—
to sort out a reasonably comprehensible recounting of
Constantia's family history?

In addition to providing Harriet with a lengthy written history of the Friedensfeld dynasty, he had also
explained in greater detail first how he had tracked Constantia to and around London, frequently losing sight of
her for weeks or months at a time and never getting
close enough to introduce himself, and then how he had
followed her from London to Rylemoor. Though that
part of the story did not in fact involve chasing her from
a London alleyway nor breaking chairs in a roadside
pub—Constantia had felt a twinge of guilt at the realization her fearful imagination had turned every chance
event against him—it had nonetheless been a thrilling
tale. Quite by happenstance, he had learned of an accident involving a young woman matching her description and had sought out the physician who had treated
her injuries. Once he had managed to ascertain Lord
Ryland's identity and whereabouts, he had embarked
upon the difficult journey across the countryside on
foot, having long since spent every penny he'd been
given for his search. He had arrived in the vicinity of
Rylemoor only the day before, encountered Edwina,
and had returned tonight intending to plead his case
to the earl. But, spying Constantia dressed for travel
and carrying her valise, he had attempted to follow her
instead, then lost his way in the darkness amid the
cavernous abbey ruins. She trembled to think that if she
had once again eluded him, or if Alistair had not checked
his swing, she might never have learned the truth.

"Mr. Schenk must be allowed to retire," Edwina gently insisted. Certainly, he had earned his rest. Without waiting for Harriet to translate her sister's words, he rose and followed Edwina gratefully out.

Seeing that her previous statement had not yet produced the desired result, Danielle folded her arms across her chest and spoke more sternly: "Harry. Bed."

Harriet rose with a halfhearted protest. "This will all still be here in the morning," Constantia assured her, lifting her head from what she had been reading long enough to cast a glance over the papers spread across the table.

Although truth be told, even she wasn't quite sure she believed it. She could not entirely shake the feeling that if she allowed herself to fall asleep, she would wake to discover this had been a dream.

"You as well," Danielle said, when Constantia did not stand and join them. "I'm not leaving you hear to brood over this affair all night."

Brood? Was that what she'd been doing? It was, well, more than overwhelming to try to take it all in. And a good deal of the story made her sorrowful in ways she hadn't expected.

But most of all, she was not sure how to begin to reconcile the woman shaped by the vicissitudes of a hard life, a woman whose experiences had formed a whole suit of rather spiky armor around her, with the woman Herr Schenk claimed she really was.

Out of habit, she shuffled the papers and books into neater stacks, not for the first time wishing her thoughts were so easy to compose. Eventually, though, she got to her feet and snuffed the last brace of candles from the dozens that had been lit at the start of the evening.

"Come on," Danielle said. "I'll show you to your room."

It took a moment for those words to sink in. "My . . . room?" She was tired, yes, and a bit befuddled. But she was reasonably sure that after more than a fortnight at Rylemoor, she could find her way to the schoolroom.

"Your new room," Danielle clarified. "Edwina feels it would be a shocking dereliction of her duty as hostess to allow a princess to continue sleeping in that broom cupboard upstairs." There was something slightly wry in her voice. Constantia opened her mouth to protest, but when it turned into a yawn instead, she realized arguing would be futile and followed Danielle out.

Harriet was already several paces ahead of them, and Constantia was surprised when Danielle led her in the same direction, toward the east wing. But she supposed it was to be expected that the guest chambers would be placed near the family apartments, in the part of the house that had been best maintained over the years. And after all, now she was no longer masquerading as a teacher; she *was* a guest.

Only a guest.

"I have not had an opportunity to praise your portrait of my brother," Danielle said as they ascended the stairs.

Constantia nearly stumbled. The unveiling of that picture seemed to belong to another lifetime. "You were pleased, then?"

They had reached the landing, and Danielle paused, appearing to have to consider her answer. "It is an exceptional likeness, very much the man I know my brother to be. Charming, kind, generous to a fault." Even Constantia, who had a great deal of confidence in her abilities, doubted she had conveyed so much with brushes and paint. "But I will confess," Danielle went on, "I cannot find pleasure in anything I am sure will bring him misery."

"Misery?" Constantia echoed.

"Marriage to a stranger, some merchant's daughter he does not love—what else would you call it? That is what your portrait will ensure." She took a few steps down the corridor and paused again. "But of course, you did what you were paid to do. If my sisters and I have convinced ourselves that you care too much for our brother to help seal his fate, well . . . I suppose we have only ourselves to blame. We did not know when all this began that you are the infamous Miss C."

The words stung, though she knew the lashing was deserved. "I certainly do not wish to see your brother miserable," she insisted. "But I did not consider myself as having the authority, the right, to go against what both he and your aunt seemed to think best. Difficult situations are often difficult to remedy—"

"He cares for you, you know." Danielle turned and searched her face, probing for a reaction to those words. "A great deal."

"And I—" she began, then broke off with a blush.

Care did not begin to do justice to her feelings for Alistair.

Oh, if only he hadn't left.

Danielle stopped before a door and handed her the candle. "I'm just here," she said, and Constantia could have sworn there was a smile about her lips as she added, "You're the last door on the right."

She took the remaining steps down the corridor slowly, her mind too busy sorting through the events of the last hours to also propel her feet. So much had changed—*everything*, one was tempted to say. But she wasn't sure she ought to go that far until she'd had a chance to tell Alistair all that she'd learned and ask him—

The last door on the right swung open to reveal a large chamber with a heavy four-poster bed. It also revealed the subject of her thoughts, clad in a dressing gown and sitting in a leather wingback chair before a fire blazing on the hearth, a book propped open on his knee.

She was torn between warring instincts: to acknowledge her mistake and withdraw from a chamber that obviously belonged to the Earl of Ryland, or to draw closer to the warmth and coziness of the fire—and to him. "Oh. I'm sorry for intruding," she said, frozen in indecision on the threshold. "I must have misunderstood Lady Danielle's directions."

"Danny sent you to my door?" He had risen and turned toward the firelight so that she could watch amusement play about his lips, a half smile very like the one she had just seen on his sister's face. "Then I doubt there was any mistake."

"You can't mean—? Surely she wouldn't—"

He shrugged. "I did warn you that my sisters were mischief-makers. Long before the monthly encouragement of Mrs. Goode."

Constantia glanced over her shoulder, into the empty corridor, and asked in a low voice, "You don't think she, er, *suspects*?"

"That we . . . ? No. None of them believes their dour elder brother capable of courting scandal in quite such a dramatic fashion."

And that, she supposed, was partly her handiwork too.

"Why did you leave?" she asked, standing with one hand on the door, torn over what to do. She thought of how he'd wrapped her in his arms earlier that evening, how he'd attacked a much bigger man in the darkness just to keep her safe. She wanted him by her side now. Forever.

But what he wanted mattered too.

"I could ask you the same," he replied, laying aside his book and coming closer. "Though I suppose I already had your answer, didn't I? Then let us say I suspected you would prefer to grapple with the implications of Schenk's story on your own terms, and that there might be aspects of your history you would not wish others to know."

"But Lady Harriet has heard—"

"I cannot say the same for all my sisters, but Harry is no gossip."

She believed it. "And if I wish for you to know everything Herr Schenk told me?"

"Then you may tell me," he said, the ghost of hesitation in his voice.

"Tonight?"

His eyes narrowed slightly, the tiniest hint of a wall going up between him and a truth he was obviously reluctant to hear. "Just as you wish."

Chapter 24

Constantia reached behind her and closed the door, and he gestured her to the chair opposite his, beside the fire. "In case it's of use to you, I compiled a list of solicitors who could be trusted to look into Schenk's claims," he told her, nodding toward a writing desk a few feet away. She could see at least two pieces of paper covered with his precise hand. "And then I decided to brush up on my German history." He gestured with the closed book. "Did you know that the principality of Friedensfeld has been defunct since—?"

"The mid-eighteenth century, yes," she said, suddenly wishing she had brought along Herr Schenk's notes—or rather, Harriet's translation of them. "After a series of skirmishes along the border with the Duchy of Knechtsburg, in which the Friedensfelders suffered many losses, the then-prince, my great-grandfather, was driven into exile. Herr Schenk wept as he told me the story. The family has remained in Transylvania ever since, allowed to retain their titles, but forfeiting much else."

Alistair looked impressed by the amount of knowledge she had acquired in so little time. But also a little grim.

"Shortly after his father's death in 1780, my father, Prince Christoph, embarked on a grand tour of sorts, to study art. Italy, Paris, eventually London, where he met my mother, painted her portrait, and, evidently, showered her with gifts." Reaching up beneath her hair, most of which had long since escaped the elegant coiffure over which Georgiana and Frederica had labored so earnestly, she plucked the earbobs from her ears. She hadn't known where else to keep them. "Do you"—she fiddled absently with them, making the firelight dance across the gems—"do you believe my parents really were married? Wouldn't there be some record—something in an English church?"

He mused on that question for a long moment. "Perhaps, when you're some sort of prince, a royal proclamation is all the authority you need. Truth be told, I'm far more interested in how you and your mother came to be left all alone." His jaw was set in a hard line; she ought to have known he would have little patience for a man who failed in his most important duty, who hadn't done everything he could to protect his family.

Fortunately, that wasn't the whole story.

"Herr Schenk said that his brother, my uncle, wrote to urge his return by lying about their mother's health. That when he arrived and realized what his brother had done, he knew trouble was afoot, which was why he issued a proclamation that very day. He wanted to ensure that my mother would be taken care of if anything happened to him. But of course, my mother never knew anything about it, because within a week, my father was . . . dead."

He leaned forward and encircled her hands with his. "I don't know what sort of condolence to offer under circumstances such as these. I am sorry you will never know him, but he left you with a marvelous gift." Surprise must have flashed across her face, for he added, by way of explanation, "Your artistic gift—the one you share with him."

She nodded and gnawed on the soft flesh behind her lower lip. For just a moment, she had thought he must have guessed the rest. "There's something else."

"Oh?"

"If we didn't misunderstand Herr Schenk, or make a terrible mistranslation, it seems that when the family went into exile and forfeited their lands, they still escaped with a sizable fortune in gold and gems. And in that proclamation, well, my father left it all to me." She had been trying all evening not to think about how different her life would have been if Herr Schenk had caught up with her sooner. Far fewer struggles and hardships. No damp cellar room beneath a modiste's shop.

No Alistair either.

"That's marvelous," he exclaimed, though his hands went slack. "You will finally be free to paint what you choose, to have whatever sort of life you'd like."

"Mm-hmm," she agreed, still worrying her lip. "Alistair? What if . . . what if I decided what I really want is a home? Here? With you?"

The almost imperceptible cloud that had formed on his brow a few moments earlier slowly cleared as the meaning of those words sank in. "Constantia, are you—are you asking me to marry you?"

He was a proud man, she knew. Was she no better than those Bristol merchants' daughters, trying to buy his hand, but in the process losing his heart?

"Should I get down on one knee?"

He shook his head, never taking his eyes from hers as he slid from his chair onto the hearthrug at her feet. "No, I believe it's I who should be kneeling in the presence of royalty."

"Alistair," she chided, trying to slip her fingers from his grasp.

But he paid her no mind. "Promise me you're not doing this because you think you should. Because you feel some ill-conceived responsibility for the situation in which I've found myself."

"I'm far too selfish for that. I'm doing it for myself. Because every moment I spent on that portrait forced me to confront how much I w-wanted you." She stammered out the word, knowing his eyes would flare hotly at it. "How much I love you."

He lifted his hand to cup her head and draw her closer even as he rose up on his knees. The intensity of his dark gaze was softened by the sparkle of unshed tears as he tipped his forehead to hers.

"Are you certain you want to say yes?" she asked, swallowing against the prickle of tears in her own throat. "I'm not much like the ideal bride you described to me." A wry laugh pushed past the tears. "Other than rich."

"And pretty, and intelligent, and good with my sisters," he reminded her.

"But totally inexperienced in the duties of a lady. Sometimes messy. And a little wild."

His dark eyes flared. "Perhaps I've decided I like wild."

At that, she laughed and tossed her head; her hair tumbled around them. "I intend to keep painting," she warned him. "Under my real name. I mean to refurbish the studio—"

"I wouldn't have it any other way."

Their lips met with a combination of sweetness and heat that until recently she hadn't known existed. It was a kiss rich with passion and promise, and when her tongue slicked daringly over his, he groaned.

Dragging his mouth over her jaw to her ear, he whispered seductively, "I am eager to serve as your consort, Princess Constantia."

He was teasing, of course, but still the title sent an unexpected shiver of delight down her spine. Or perhaps that was simply the heat of his breath.

"I fear a princess without a principality hasn't any real power," she retorted, reaching out to trace the open collar of his dressing gown. The V of bare skin displayed there was dusted with dark hair and deliciously warm.

His answering laugh was more than a little wicked. "Oh, my love, I wouldn't say that."

With one hand still on her nape, he held her in thrall to the kisses he pressed down on her throat and over her collarbone. His other hand slipped beneath the hem of her skirts and slid up her calf, raising the layers of wool and linen as he went. Then he bent his head and kissed a spot just above her knee. The forbidden excitement of his lips in such a place set up a desperate throbbing at the joining of her thighs.

Releasing her neck, he grasped her hip instead and tugged her forward several inches, her bottom sliding easily over the smooth leather seat. The sudden movement drove a squeak of surprise from her. She wasn't alarmed, though she thought perhaps she should be, given the fiery expression in his eyes when he looked up at her from between her spread knees.

"Well, your highness? Will you let me worship you as you deserve?"

Despite her scattered wits, she managed what she thought was a very regal-sounding "You may."

With teasing kisses along the sensitive skin of her inner thighs, he made his way to her mound. His breath was hot against her private curls, the feel of his mouth there like nothing she could have imagined. When his tongue slid into the seam of her sex, she thought she might die of the pleasure. Her heart banged against her ribs, and she dug her fingers into the arms of the chair, trying to keep herself from flying apart, trying to drag herself closer to him.

At that, his low chuckle vibrated through her most intimate places. Hooking her knees over his shoulders, he opened her more fully to his passionate onslaught. The shockingly decadent sounds of his mouth and tongue against her slickness brought a flush of heat to her chest. Without conscious thought, she moved her hands to his head and drove her fingers through his thick, dark hair, pulling him closer still. His lips found that little bundle of nerves and he began to suck, ratcheting her need higher and higher until she shattered, her release almost painful in its intensity. Her thighs trembled and clenched around his head as he gentled his ministrations, easing her through the crisis until she shuddered once more and finally slumped, spent, in the chair.

"Don't fall asleep, Princess," he teased, nuzzling her inner thigh with a wet kiss. "I need you in my bed."

With what seemed to her extraordinary energy, he leaped to his feet and helped her to stand on rather wobbly legs, then divested her of her clothing more quickly than she would have imagined possible.

"You were beautiful tonight in that gold dress," he murmured as he bent to kiss her. "But not more beautiful than you are out of it."

She had felt beautiful then, with his sisters fussing over every detail of her appearance as no one ever had. But nothing compared to the way she felt in this moment. Worshipped, as he'd said. Adored. Loved.

When she reached for the tie of his dressing gown, she discovered he wore nothing beneath. "Somehow," she said, her voice breathy in spite of her intent to tease,

"I imagined you the sort of man who would wear a nightshirt."

"Did you?" He shrugged, once, and the heavy silk slithered to the floor. "Well, my dear, it turns out I'm not nearly as dull and proper as certain people have made me out to be."

She lowered her eyes at that, but only to rake them over his body. "It seems I still have much to learn," she said, reaching for him.

"And here I thought you might be rather sh-shy." He hissed in a breath when her fingertips brushed along the heated length of his member.

"Whatever gave you that impression?"

"The, uh, the second portrait, shall we call it?" His eyes gradually lost their focus as her touch grew more insistent. "You drew me with a sheet draped over my middle, and that's not quite how I remember posing for you."

"Oh, *that* picture." A tiny flicker of alarm passed through her as she recalled when and where he'd seen it. "Oh, my goodness. Is it still lying in the studio for anyone to see?"

"No." His hand encircled hers, firming her grip, teaching her how to stroke him. "I, um, I went back for it later. While you were working in the library. It's safely stowed away."

Relief and amusement escaped her in a shivery breath. "Excellent. Then I can finish it properly." She watched their joined hands slide over his cock. "Once I've had the chance to study my subject more carefully."

"I'm all yours, whenever you wish." His breaths were coming more rapidly. "But right now, I need—"

She thrilled at the wolfish eagerness with which he prowled closer, propelling her backward until they reached the bed. When she turned, he dropped his head to nip the place where her neck joined her shoulder. His arms came around her and his hands covered her small breasts, his thumbs brushing lightly over her nipples.

Then, as she prepared to climb onto the high mattress, the movement of her hips seemed to snap the thin tether on his desire. His fingers dug into the soft flesh of her bottom and in another moment, she felt his shaft at the entrance to her body.

"Yes?" Part growl, part desperate plea.

"Yes." She canted her hips backward and he filled her on one long, glorious slide. Gripping the coverlet, she tried to capture every sensation, the hair on his chest as it tickled across her back, the heat of him, inside and out, as he drove into her again and again, pushing her toward another shattering climax. One of his hands cinched her hips to his as he spent, while the other slid languorously up her spine. "Definitely not dull or proper," she said with a soft, wondering laugh as he dropped a kiss onto her shoulder.

"No," he agreed, and felt his lips curve into a smile. "Because I've wanted to do that since that night at the pub, when you asked me to help you out of your dress."

"Ah," she said, recalling the state he'd been in the next morning. Perhaps he was a bit wild himself, a bit rakish after all? "But it's probably for the best that you held off until we had a sturdier bed."

Laughing, he withdrew, but he did not let her go. "Stay with me," he said, sweeping back the covers.

"What will your aunt think? Or your sisters? Or—oh, good heavens—the rector?!"

He hoisted her into the bed with surprising ease, then snuggled in beside her. "They'll think that I'm the luckiest man in the world."

Chapter 25

For just the second time in his life, Alistair awoke in the morning to the pleasure of finding Constantia in his arms. And for the second time, he held her close a moment longer than he should before hoisting himself from bed. Oh, he wanted to stay—just as he had wanted to once before. But he'd kept her up half the night making love and talking and making love while talking. She had earned her rest.

By rights, he ought to have been exhausted too. But an unusual energy, an unfamiliar excitement buzzed in his veins.

He was in love. He was loved in return.

Of course, a man schooled in practicality and self-restraint did not easily shake off his skepticism. A princess? A fortune? Those were fairy tales on which it wouldn't pay to rely. But love? Love was real.

He and Constantia made one another happy. And whole. They were going to marry, no matter what.

Of that, he had no doubt at all.

So while she slept, he rose and dressed. The storm

had passed, and if he knew his guests, some of them would be ready to depart at dawn.

As he had expected, he found the rector and his wife with Forster in the entry hall awaiting their carriage, which had already been ordered.

"Just the man I hoped to see," Alistair said, approaching the rector with hand outstretched. "I wish to marry Miss, er—the, uh—well, Constantia." Lord, it would be easier when she was Lady Ryland. "As soon as possible."

The rector's wife smiled with her merry, twinkling eyes. "Of course you do. Every man should find a woman who sees in him nothing but the best."

"Very well, very well," said the rector, shaking Alistair's hand as he nodded to his curate. "Samuel here will read the banns this Sunday."

Four weeks would be an eternity. He might have pleaded for a special license, but that would have meant going to the bishop and more time spent away from his bride-to-be. And there were plans to make, shopping to be done, Christmas to celebrate—he must hope that keeping busy would make the time go by fast enough.

Alistair nodded and turned to Forster. "If it suits you—and unless I'm very much mistaken, I believe it will—you might as well read out another set of banns at the same time."

Forster jerked back his head in surprise. "You don't mean—?"

"You and Eddie." He lifted his brows in something he hoped would pass for sternness, though there was too much joy in his heart to manage the real thing. "Or did I mistake your intentions toward my sister?"

"God, no," the other man exclaimed, which prompted a little cough of disapprobation from the rector. "Thank you, Ryland." Forster now gripped his hand and was shaking it vigorously. "Thank you very much."

Someone summoned Eddie, who appeared, still in her wrapper, to hear the good news. After the three guests had been successfully dispatched, she turned to Alistair, her eyes shining with tears of happiness and gratitude, and sniffled, "I'll just order breakfast, shall I?"

"A big one, if you don't mind," he called over his shoulder to her as he headed toward the library.

He'd worked up quite an appetite last night.

In the library, which he'd assumed would be empty at this early hour, he found Harry already hard at work. "You know," he said, bending to plant a kiss on her head as she leaned over the table, "I actually doubted you when you said you were keeping up with your German studies. I've never been so glad to be proved wrong."

"Well . . ." She sent him a sidelong glance. "I never believed you when you said you'd let me have drawing lessons someday. So, I suppose we're even."

He laughed, then twisted a piece of heavily-inked paper toward himself, though he couldn't read it. "Harry? Do you think this business might be a ruse?"

To his surprise, she laid down her pen and looked up, giving the question serious consideration. "I don't," she concluded after a few moments of thought. "Who would bother? All this time and effort"—she waved a hand over the paper-covered table—"and to what end? I think, in spite of how unbelievable it sounds, Herr Schenk is who he claims to be."

"Which means Constantia is who he says."

"A princess." Her voice was breathy and full of wonder, an unexpectedly sweet reminder of the little girl she had once been. When had his sisters all grown up?

He squeezed her hand, nodded, and intended to retreat to his desk, but another question niggled at him. "I understand that sometime after I left last evening, Schenk said something about money?"

Harry shuffled through two stacks of paper, finally found whatever it was she sought, and slid a page toward him, using the nail of her first finger to underscore a number. A low whistle escaped between his teeth. "But that won't be British pounds," he reasoned aloud.

"He told her last night that her father did everything he could to protect the family fortune from his brother, whom he'd always suspected of treachery. Unless my German's truly terrible, the money has been sitting in a British bank for years. So, yes." She tucked the paper back into its stack with a decisive motion, as if she considered the matter settled. "That's in pounds sterling, brother dear."

Good God.

"Have you . . . have you mentioned this to any of your sisters?"

A frown of confusion dug into the space between her dark brows. "Why would I? It's Miss Coop—er, I mean, well . . ." The title of princess didn't rise naturally to anyone's lips, it seemed. "It's *her* money," Harry finished, as if that settled the matter.

It was. And his dear Constantia wanted to share it with him.

He sat down behind his desk, staring for a long moment at those hated ledgers, before slipping two sheets of foolscap from the center drawer and dipping his quill. *Dear Lady Stalbridge,* he began. Much of the story would have to come later; it was Constantia's to tell. But the countess deserved some explanation, some reassurance. After what he suspected had been weeks of worry following his last letter to her, she deserved some share of the joy.

And when that was written, he started in on the second sheet. Unless he saw it in Alistair's own hand, Miles would never, never believe what had transpired. Remarkable, really, how similarly their lives had turned out, in spite of their many differences. Each of them had fallen in love with one of Mrs. Goode's Misses, in spite of that young lady's rather unflattering depiction of him—in words, in Miles's case, rather than pictures.

Perhaps a guide to misconduct wasn't such a bad thing, after all.

As he sanded and sealed the paper, Alistair smiled rather impishly to himself. He had mentioned nothing of it in his brief note, of course—a gentleman didn't kiss and tell—but Alistair felt certain he finally had one up on his friend. Miles, for all his wild times and rakish ways, had never taken a princess to his bed.

Then, stomach rumbling, he handed off the letters to Wellend for posting and went to breakfast. Harry, who was focused on her translations, promised to join him in a little while.

In the family sitting room, which also served as the breakfast parlor, he found Edwina, Danny, and Aunt Josephine.

"Ryland," said his aunt, her voice as sharp and bitter as the coffee in her cup. He gave her an answering nod. "You look a wreck," she went on as he filled a plate with eggs and sausage and toast. "But I suppose one can't wonder at it. I doubt any of us slept well after that ridiculous drama last night. Well, let's put it behind us this morning, shall we?" she said. As he sat down across from her at the large round table, his back to the door, she withdrew a folded piece of paper from her sleeve. "I've taken the liberty of compiling a list of eligible young ladies in and around Bristol who—"

"Alistair won't be needing that," Eddie said quietly.

Reflexively, Aunt Josephine curled her fingers around her lorgnette, which was lying beside her plate. "I beg your pardon, Edwina?"

It was Danny's turn to chime in. "My brother won't be needing your list." She smiled knowingly at him around her teacup as she lifted it to her lips and drank. "He's marrying a princess."

"Princess," Aunt Josephine scoffed. "Your brother may be dull, but he's sharp enough to know a swindle when he hears one."

Alistair enjoyed a few mouthfuls of his breakfast

before replying, determined not to let his aunt spoil another perfectly good meal. "A German envoy, a royal proclamation, crown jewels—rather elaborate for a swindle, don't you think?"

"So she managed to hire some . . . refugee"—she fairly spat out the word, then paused for a shudder of distaste—"from the Continent, had him tell a tall tale, and then flash around a sheet of parchment and a pair of earbobs made of paste. I should have thought that you of all people would recognize it for what it is: utter madness." She tapped one bony finger against her temple. "Perhaps it's something in the paint that twists their minds."

"I wouldn't doubt it," Constantia said from just inside the doorway.

Her voice struck his aunt like a bucket of cold water on a hot summer day, and she began immediately to sputter.

Ignoring her, Alistair rose and welcomed his beloved into the room with outstretched hands. The kiss he'd first intended for her cheek was quickly diverted to her soft lips instead.

She looked remarkably beautiful to him in the morning light, clad in the same simple woolen dress in which she'd come to him last night, rather the worse for wear for having lain in a heap on the floor of his bedchamber for hours. Her hair was a tumbled mass of curls, though somewhat smoother and glossier than usual, thanks to his sisters' efforts the evening before.

"I suppose you've come down this morning expecting to be paid for that travesty of a portrait?" Aunt Josephine sneered.

"You may keep your money, Lady Posenby," Constantia answered calmly. "And that painting, too, for all I care." She darted a mischievous glance his way that told him she preferred a certain, er, less formal drawing she'd made. Then she twined her fingers with his and gripped his upper arm with her other hand. "I have everything I really need."

"You don't mean—? Surely you're not suggesting—?" Aunt Josephine scrambled to her feet, making the dishes on the table rattle. "Ryland, you can't possibly mean to marry that woman."

"I do." He looked down into Constantia's eyes and covered her hand with his. "In fact, I've already spoken to the rector this morning. I hope that meets with your approval, Princess?"

For answer, the corners of Constantia's mouth curved in an ever so slightly crooked smile.

"I will not stay and be a part of this travesty," declared Aunt Josephine, snatching her lorgnette and her list from the table. "I intend to leave for Bath this very hour. Come, Danielle."

"No," he said, not lifting his eyes from his bride's. "Go if you wish, by all means, Aunt. But Danny's staying here."

Danny flew from her seat to embrace him, and her new sister too. In half a moment, Eddie had joined them. With a snarl, Aunt Josephine stormed from the room, and snarled again when she met Harry and Herr Schenk on the threshold.

The pair of them entered—the big German had to duck his head—and looked about, rather bewildered. "*Alles in Ordnung?*" the envoy asked, after greeting Constantia with a deferential bow.

That question required no translation. "Order? Never," Alistair answered with a laugh. Extracting himself, he took the other man by the arm and led him toward the sideboard. "Harry, how do you say *breakfast*?"

Harry thought for a moment. "*Frühstück?*"

It was, Alistair thought, the most absurdly joyful, joyfully absurd word he had ever heard. The six of them were still laughing merrily over everything and nothing when Freddie and Georgie appeared in the doorway and asked, in wide-eyed unison, "What did we miss?"

The Countess of Stalbridge sat cross-legged on the bed while having her hair done. That she was in the nursery, that the mattress lay on the floor beneath a tent made of the former dining room draperies, and that her stylist was a girl of not quite seven, only made the moment more perfect.

Ferncliffe's nursery décor had been a hurried attempt on Oliver's part to make the empty attic a welcoming and magical place for the Earl of Stalbridge's niece and nephew, who had arrived on their guardian's doorstep far sooner than expected.

Oliver's unique gifts in such matters were attested to by the fact that the children had absolutely refused to permit a single change to his makeshift design. They loved to fall asleep beneath a "starry sky" of dark blue silk poked with holes, and to entertain their adult family members—Oliver, who was no relation to the children at all, had been bestowed with the honorary title of cousin on the very day of their arrival—in a cozy space that was wholly without pretension, and wholly their own.

While Luca, who was five, pretended to read aloud from yesterday's newspaper, Isabella arranged Tabetha's hair to highlight the distinctive silver streak that ran through its dark length. "Uncle Kit," she exclaimed when the earl entered the nursery and peered beneath the tent. "Come see how beautiful Aunt Beth looks!"

Kit grazed warm eyes over his wife. Her hair, normally pinned in a sleek coil, now hung over one shoulder in a messy braid. He smiled. "Beautiful indeed. Always." Then he stood so he was only visible to them from the knees down, held open the flap of the tent, and announced, "Cousin Oliver is here, and he's positively weighed down with Christmas presents. I wonder who will help him?"

Two noisy squeals and less than half a minute later, he was alone beneath the tent with his arms around Tabetha. "How disappointing," she teased, as Kit nudged her braid aside to nuzzle beneath her ear. "Now I'll never hear the end of that article Luca was reading to me."

"So this is where my newspaper's disappeared to. Had he got to the review of the art exhibition yet?"

She giggled girlishly when he found a particularly ticklish spot. "You do realize he can't actually read?"

"Mm." Kit brushed a kiss across her cheek as he reached for the newspaper. "Lucky for us both, I can. *If*

I remembered my spectacles." He patted his coat pocket, found them, and put them on. "Ah, here we are. It was this bit in particular I thought might interest you: 'Placing second in the watercolor category, a whimsical composition entitled *Ladies Reading, With Swords*'— hmm, I'd like to see that—'signed only with the initial *C*.' You don't suppose that's your mysterious Miss C., do you?"

Tabetha considered the possibility. "Miss Nelson did mention that she'd told them something about entering a painting in an exhibition. Oh, if it is Constantia's work, I hope the good news has made its way to her."

"It really doesn't seem right for you to look so beautiful, even when you're worried," he told her, brushing a few stray silvery strands away from her blue eyes.

She lifted one shoulder in mock despair. "I'm afraid it can't be helped. I'm beautiful always, remember?" He laughed then, and so did she, though she truly was concerned for Constantia. "She's always been such a private person. Do you suppose it would be meddling overmuch in her affairs if I were to write another letter to—?"

"Letter," Kit echoed. "Good heavens. Your beauty has me so distracted, I almost forgot. Oliver asked me to give this to you." Once more, he reached into his breast pocket. "He said it was delivered to the house in Town last week, and he thought rather than forwarding it on, he would bring it to Ferncliffe himself when he came."

There was something vaguely familiar about the precise, masculine handwriting. With trembling fingers— she'd not entirely got over the shock of last month's threatening letters, despite the fact that all had turned out well—she broke the seal and unfolded the paper. "It's from Lord Ryland."

"Oh?" Kit leaned back against the mattress and tugged Beth down beside him. "What's he say?"

"Miss Cooper is safe! She's been in his care all this time, just as I hoped, and—oh, my! Oh, I certainly didn't expect that! He says they're to be married in a month."

"Well, well. Another Miss becomes a Missus. I suppose we ought to send a nuptial gift."

"Mm, yes," she agreed absently, suddenly conscious of the fact that her husband's arms were around her and they were alone. The letter fluttered to the mattress as she turned in his embrace. "I think I really must do something different with the magazine, don't you?"

He made a sound that might have been agreement but was more likely a response to her plucking off his spectacles and tossing them aside. "Tomorrow will surely be soon enough to decide, my dear."

Epilogue

The following spring . . .

Alistair had not intended to return to Haythorne
House quite so soon. But the noise at Rylemoor—
a combination of workmen making repairs and Freddie
and Georgie's repeated pleas to be allowed to join some
of their friends in Town for the end of the Season—had
at last driven him to write to his tenant and ask whether
an earlier than planned end to their lease would be a
great inconvenience.

Fortunately, his tenant's daughter had succeeded
quickly and well in her matrimonial efforts and was
already settled in her new home. The man and his wife
had been thinking of summering in Brighton to be
closer to her. And so, with remarkably little fuss, the
house in Marylebone was once more Alistair's.

The house . . . but not the library.

Or rather, the library was no longer his sole province,
as three-quarters of it at least had been given over to
his wife.

"It really is very sweet of you to let me paint here,"

Constantia said. She was blocked from his view by two easels, a half dozen canvases turned this way and that, a tall, narrow-mouthed tin filled with a spiky assortment of brushes, and a large mahogany and brass chest of shallow drawers containing cakes of watercolor paint, one in each of the seventy-six colors sold by Rudolph Ackermann.

"Really, it's a far better use of the space," Alistair answered honestly from his corner. He had never before realized how bright and airy the room could be. He admired the gauzy new curtains fluttering in the breeze of an open window. The plant he had long since given up for dead, she had moved to the windowsill, and he saw with amazement that it was beginning to turn green. "But I do think I may have to consider getting a smaller desk."

At that, a pair of mischievous hazel eyes peered around the corner of a canvas. Those eyes were crowned by a tangle of red curls pinned up by, of all things, a paintbrush, fortunately free of paint. "Don't do anything rash, my love. That one looks delightfully"—her fair eyebrows lifted suggestively—"sturdy."

Alistair was just on the point of asking his wife whether she would like to test that proposition when Harry waltzed in with the morning post and handed off most of the stack to him. "Latest issue of the *Magazine for Misses* is here," she announced as she threaded her way to the sofa, plopped down, and began to page through it.

"Ooh," said Constantia, rattling a brush in a can of water, "what's Miss Busy B. have to say this month?"

"As if you don't already know," said Alistair a bit grumpily as he began to sort through the letters, dividing them into neat stacks of invitations and bills, and plotting to disorder them by tumbling his wife on the desktop at the first opportunity.

His not quite gloating note to Miles had produced one entirely unexpected outcome: It had established a regular correspondence, some might even say friendship, between their wives.

"Well, yes," Constantia acknowledged. "But there's nothing quite like seeing it in print—and I have it on good authority this column might be one of her last." Daphne was in the process of completing a book advocating for new—and in some circles, controversial— methods for the education of young people, especially girls. In addition to many other notable women, the Princess Constantia von Friedensfeld had contributed handsomely to support its publication.

"What a shame. I miss the theatrical reviews, too," said Harry. "Oh, but here's a description of Lady Clarissa Sutliffe's pianoforte concert last week—what an event that was. Who would have thought her father would ever allow it?"

"Yes, society has certainly seen its fair share of changes since the *Magazine for Misses* began its run," said Constantia, who had once more retreated fully behind her canvas.

The Unfashionable Plates continued to be the magazine's most popular feature—and the only pages at which Alistair steadfastly refused to look. "Don't you think I've learned my lesson?" Constantia had asked him once, as she'd put the finishing touches on her first contribution as "Miss C." since becoming Lady Ryland.

"Do you know," he'd told her with a kiss, "I rather hope not."

"Mrs. Goode must find it difficult to keep up with everything," Constantia mused now, bringing him back to the present moment.

"Speaking of," said Alistair as his eyes lighted on the next letter in his stack. "Here's something for you— from Mrs. Goode herself."

The letter was really from Lady Stalbridge, of course, but Harry didn't need to know that. She had gleaned a great deal too many secrets about the magazine already.

"Oh! Will you read it for me, please, Alistair? My fingers are quite covered in paint."

"Of course they are, dear," he said as he broke the seal and scanned through the letter's contents once and then again.

"I meant aloud," Constantia prompted when he did not speak for several minutes. A tuft of red-gold hair poked around the edge of a canvas. "Is everything all right?"

"I'll let you be the judge of that. 'My dear Lady Ryland,'" he read.

After some months of deliberation and discussion with my family, I have reached the conclusion that it is necessary to make some changes in the management of the Magazine for Misses. I write to ask whether you would consider sharing the editorial duties with me—

He paused when he heard something clatter to the floor.

"Truly?" gasped Harriet, closing the magazine and laying her hand reverently on the cover, obscuring one of the two caryatids that framed the title. "Would that make you the new Mrs. Goode?"

"Certainly not," said Constantia, bending to retrieve her brush. "There will only ever be one Mrs. Goode. But to think that she . . . That I might . . ."

Alistair, better than anyone, knew what the magazine meant to Constantia. How she had drawn courage from its mission to entertain, to educate, and most of all to empower young women, to teach them the strength of their own voices and to give them confidence in their choices.

However, he had not known until that moment, when he heard the eagerness in her voice, that she had also dreamed of one day doing more than illustrating it.

"I have the most marvelous idea," said Harry. "If the magazine needs a new advice columnist, and you're the one who gets to help decide who it should be, you should pick Danny. She's wonderfully good at ordering people about."

From the corner, Constantia laughed. "I suppose she is a bit like Miss Busy B., now you mention it. But if Danielle were to contribute to the magazine, I always thought she might do an excellent job of speaking to another set of readers—those who find themselves in the sorts of situations in which she once was. You know, ladies' companions and the like. We could call it Miss D.'s—"

"Degradations?" muttered Alistair. The mortification of what his sister must have had to endure all those months with Aunt Josephine still had not lost its sting.

"Or Decapitations?" suggested Harry in an alarmingly bloodthirsty tone. It seemed she hadn't forgiven their aunt either.

"I was thinking 'Miss D.'s Directions for Managing Difficult People,'" said Constantia, with a tinkling laugh.

"I'm going to tell her, right now," Harry announced, bouncing to her feet and hurrying from the room. Constantia made no attempt to stop her.

Alistair stood too and approached the corner where his wife was painting. "So, you're considering it?" he said. "The added responsibilities won't interfere with your art?" She was already juggling several portrait commissions and entries in two exhibitions.

"I could do a bit of rearranging. Perhaps some retrenching." He heard the swish of the wet brush as she dragged it across the canvas. "What would you say to Harry taking over as Miss C.? She would bring a fresh pair of eyes to the magazine."

Harriet alone had continued her drawing lessons since the wedding and had made remarkable progress. "She would, at that," Alistair had to acknowledge.

"And I know some of the strain Lady Stalbridge has felt had to do with, well, geography. She desires to spend more time in the country, with her family." At last, Constantia emerged from behind the easel, wiping her hands on a paint-stained rag. "While we've already discussed living mostly in Town."

"We have."

While she had been busy painting, he had taken a more active role in the Lords and found that politics suited him. It had felt good to be of use, speaking out on behalf of those who were vulnerable, the plights of orphans and refugees in particular. He had been advised on the latter issue by Dieter Schenk, who had decided, after years of displacement and wandering, to stay in London.

Rylemoor Abbey would, of course, always be Alistair's home. But now it was Samuel and Eddie's home too. After their joint marriages had been celebrated, Samuel had agreed enthusiastically to Alistair's request that he take over managing matters in Devonshire. And truth be told, a small country estate didn't require as much attention as a large one; rather than repurchasing extensive farmland, Alistair and Constantia had chosen to invest her fortune in several modern enterprises, and those investments were already paying off. They would support the earldom's dependents well into the future.

Lord and Lady Ryland were now at liberty to enjoy all that the metropolis had to offer.

Hungrily, he raked his eyes over his wife. He knew he was imagining a slight swelling of her belly—it was far too soon for that. She'd only told him of her suspicions that morning. Still, he wanted to wrap his arms around her, around them, and caution her against doing too much.

But he knew that however busy he and Constantia were, their child—their children—would never want for familial affection and attention. They would grow up surrounded by doting aunts, and soon more uncles, if the number of suitors trailing after Freddie and Georgie was any indication. Eventually cousins. And they would know the steady but quieter love of their great-grandparents, the Marquess and Marchioness of Brookworth, who were a far cry from Constantia's ruthless imagining of them and had been thrilled to learn of the existence of a granddaughter they'd believed lost to them, along with their daughter, so many years ago.

"You should do it. Because I want everyone to see you as I do, a woman fulfilled by her work and happy in her life. And especially if this baby is a girl," he said, running his palm over her still-flat abdomen, "I want her to grow up knowing just how much a determined miss is capable of achieving."

At that, she dropped the rag and threw her arms around his neck. He suspected he now had paint on his cravat. "But if it's a girl," she cautioned, looking up at him with bright eyes, "we do run a greater risk of her falling in love with Miles and Daphne's son someday."

Geoffrey Alistair Deveraux, Lord Lyne, was at present only a few weeks old.

"I don't doubt but what he's destined to be a heart-breaker, given that he'll grow up surrounded by the combined influences of his father's charm, his mother's intelligence, and his godfather's devastating wit," Alistair teased, brushing his mouth across her upturned lips.

"Our daughter will have to be strong, to withstand all that."

"Oh, she will be."

Out of habit, he nudged a wild red curl from her brow and watched it spring right back to the place where it had been. He could feel even more chaos encroaching, straining the seams of his previously well-ordered life.

Reaching up, he plucked the paintbrush from her hair and sent its glorious waves tumbling around them as he set his mouth to hers for a more thorough kiss.

He wouldn't have it any other way.

Don't miss Julia and Graham's story!
THE LADY PLAYS WITH FIRE
by Susanna Craig

**In this *Bridgerton*-era *You've Got Mail*,
the clever, popular, and deliciously shocking ladies'
periodical *Mrs. Goode's Magazine for Misses* only
employs women who are equal to the challenge—
and for one biting theater critic, that challenge
happens to include romance.**

As the daughter of a clergyman, Julia Addison
knows she'll never be able to fulfill her lifelong
dream of acting on the stage. But writing forthright
reviews of the Season's most popular plays for *Mrs.
Goode's Magazine for Misses*, popularly known as
Goode's Guide to Misconduct, is surely the next best
thing. Even better, she's got a ticket to Ransom
Blackadder's latest irritating satire about English
society. Best of all, she's sharing a theater box with
the gruff but handsome Lord Dunstane, which is
enough to make Julia call for an encore . . .

Graham McKay, the Earl of Dunstane,
rarely leaves his home in the Scottish Highlands.
Why would he? Nothing about London has ever held
his interest—until he meets Julia. But when Graham
realizes she is the critic who panned his last play—
and she discovers he is in fact the man behind
Blackadder's wicked pen—will it bring down the
curtain on their romance—not to mention the
magazine that published the humiliating review?
Or can an unexpected collaboration set the stage
for a scandalous love affair?

**Keep reading for a special excerpt
from Julia and Graham's story**

THE LADY PLAYS WITH FIRE

Chapter 1

London, September 1810

As the carriage crept along crowded West End streets, Julia Addison's anticipation grew, until the butterflies dancing and fluttering inside her might have been mistaken for a herd of dashing, leaping stags. Tonight marked the official start of her second London Season.

But it wasn't a ball or a rout or a dinner party that had set her nineteen-year-old heart racing. *That* part of the Season was yet to come, and nothing she, as a lady's companion, was likely to participate in. What marked the true beginning of the Season in Julia's mind was not even the opening of Parliament. It was the fresh bill of operas and ballets and, most important of all, plays to be performed each autumn and winter at the Theatre Royal, Covent Garden, this year to be observed from Mrs. Mildred Hayes's reserved box on the second tier, overlooking stage left.

Mrs. Hayes sat on the carriage's forward-facing seat,

the tip of her cane planted on the floor between her feet, both hands resting on its polished silver handle, her relaxed body swaying easily with the vehicle's desultory progress. Her eyes were closed.

Julia marveled that anyone could sleep at a time like this. The noise surrounding them was terrific: the clatter of hooves and harness, the rattle of iron-rimmed wheels over cobblestones; men, women, and children along the pavement hawking goods and services ranging from the practical to the profane; and the shouted oaths of carriage drivers—occasionally including their own.

As she peered out the window, a sedan chair hurried by, easily threading its way through the snarl of traffic. Julia envied its occupant. No matter how burly the men hoisting the poles, Mrs. Hayes could never consent to put her trust in such a contraption. So, they lumbered through the crowded streets in Mrs. Hayes's old-fashioned barouche, traveling at a snail's pace, even as the minutes flew by.

They would be late. At half past six, the curtains would rise on the celebrated Mrs. Siddons acting the part of Desdemona in *Othello*, and Julia might as well be back in the little stone rectory in Oxfordshire, where she had had grown up, for all she would see of it.

No, *there!* The head of Bow Street, just visible in the distance. If she hopped down now—she wouldn't even need to signal the driver to stop, they were moving so slowly—she could make it the rest of the way on foot in a matter of moments.

"Settle yourself, my dear. We'll only be fashionably late."

Julia had reached for the door handle without realizing it. Now a spasm of guilt drew her primly back into her seat. Of course, Mrs. Hayes couldn't be expected to walk so far. The staircase to the boxes would be trial enough. And even aside from her rheumatism, such bustle did not suit her notions of either propriety or consequence.

Mrs. Hayes had spoken those words of reassurance without even opening her eyes, Julia realized. The jewel-handled lorgnette Julia had long known to be an unnecessary aid to Mrs. Hayes's vision, not quite an affectation. But surely she was not possessed of the gift of second sight?

"I do beg your pardon, ma'am." Julia folded her hands in her lap and refused even to glance toward the window, though the increasing gloom of the carriage's interior was a telltale sign of the lateness of the hour. "I must learn to curb my impatience."

A smile carved Mrs. Hayes's wrinkled cheeks, her round face a pale circle against the leather squabs, rising above her black bombazine gown. "I understand your eagerness—though when I was your age, I fear the audience would have held at least as much of my attention as the actors. Well . . . *most* of the actors." A twinkle revealed that her eyes were not as tightly closed as Julia had thought.

Mrs. Hayes, who had been a widow far longer than she had been wife, was rumored to have had an affair with Mr. Garrick, one of the leading actors of her day. Most of the time, Julia found the story impossible to believe. But at the moment—her fancy helped along by the magic of the evening and Mrs. Hayes's mischievous expression—she wondered whether it might not be true after all.

"One cannot avoid looking at the audience, ma'am," Julia conceded, try though she might to focus all her attention on the stage. Enormous chandeliers lit the house throughout the performance, and most people— dripping with jewels and swathed in showy silks and sparkling taffetas— attended the theater less to see than to be seen.

"Surely even you will agree that sometimes it is the more interesting show."

Grudgingly, Julia dipped her chin. "Sometimes." Not every item on the bill could be equally entertaining.

Though, truth be told, she had never seen a gentleman in the audience who could hold her attention, who made her breath catch and her pulse quicken, like the actors who trod the boards. From the first time she had seen a traveling troupe spout their lines from a makeshift stage on the village green, she had wished for some way to join them— an impossible dream for almost every woman, but most especially the daughter of a clergyman.

The sharp turn onto Bow Street caught her off guard, so absorbed had she been by the image in her mind's eye: a fantastical vision of herself as a celebrated actress, the audience in her thrall. "Nearly there now," she said to Mrs. Hayes, who surely knew the route at least as well as Julia.

A moment before, everything had seemed to stand in the way of their pleasure. But now, every lurch brought them closer, as each carriage in line ahead of them disgorged its passengers, and the distance between Julia and the theater doors dwindled, measurable now in mere yards, in feet, in inches.

With her eyes raised to the theater's grand façade, Julia descended first, the better to assist Mrs. Hayes. She turned back just as Mrs. Hayes appeared in the carriage's opening, reaching for the cane with one hand and wrapping her other securely around 'the older woman's left arm as a liveried footman took her right. Together they helped Mrs. Hayes down the two steps and onto the pavement. Once she had shaken the creases from her skirt and straightened herself, she gestured for her ebony walking stick and Julia restored it to its rightful owner. The usual *clickity-clack* of its silver tip against the ground was inaudible over the noise of the crowd as they made their way inside.

True to her word, Julia spared no more than a glance for the crush of patrons surrounding them on every side. Once through the doors, they made their careful way up the sweeping staircase to the elegant saloon that ran behind the private boxes, decorated with marble sculptures in the Grecian style and tufted benches upholstered in crimson velvet. Cologne was thick on the air, not quite masking the lingering scent of tobacco, the cheroots the gentlemen had extinguished outside, just a moment or two before. Conversation

buffeted them like waves, a greeting here, an exclamation
there. The plumes on Mrs. Hayes's turban nodded to
her left and to her right, but she never paused for more
than a moment, nearly as eager now as Julia to reach
their seats.

Every indication gave her hope that they had not
missed the start of the performance, though it must
surely be nearing a quarter of seven. Heavy crimson
velvet draperies guarded the entrances to the individual
boxes, giving the occupants some degree of privacy
and muffling the incessant noise from the saloon. A
good number of them still stood open, awaiting the
occupants' arrival. As no usher stood nearby to assist,
Julia stepped ahead to sweep aside the curtain to their
box for Mrs. Hayes.

Curious. The cord that fastened the curtain shut
during the play had been secured from the inside. She
supposed it had accidentally fallen into place, somehow.
She would have to slip her hand around the corner of
the door frame to release it.

As her gloved fingertips found the curved metal hook
and fumbled to slide the silken loop over it, the curtain
was wrenched open by someone unseen, and a strong,
warm hand encircled her wrist.

"And just what do you think you're doing?" demanded a man's voice in an unmistakable, though not
unpleasant, Scottish accent.

Against the glare of light from the theater beyond,
she could make out little of the man's appearance
beyond the fact that he was tall, with brownish-red hair
the color of burnished copper. She was still trying to

blink him into focus, and to rein in her clattering pulse, when Mrs. Hayes spoke.

"We are trying to enter our box, good sir," she said in a firm voice, accompanied by a sharp rap of her cane against the floor. "And I will thank you to unhand my niece."

Mildred Hayes was not Julia's aunt. At best, she was Julia's aunt-in-law, if such a relationship could even be said to exist. Not quite two years ago, Mrs. Hayes's actual niece, Laura, had married Julia's brother, Jeremy, Viscount Sterling, and moved with him to Wiltshire. Mrs. Hayes, however, had been determined to remain in London. Not wishing to abandon her elderly aunt, Laura had suggested her new sister-in-law might take her place as Aunt Mildred's companion.

Relatively few young ladies of nineteen would have jumped at the chance to serve at the whim of a widow who, in spite of her professed Town habits, actually lived quite retired in Clapham. But Julia, faced with the prospect of returning to quiet country life at her brother's estate, had readily accepted Mrs. Hayes's offer. Mrs. Hayes had a reputation for being liberal-minded and good-natured.

Most important of all, she loved the theater almost as much as Julia herself.

Julia's brother had taken her to plays now and again, when he could spare the time and the coin. She had treasured the memories of those evenings in Haymarket and Drury Lane: straining for a view of the lavish costumes and fancying she could still catch a whiff of greasepaint, even from the cheapest seats in the house.

Then, she had never dared to dream of what Mrs. Hayes had since provided: tickets for the Season, every performance within her grasp.

And speaking of grasps . . .

The unknown gentleman released her reluctantly, as if she were a thief he had fully intended to turn over to the authorities.

Once freed, she longed to rub her wrist, not because it hurt—he had been neither rough nor careless, despite the quickness of his movement— but to rid herself of the sensation of his unwelcome touch.

The impatient tap of Mrs. Hayes's cane had given way to a sniff of derision as the widow snapped open her lorgnette and eyed the gentleman suspiciously through it. "Who the devil are you? And what are you doing in my box?"

"*Your* box, madam?" The words were punctuated with a mocking laugh. "I think you'll find you're mistaken."

All of Julia's blinking had managed to bring the man into better focus, though his features were still cast in shadow by the glare of light behind. He was not quite thirty, she guessed, impeccably but not ostentatiously dressed, with surprisingly broad shoulders that seemed somehow in contradiction to his aristocratic bearing.

Julia turned and began to murmur to Mrs. Hayes. But before she could request to be allowed to fetch an usher, Mr. Pope, the box manager, appeared beside them as if summoned by the imperious snap of someone's fingers. Someone's strong, warm fingers.

Despite her earlier resolve, she wrapped her other

hand around the wrist he had held, however briefly, in his implacable grip, hoping her movement was disguised by the folds of her skirt.

Mr. Pope bowed to the gentleman, as if Mrs. Hayes were suddenly beneath his notice, however respectable she might be. "May I be of some assistance, my lord?"

My lord.

Julia narrowly managed to avoid rolling her eyes. She had no good opinion of noblemen—her brother excepted, and then only because he had inherited the title unexpectedly, without the encumbrance and expectations of a fortune to go with it, and not until he had been almost a grown man, past the age of spoiling.

"Yes," said Mrs. Hayes. "You may explain to this"—she tossed another dismissive glance toward him, her lorgnette only half-raised to her eyes—"*gentleman* that he is in my box, and then do me the kindness of escorting him from it to his proper seat."

The color that flushed into Mr. Pope's cheeks was visible, despite the uncertain light in the area between the saloon and the rear of the box, still half-shielded by the curtain. "I, er. . . ."

"Aye, Mr. Pope." She heard a thread of humor in Lord Scottish's voice now, as he widened his stance and crossed his arms behind his back. "Why don't you explain matters? I confess I'm most eager to hear what you have to say for yourself."

"I, er . . ." he stammered again, glancing downward before turning toward Mrs. Hayes. "This is Lord Dunstane's box and always has been. But as he comes to

Town so rarely—almost never—I, uh, I took the liberty of selling the tickets again to you, ma'am."

The reselling of tickets was a common enough practice. When those with a private box had already seen a performance, or were unable to attend, the box manager was employed to sell the tickets again to another interested party. But what Mr. Pope had done was a clear violation of both theater policy and good manners.

"Pocketed the double profit yourself, I daresay," added Lord Dunstane. To Julia's astonishment, he now sounded not angry, but almost amused.

The pink in Mr. Pope's cheeks darkened to crimson. He did not refute the accusation.

Mrs. Hayes gripped the handle of her cane more firmly. "I see. Then you must forgive us for the intrusion, my lord. We, of course, had no idea."

She had taken a box this year with every intention of asking friends to join them throughout the Season; thankfully she had not done so tonight. Now Julia thought with some embarrassment of the invitations that would have to be rescinded: Lady Clearwater and her daughters next week; later, Mama and her husband, Mr. Remington, and Mr. Remington's particular friends, General and Mrs. Scott.

"Perhaps Mr. Pope can find us another box," Julia suggested.

"Unfortunately, the performance for the next several evenings is . . ." the box manager began. Julia could guess what he was hesitant to say.

Sold out!

She had seen the placard, plastered over the playbill displayed outside the theater. Even if she had not, she might have guessed the state of things from the crush of carriages on Bow Street and the noisy crowd mingling in the vestibule. The size of the audience, the chaos of getting everyone properly seated, no doubt explained the delay in starting the performance.

"I paid for tickets for tonight, Mr. Pope," Mrs. Hayes reminded him, holding up the thin ivory disk that was marked with Lord Dunstane's box number. "Tickets you *will* find some means of honoring."

Mr. Pope glanced downward into the pit, where patrons seated on long benches could be squeezed together to accommodate another person or two.

This silent suggestion was met with a *harumph* of displeasure. "Oh, I think not, sir."

"I could easily find you places for next week," Mr. Pope suggested.

Next week? Julia gulped. Not that she had grown so spoiled she imagined she would suffer some irreparable harm by waiting a few days to see *Othello*. It was not her own disappointment she was struggling to swallow.

Under the name "Miss on Scene," she wrote reviews of theatrical performances for *Mrs. Goode's Magazine for Misses*, and this month's deadline was tomorrow. Lady Stalbridge, the magazine's editor, was expecting Julia's contribution by midday at the latest. Lady Stalbridge, the readers, and the magazine would all lose by Mr. Pope's double-dealing.

A sudden hush had fallen across the theater, which

caused the noise in her throat to be surprisingly audible, easily mistaken for a soft sob. Lord Dunstane settled his light eyes on her, taking in every detail of her appearance, her age, the modest quality of her sprigged muslin gown. *A poor relation*, his sardonic gaze said clearly, *doomed to a future as a lady's companion*.

And yet, he did not immediately look away—at least, not until Mrs. Hayes's pronouncement: "Unacceptable. We shall simply have to join Lord Dunstane here. As he's alone, I'm sure he won't mind."

With that, she began to move deeper into the box, her cane clearing the path ahead of her, both Mr. Pope and Lord Dunstane looking on, dumbfounded.

When neither of the men made as if either to assist or prevent her, Julia stepped forward and laid a hand on her arm. "We mustn't presume, ma'am . . ." she began.

But Mrs. Hayes kept going. "*Hmph.* Can't see that *we* are the presumptuous ones. Now, help me to that seat, child." She pointed with the tip of her cane.

Though well-positioned, the box—*their* box, as Julia had been thinking of it until a few moments ago—was one of the smaller ones in the theater, holding just six seats in two rows of three. Lord Scottish was evidently not the sort who reserved a box with the intention of inviting a dozen of his closest friends to chatter their way through the performance.

After Mrs. Hayes was seated in the front row closest to the stage, Julia moved to take one of the blue-upholstered chairs in the back. Lord Dunstane spoke from behind her. "You'll be more comfortable—see better—from the seat beside your aunt."

With a mute nod, more surprise than acquiescence, she accepted the middle chair. In another moment, he had taken the spot to her right. Of course he would expect to have the best view—or at least, the best remaining view—from his own box. She refused to turn her head in his direction, not even when a wry laugh gusted from his lips, as if he were incredulous at his own misfortune.

She wanted, uncharacteristically, to fidget. But why should Lord Dunstane make her agitated? After tonight, he would doubtless never give her another thought. *Sooner, in fact*, she thought, when she recollected his glance of disdain and pity. Once the performance began and gave them all something else to think about, he would forget her existence entirely.

Nevertheless, she could not remember ever having been so aware of the strange intimacy of a theater box, where people sat, almost shoulder to shoulder, snug within their private world and yet on display to anyone who cared to look.

And people *would* look, from below or across the way, everyone eager for a glimpse of something new or unexpected.

Lord Dunstane—a striking-looking Scotsman who came to London so infrequently that Mr. Pope had believed his deception would go undiscovered, but who nonetheless reserved a box at Covent Garden for performances he would never see—certainly fit the bill.

For just a moment, Julia considered slipping into one of the empty seats at the back of the box after all. But before she could make her move, the curtain rose.

Visit our website at
KensingtonBooks.com
to sign up for our newsletters, read
more from your favorite authors, see
books by series, view reading group
guides, and more!

Become a Part of Our
Between the Chapters Book Club
Community and Join the Conversation

Betweenthechapters.net

Submit your book review for a chance to win exclusive
Between the Chapters swag you can't get anywhere else!
https://www.kensingtonbooks.com/pages/review/